The Legacy of The Boc

Book 2 of The Gnome Door Chronicles

By Tom Dillman

FIRST EDITION

ISBN: 978-1-952352-16-4

Published by:

Crave Press
www.cravepress.com

Chapter 1

Lady Coramina wondered to herself if maybe Korin had been right. Perhaps she had taken on more than she had bargained for. He had warned her to be careful what she wished for.

But the king had finally said yes. After months of pleading, subtle persuasion, and a bit of arm twisting by both Coramina and the princess, the king had reluctantly agreed to allow one of the more spacious, unused rooms in the north tower to be converted into a proper library. The archives would be moved from the bowels of the castle to a clean, warm, and, most importantly, dry location. No more trudging down through those damp catacombs to perform her duties as court scribe.

The last two weeks had been a whirlwind of activity as she personally took charge of overseeing the transporting of all of the castle's old volumes and records to their new quarters. Getting the most delicate of the old manuscripts safely from one end of the castle to the other had been an exhausting job. She was tired and dirty, and her shoulders ached from lugging around old volumes. Why did those old scribes insist that their books had to be so big and heavy?

Next would come the monumental task of reorganizing and cataloging. But that was a problem that would have to wait until another day. For today, only a small pile of old books remained in the original archive room. Everyone else had already gone home. All that was left was a quick review of these last few books to determine where to file them in their new quarters, and she could also retire for the day. If only her husband, Korin, was home, she thought to herself; she could have him rub some of the stiffness out of her shoulders. But he was away from the castle on duty with Princess Ashley, and he wouldn't be back for the next two days. She would just have to settle for soaking in a hot bath. It wasn't as soothing as Korin's skilled hands, but it was the next best thing. Maybe she'd even have a small glass of that sweet wine the princess had given her to try. The princess did have excellent taste in wine.

When this move was finally complete, Coramina was going to ask Korin to take her away for a few days. She smiled to herself as she remembered when they had accompanied Cooper, his granddaughter Susan, and the princess on a trip to the Glade of the Golden Willow. The weather and circumstances had been just right, and they were fortunate enough to be present when the fairies danced. If she closed her eyes, she could still picture the amazing spectacle. Everyone should have the chance to see that at least once in their life, she thought to herself. Those first two days of that trip had been the most pleasant time that they had spent together in many years, but that was almost three years ago. They were both overdue for a vacation.

Both she and Korin were completely devoted to their duties, she as court scribe and assistant to the princess, and he as the captain of the princess's personal guard, but as the years went on, they found that those quiet moments together were becoming much more important to both of them.

"Well...this last pile of books isn't going to get sorted all by itself," she said aloud, even though there was no one there to hear.

The first two books on top of the pile were just old ledger books documenting the day to day commerce at the castle. Coramina reached for the third book. It was a ragged old leather-bound volume, and she didn't recognize it. As her hand touched the book, a spark jumped to her finger. She yanked her hand back reflexively, both from the surprise and from the sudden tingling in it. Just a bit of static. As she rubbed her hand, she dismissed it as nothing, no different than if she had walked across the carpet and touched something metallic. But, a moment later, as she held the strange looking volume and began to examine it, the buzzing started in her head. Very faint at first, but slowly getting louder.

Besides being the scribe, Coramina was also the court psychic and, as such, she was much more receptive to certain things than most people. Within two minutes, the buzzing had increased until her temples were pounding, and the room started to spin before her eyes. She dropped the book and stumbled from the room, vomiting violently by the time she got twenty yards down the hall.

Out in the hallway, Cora nearly bowled over Tia, one of the girls from the kitchen staff. When Coramina didn't arrive in the dining hall at her usual time, the kitchen matron assumed that she had lost track of the time and sent Tia to see if she wanted dinner brought up to her. Fortunately, Tia was a sharp girl and had her wits about her. She quickly called down the hall for a guard to come and help her. Between the two of them, they got Coramina back to her quarters and into bed and sent for a physician. Tia stayed with Cora until the healer arrived. Matron would demand an explanation for her absence, but Coramina was well-liked and, under the circumstances, Tia knew that she would be forgiven. As she was leaving to return to the kitchen, Cora grabbed Tia's hand and whispered, "Send for the orcanus!"

"Well, Pinkie, what should we make of this?" Shirell asked the little snicker. Pinkie was her constant companion anytime she was at the Guild Hall that had become her home in the last few years. "An urgent request for me to come to Kestriana, the castle of the elf king, and from Lady Coramina of all people."

She liked Coramina. Shortly after accepting the title of orcanus, leader of the Guild of Conjurers, she had been obligated to spend two weeks with the court scribe chronicling all that she knew of Marcus, the shadow mage, brother to the king, and her former teacher.

Coramina was soft-spoken and patient and had helped to turn what could have been a tedious task into a somewhat pleasant experience. By the end of the second week, they were on pretty friendly terms. Cora had even coaxed Shirell into revealing a bit of her own personal history, something that Shirell usually guarded fiercely. Coramina had gone a long way toward dispelling Shirell's long-standing dislike and mistrust of elves, even though she was half-elf herself.

Shirell was still divided in her feelings regarding Princess Ashley. For Shirell's help in defeating and capturing the shadow mage, the princess had generously secured for her an old lodge that had been reconditioned to house the new Guild. The lodge was far enough from the city to free them from the prying eyes and political machinations of the High Council. Then she had supplied workers to renovate it and staff to man the new hall. Ashley had given Shirell numerous reasons to trust her, even saving her life when the Mage had attacked her while she slept. But after years of holding the princess personally responsible for her mother's death at the hands of the gremlin army, it was still difficult for Shirell to be friendly towards her.

As leader of the Guild, diplomacy was an important part of Shirell's job. Old Horus was a skilled wizard, and he was even

4

a reasonably good teacher once you got past his quirks. But too many years of living by himself had made him rather eccentric. His social skills, which had always been somewhat lacking, had become almost non-existent as he got older. She had had to learn to be diplomatic on the fly.

She had really wished that Cooper, the guardian of the Gnome Door, would have agreed to become the new orcanus, or at the very least, joined the Guild. She would have immediately made him her second-in-command.

It was many years since the end of the Gremlin Wars, but Cooper's name was still well known and respected, not just among the elves, but also with the gnomes and travelers from the other races that passed through his portal from time to time. He would have made an excellent emissary, representing the new Guild while retaining a link to the Guild of old. Plus, he would lend it a lot of credibility. But he had graciously declined, stating that he preferred to remain as the guardian of the Gnome Door.

"Well Pinkie, I guess I'm going to Kestriana." Shirell smiled as the little snicker chattered at her. "Yes, I know that I was already planning to go there anyway. Cooper and his granddaughter, Susan, are coming for a two week stay, and I promised them that I'd come during their visit. Susan has just turned fourteen and grown about a foot taller than the last time we saw her. She is quickly becoming a fine young woman."

Susan and her grandfather had been two of her strongest supporters when Shirell took on the monumental task of rebuilding the Guild. They had also become two of her closest friends.

At the mention of Susan's name, Pinkie began to excitedly run circles around her, leaping from one piece of furniture to the next.

"Yes, I know that you want to come, and I'd love to take

you with me, little one, but you've been banned from Kestriana," said Shirell, scratching Pinkie under the chin. "Remember the last time you were there? You teased the chancellor's fat little dog until he chased you right out an open window. Lucky for you, there was a cloth awning just below the window and he wasn't hurt. But he was stuck there for an hour until someone could finally get him down. I've never seen the chancellor so angry. Fortunately, Susan has promised to come here and visit you while she's here. Maybe Cooper will come, too. I'm sure that, if necessary, he'll come and help in dealing with Lady Coramina's problem. Now, I need to pack a few things, so scoot."

Pinkie reluctantly went and sprawled on top of the tall wardrobe in the corner to watch as Shirell began placing clothes in a travel bag.

Chapter 2

Even after experiencing it numerous times, Susan still had to struggle to contain her excitement every time she passed through the Gnome Door. Although the sensation only lasted a few seconds, it was like nothing else she had ever felt.

There was that intense tingle as the magic of the fairy mists ran from the top of her head down to her toes and then back up again. For a split second, everything blurred before her eyes; then suddenly, her vision cleared and she and her grandfather were standing on the grassy hillside on the other side. She quietly hoped that she never got so used to it that it didn't give her that thrill.

As her eyes adjusted to the bright sun, she saw Bodkin and her brother Pen instantly start towards them. The two girls hugged each other warmly. Both had grown since the last time they had seen each other. Bodkin still had the petite build of an elf, but she had added muscle tone and strength. Her training with the forest wardens had given her the strength and agility of a world class gymnast. Susan, on the other hand, had shot up tall and straight, like her grandfather, and she towered over Bodkin by half a head.

Off to the right, Princess Ashley stood next to a half dozen mounts — two full size horses and four takis, the smaller pony-like creatures that bred wild on the grassy slopes of the highlands.

Takis were almost as fast as a full-sized horse, but only ate half as much. Most elves rode takis, but they were a bit small for full grown humans. They were the perfect size for Susan and Bodkin.

Ashley smiled warmly as Cooper approached. "Dear Cooper, it is wonderful to see you," she said as she gave him a small kiss on the cheek. "I'll give you a proper kiss later, after the girls have gone off on their own," she whispered in his ear.

A smile was his only response as he returned the peck on the cheek. "Hello, Ashley. Something important must have happened if you came with mounts. You brought takis for the girls, I see. Good, they both love riding those ponies."

"Yes," Ashley responded sheepishly. "You've remembered that I never really liked riding horses. I'm sorry, I just don't trust these creatures, but we would like to get you to Kestriana as quickly as possible, so they were a necessary evil. I know that we're imposing on your visit, but Coramina has stumbled upon a magic artifact that we'd like you to take a look at. Shirell has already been sent for and, even now, she should be on her way."

"As much as both Susan and I are always anxious to see Shirell, I would remind you that this is supposed to be just a quiet visit," Cooper answered with a sigh. "And Susan's mother will be furious if we get her involved in anything dangerous."

"I won't ask you or Susan to do anything that you don't think is safe. Besides, Elana's one to talk. I seem to remember that my dear niece always liked the thrill of a little danger and risk."

"Which is exactly the reason that she doesn't want Susan exposed to it. She recognizes that same reckless spirit emerging in her daughter. The temptation is too great. As you undoubtedly remember, more than once, Elana had close calls that could have turned out very badly. I'll agree to take a quick look, and then we turn the artifact over to the orcanus. We're traveling pretty light,

8

so if you're in a hurry, we'll get the two girls moving and you can fill me in along the way."

It didn't require much coaxing to get the two girls mounted and ready to go. Both Susan and Bodkin were excited to visit the castle and anxious to see Shirell. In less than five minutes, they had said their goodbyes to Pen and were on their way.

The ride to the castle was uneventful for the most part. Both girls had riding experience, and the takis kept up a smooth and steady pace that ate up the miles quickly. Before they knew it, the towers of Kestriana came into view. A half mile from the castle, Susan and Bodkin decided to race the last stretch to the gate.

As the girls spurred their takis, Cooper leaned over to Ashley. "I told you that she has her mother's spirit." Then, with a grin he added "C'mon, they've had a little bit of a head start, let's see if we can catch them." Cooper leaned low over his horse's neck and urged him up to a full gallop.

"Cooper! No! You know I hate racing on these animals!" yelled Ashley as her horse followed the others and broke into a run, leaving her struggling to regain control and shouting at Cooper.

Cooper's mount was a big mare that loved to run. A hundred yards from the castle gates, he caught up to the two girls on their smaller ponies. Ashley arrived a moment later, looking disheveled and very un-princess like.

"That wasn't funny!" she snapped at Cooper with fire in her eyes. "I should have you banished."

The two girls giggled at her and she shot them a look that would melt glass.

"Your father tried that already," responded Cooper with a smile. "Besides, I knew that you were never in any real danger.

You've had plenty of training with horses. I was sure that you'd be fine. And, if you banish me, who would help you with your artifact? I'm sorry if I made your horse run. Here, let me help you down and we'll go see if Shirell has arrived yet."

"Don't touch me, I'll get down myself. You're a horrible person, and I don't wish to speak to you anymore. Come along, girls. Let's go find the orcanus." With that, she stormed off into the castle, her long hair flying wildly behind her.

They found Shirell in the dining hall. Coramina was with her, and the two women were sampling pastries that had been put out by the kitchen staff while they waited for Cooper and the others to arrive.

"Your pastry chef is an artist, Princess. Everything here is wonderful," said Shirell as Ashley came into the hall with Susan and Bodkin trailing close behind. The Princess had calmed down a bit on her way through the castle, and after carefully selecting one of the treats from the platter and popping into her mouth, she was back to her usual self.

"She is the best in the kingdom. Try the little round cookies; they're excellent."

Cooper arrived a moment later. Ashley continued to treat him indifferently, but her anger over the stunt on horseback had faded. The next ten minutes were spent exchanging pleasantries and catching up. Finally, they all settled at the end of one of the long banquet tables, and Coramina related all that had happened with the mysterious book.

When she finished, it was agreed that Cooper and Shirell would go to the archive room, examine the book, and report back to the princess. They would determine how to proceed based on that they found.

A half an hour later, the guardian and the orcanus were standing in front of the entrance to the old archive room. They cautiously drew back the bolt and slowly opened the door. Everything was just as Coramina had described it. The room was empty except for a half dozen books stacked on a small table in the center. The volume that had affected Cora lay on the floor, exactly where she had dropped it.

Cooper had borrowed a pair of heavy gauntlets from the captain of the guards and carefully knelt and retrieved the book. Shirell set the other books aside so he could place it on the table where they could examine it.

The cover of the book was old leather, weathered and battered, and so dark that it was almost black. The front had been embossed with ancient symbols and runes.

"Horus has been teaching me to read runes, but I don't recognize anything here." Shirell traced one of the symbols on the cover of the book with a gloved fingertip.

"I can't read it either," said Cooper with a sour expression. "But I believe I recognize it, and I don't like what I see. If my guess is correct, the runes are Boc-Tan, the ancient script of the Boc clan. And it's almost certainly a warning about the dangers of opening the book."

"Boc clan? I've never heard of them."

"That's not surprising. They're not spoken of much anymore. Centuries ago, the elves were divided into clans. They sometimes fought each other, and other times they traded back and forth. From time to time, the clans would need to band together to protect themselves from a common enemy, evil wizards, gremlins, or marauding bands of gnomes. And like people everywhere, some younger members of the clans ignored tradition, fell in love, married from one clan to another, and eventually they all became one. Some of the older elves still observe clan traditions for weddings and special occasions, but otherwise, the different clans have faded into elven history and been mostly forgotten.

"Except for the Boc. The Boc never wanted to join the rest of the elf nation. They primarily lived on the borders to other lands and were almost constantly at war with the gnomes and the gremlins. They were easy to recognize; most of them had red hair and green eyes, unlike the blond, blue-eyed complexion of most elves. They came to believe that war was honorable, and their honor was all important. They considered the idea of living peacefully with the other races to be cowardly and weak. When all the other clans agreed to unite under a single king, they just disappeared.

"Representatives from the other clans were sent out to speak with the Boc, but the representatives found their villages abandoned. No trace of them was found. There were countless rumors as to what happened to the Boc. It was well known that some of them dabbled in the darkest of magics to try to find new ways to destroy their enemies. The Order of The Shadow Mages originated with the Boc. Some believe that, like the shadow mages, the Boc unleashed something that destroyed them all, but their settlements offered no clues as to their fate, and no one actually knows. Not long after that, the Gremlin War began, and no one had time to worry about where the Boc went.

"If this book came from the Boc, there's no way to know what evil it may contain. But it is undoubtedly dangerous, and we need to determine what this says before we try to open the book or learn any of its secrets."

Shirell looked up at Cooper. "How could a book like this

wind up here in the first place?"

"What better place to hide a book than in a library? Until a few weeks ago when they started to move the archives to the new rooms, some of the volumes here hadn't been touched for decades. If this book was written by the shadow mages, then I would venture a guess that your old friend Marcus knows something about how it got here."

A determined look crossed Shirell's face. "Destroy the book. Right here, right now. Marcus called himself a shadow mage, and his only goal was destruction. If this book was created by the original shadow mages, it can contain nothing but evil. We should destroy it immediately. Bury it's secrets so they can never harm anyone again."

"I am inclined to agree with your logic, and as orcanus, it is your decision on how to deal with magic artifacts. I don't believe that it will be that simple, though. If we just try to burn the book or destroy it with magic, we may release something terrible that is deliberately set inside to prevent just such a thing. The Boc would almost certainly set a trap of some sort to protect such a book. We need to find out what is written on the front. I think we need to lock this book in as safe a place as possible until we have had a talk with your old teacher."

"I was afraid that you were going to say that. You're right, of course, but he won't be very cooperative, and I doubt that we'll learn much from him."

"Yes, but me must try anyway. I'll have the princess arrange it."

Chapter 3

An hour later, Cooper and Shirell stood in the hallway outside Marcus's quarters. Even though he was a prisoner, he was still King Marinus's brother and, no matter what his crimes, Marinus would not subject a prince of the royal family to rotting in a damp cell. Rather than being confined to a dungeon, Marcus's old quarters had been modified after being thoroughly searched. Special attention had been given to the search for hidden entrances as there was still the question of how he was able to come and go so easily as the shadow mage. A long-hidden passage was found behind the fireplace and sealed. All sharp objects and anything suspicious had already been removed years ago when Marcus was masquerading as an idiot.

His rooms were comfortable, but somewhat sparse. The windows had been barred, and two guards were stationed outside at all times — one by the door, and the second one patrolling the hallway. A full-time warden oversaw and had to approve everyone who came and went, from kitchen staff all the way up to the king himself.

Cooper and Shirell were instructed to leave all weapons, talismans, and any objects of magic in their quarters before they were allowed entrance. Although Marcus was a prisoner now, for many years he was able to convince everyone in the castle that he possessed the simple mind of a child. He was still very crafty and not to be trusted.

"I think our best bet is to play off his ego. I've no doubt that he'll be condescending," Cooper said to Shirell on the way to Marcus's quarters. "I doubt that we'll be able to force anything out of him, but he may be arrogant enough to reveal something important if he thinks he's showing us how much smarter he is than we are."

"I was thinking much the same thing," answered Shirell with a nod. "I've little doubt that he still considers me nothing more than the stupid girl that used to be his student. I'm sure that he feels that he is still the master."

After a short wait in the hall, the warden came and made the required checks to verify that they carried no objects of magic or weapons. Then they were shown into Marcus's quarters.

The main parlor was roomy with little furniture. Occupying the center of the room was a table surrounded by four chairs. A chessboard, set up for the next game, occupied the far end of the table.

Although the warden had informed Marcus of their presence, he remained in the other room, forcing them to wait until it suited him to come and speak to them. Finally, he strode defiantly into the room.

"Well, I am certainly honored to have two such distinguished guests," said Marcus, his voice dripping with contempt. "The disgraced hero who has become a lowly gatekeeper and the little wild girl who dreams of being a real witch someday. Did my brother perhaps send you to play chess with me? I do hope that you're a better player than he is. He loses every time."

Shirell felt the small hairs on the back of her neck stand up as Cooper's voice turned icy and hard.

"No, Marcus, we did not come to entertain you. We came

to ask about a book that we found in the archive room. We had expected to speak to a prince of the House of Samarian, not a spoiled child. C'mon, Shirell, we've wasted our time coming here. He can't tell us anything."

Marcus's demeanor changed instantly as Cooper turned toward the door.

"No, please wait...I am sorry for such an undignified outburst. Please forgive me. The healers have told me that even after all these years, my moods are still affected by the fall from the horse. They provide me with an herbal tea that helps, but chess calms me and is a welcome relief from the crushing boredom. You're an educated man, Cooper. Please, if you would indulge me in a match, it will help me remain focused, and I will try to answer your questions as best I can."

"I doubt that I will be much of a challenge, Marcus. I haven't taken the time for chess in many years, but I'll play if that's what's required to enlist your help."

"You underestimate yourself, Guardian. My memory is still good. Your reputation was that of an excellent player years ago. My dear brother is only average at best. You can be white, so yours is the first move."

"As you wish," said Cooper as he sat down across from Marcus and slid one of the white pawns forward.

The two men played silently for twenty minutes, carefully assessing and weighing their options before committing each piece to a given move. Shirell was little more than a novice to the game, but she felt Cooper was at a clear disadvantage as she quietly watched the pieces get captured and sacrificed on both sides.

As Marcus removed a captured rook from the board, he

17

asked "So, what can you tell me about your mysterious book?"

Cooper answered without looking up from the board.

"It's old, bound in dark leather with unknown runes embossed on the front. I'm sure that you remember that Court Scribe Lady Coramina is a psychic, and after handling the book, she became violently ill. We suspect that the runes may be Boc-Tan. No one knows where the book came from or how it came to be in the archive room."

"I have heard of such books, and I'm sure that you have guessed correctly," sighed Marcus. "Even without seeing the book, I'm certain that the writing is Boc-Tan, the ancient script of the Boc. In my quest for ancient magics years ago, I searched for any information I could find concerning the original shadow mages, many of whom came from the Boc clan. It was difficult for me to search thoroughly and still maintain my masquerade as the castle fool, but I was able to discern what limited information still existed about the Boc.

"When the other elf clans agreed to unite peacefully under a single king, the Boc rejected the idea and refused to join the newly formed elf nation. Respected leaders of the old clans were sent out to try to persuade the Boc to reconsider. But when they arrived, they found empty settlements and abandoned villages. This is all common knowledge, I know, but few know what they did actually find in each of the towns.

"In every village, a book similar to the one you describe was discovered, usually in the home of the elders or in a large common building. Early attempts to open the books resulted in many lost lives. Forcing the books open, either by physical force or with magic, caused them to explode in an enormous fireball. Those with psychic abilities, like our friend Lady Coramina, were sickened by the dark magic protecting the books.

"The few remaining books were carefully collected and

taken to the Hall of Conjurers. Much of the message on the covers of the books was almost indecipherable. The Boc were very secretive about their runes and dialect. But all language is built on certain common threads, so eventually enough of the message in the runes was deciphered to allow an incantation to be created that would neutralize the books' defenses and allow them to be opened safely. I believe that it was your old friend, Poole, who broke the code."

"What did they find in the books?" asked Shirell.

"Patience, wolf-girl, I'm coming to that," sneered Marcus, as he captured one of Cooper's bishops. "Check; you only have two pawns and a knight left to defend your king. You have very few moves left, Guardian."

"Neither the game nor your story is over yet, Marcus. Please continue. What did the books say?" Cooper moved his knight to a space next to Marcus's king.

"Oh...I fear that that move has just cost you the game, but in answer to your question, nothing. The books were blank inside."

"Blank pages? Surely what was written there was just hidden, made invisible by some spell or magic."

"That, of course, is the obvious conclusion. The members of the Guild thought the same thing. They tried repeatedly to discover some hidden information, but in the end, they found nothing. The Guild was finally forced to conclude that the books were nothing more than cleverly disguised booby traps left behind to destroy their enemies when they came looking for them. The Boc were well known for their hatred of the gremlins."

Marcus moved his king to eliminate the knight.

"There are very few examples of Boc-Tan writing or translations, but in an old volume borrowed from the Guild, I was able to find all that was known, including a copy of the incantation that renders the books harmless to open. I copied it so that I could return the book to its original location before its absence was discovered. It was essential that my masquerade was not discovered.

"I offer the incantation to you freely as a gesture of my desire to be cooperative. With it, you may safely open the book and see for yourself what is, or is not, inside. The spell is written on the third page of my journal that was taken from these rooms when I was imprisoned here. The journal is small with a reddish-brown cover. It should not be difficult to find among my confiscated belongings. You may retrieve it at your convenience. I would appreciate it, though, if you mentioned my helpfulness to my brother. Then perhaps he would allow me a bit more freedom to move about the castle.

"The answer to how this Boc book came to be here at the castle, I do not know. It was believed that all the remaining books had been taken to the Hall of Conjurers and were subsequently lost in the attack of the lindworm that led to the destruction of the Hall. If this particular book has been here a long time, I can only guess that it was brought here on its journey to the Guild, and then mistakenly placed in the archives. Perhaps by some servant, who unknowingly thought that they were doing the right thing and returning it to its proper place. An individual with little psychic sensitivity could handle the book with no ill effects. I'm sure that the book would appear to be just another dusty old volume to the untrained eye."

"You are probably right," said Cooper, with a nod. "Although, it is hard to imagine that the Boc went to all the trouble of creating these books, then filled them with blank pages for the single purpose of eliminating a few stray enemies. But if the combined efforts of the Guild couldn't find anything, then I doubt that we will either."

Cooper moved one of his pawns on the board. "Thank you for your help and for a stimulating game. Checkmate."

"What?" Marcus came completely out of his chair. "That cannot be! You only have two pawns left!"

"Look for yourself. Your king is in checkmate. You have no moves left."

Marcus stared at the chessboard in disbelief. There was no denying it. Cooper had won. When Marcus looked up from the board, sheer hatred showed on his face for just an instant before quickly changing to a forced smile.

"Well...congratulations, Guardian. Clearly I have become careless playing against my brother. The game is yours. Please, while you are visiting here, come back and allow me a rematch."

"My time at Kestriana is limited, but if I am able, I will. Now, the orcanus and I must go. I will inform the king of your cooperation. You have my word on that. Thank you again for your time. Good day, Marcus."

Once they were out in the hallway, Shirell looked over at Cooper.

"Maybe you should have let him win. There was murder in his eyes when he looked up from that chessboard."

"Yes, for just a second he left the facade slip and we caught a glimpse of the real Marcus beneath. I'm certain he would've tried to kill me if he had half a chance, but I couldn't let him win. He looks down on anyone that he feels is inferior to him, which is almost everyone. You heard the way he speaks of his own brother, the king. By defeating him, even in something as simple as a game of chess, I've proven that I'm his equal. He hates the very thought of that. In his obsession to prove that he's superior, he may do something stupid or let something slip."

"You're playing a risky game, Guardian," said Shirell. "Even locked in his rooms, he can still be dangerous."

"I know. I don't trust him, and I have little doubt that he knows more about that book than he's telling us. He was much too willing to give us the incantation that serves as a key to open the book. I'm sure that he's been plotting something from the day he was locked in there. I just wish we knew what it was. As a precaution, I'll ask the princess to alert the guards to watch for any unusual behavior."

"What about the book? Can we trust him enough to try the incantation and attempt to open the book?"

"I don't think we have much choice. We have to open it to see what's inside. There must be more to it than just blank pages. But we'll need to open it somewhere safe, far away from the castle grounds, just in case the incantation doesn't work, or worse, it releases something nasty to attack us."

"That's not a very pleasant thought," responded Shirell with a nod. "How soon do you want to attempt this? I would like to resolve this as soon as possible."

"I was thinking later this afternoon. I'm meeting the princess for lunch. I'll fill her in on what Marcus said."

"A lunch date with the princess?" said Shirell with a grin. "Sounds romantic. And you've only been here a day. I see that you're not wasting any time."

"Now you sound like Susan. But for your information, it's just a casual lunch. Susan and Bodkin will be joining us. You're welcome to come also. Both girls admire you and would love to see you."

"Thank you. I can't tell you how inviting that sounds, but as orcanus, it is customary for me to appear before the king while I'm here. I'm scheduled to meet with him at noon. Shall we meet in the archive room around three? We could take the book out to the edge of the forest to try and open it there."

"Three o'clock should be fine. There is one other thing that I need to ask about. Why does Marcus call you 'wolf-girl?' I don't want to pry into your past, but it could offer some insight into what he's thinking. If he's underestimating you, that could work to our advantage."

"Well, you already know part of the story. I was trapped inside of the Hall of Conjurers when it was destroyed. By the time I escaped from under the wreckage, I was starving, almost naked and half mad from the kuri-aken. I was nearly helpless when I was discovered and cornered by a pack of nightshade dogs. Normally, they would have torn me to pieces and had me for their dinner but one of the she-wolves wouldn't let them.

"She had recently lost a cub and, for some reason, instantly adopted me as it's replacement. She placed herself between me and the rest of the pack, drove them off and saved me. I've always had a special way with animals, and we bonded. She brought me food and protected me until I was able to take care of myself. She was dark gray and moved like a ghost. I called her Shadow. We lived in a makeshift shelter, scavenging food where we could, and hiding from marauding patrols from the gremlin army.

"That's where Marcus found me. He took me to a cabin at the edge of the Dark Woods where there was food and clothing, and he made me his student.

"He would just appear some days and show me some technique or spell, then vanish for days at a time. When he returned, he expected me to have practiced this new lesson and perfected it in his absence. If I failed to do a spell correctly or mispronounced an incantation, Marcus would berate me, calling me a 'stupid wolf-girl' and saying that he would have better luck training the wolf. A few times, he became so angry that I was sure that he was going to strike me.

"But Shadow was always there watching him, sometimes just appearing out of nowhere. For all his magic, I believe that Marcus was always a little afraid of her. His words did have the effect of making me angry enough to work harder to make sure that I did it right the next time, but I came to hate those words more and more each time, and he knew it. Shadow stayed with me for many years.

"Then one day, after she had become old and sick, she just disappeared into the woods and never returned. Finally, when I had had enough of his abuse, and without Shadow to keep me company, I saw no reason to stay. So, I just left. I didn't know if he would come after me or not, but I refused to remain there any longer. After I left, I stayed far away and hoped that he would not consider me worthy of pursuit.

"The next time that I saw him face to face was when he attacked your party in the Ice Caves. I'm sure that his comment today was just his way of telling me that, in his eyes, I'm still nothing more than a mere student, unworthy of the title orcanus."

"Don't let the things he says get to you," responded Cooper. "You've worked very hard to rebuild the Guild. You've earned that title."

"Thank you, your support has always meant a lot to me. Now, let's forget about Marcus for a while. Tell me about Susan."

Chapter 4

Shortly after three, Shirell arrived at the archive room to find Cooper patiently waiting for her.

"Were you able to find Marcus's journal?"

"Yes," said Cooper, as he held up a small book bound in reddish-brown leather. "The warden took me directly to where Marcus's possessions were stored. There wasn't much there. Many of his belongings were destroyed years ago when he faked his death, so I was able to find the journal rather quickly. Both the book and the incantation were exactly where Marcus said they would be. I don't like it when Marcus offers to be helpful. It's not in his nature to be straightforward about anything. I can't help thinking that he's somehow playing us for fools. I just haven't figured out how."

Cooper produced a large ornate key from his pocket. The tumblers clicked and the door swung open soundlessly on ancient, but well-maintained hinges. The mysterious book was exactly as they had left it on the small table in the center of the room.

As they entered, Cooper noticed that there was an unpleasant feel to the air in the room. Nothing tangible, just a sense of unease that seemed to hang in the air, a certain dreariness that made the room feel damp and forbidding. As he glanced around, he noticed that others had sensed it too. There were no cobwebs anywhere. Such a dusty old room, and yet not a single spider in the corner or a fly buzzing around the walls. It was clear that even the smallest of the castle's inhabitants wanted nothing to do with this strange book or the room it inhabited. Cooper loaded the book carefully into the backpack that he had brought with him and slipped the backpack over one shoulder. After locking the door on the way out, they started down the hallway toward the far end of the castle. Their footsteps echoed noisily through the empty passages of the castle's lower levels. At the end of the hall, Cooper turned down a corridor that looked like it hadn't been used in years.

"Where are we going to try to open this?" asked Shirell.

"The princess and I consulted with the castle groundskeeper and the captain of the guard. There's a small secluded clearing a few hundred yards west of the castle. Its location is kept secret and only known to a handful of trusted individuals. They believe that would be the safest place to try opening the book. We can exit the castle unnoticed through a small side door that's kept bolted from the inside and can only be accessed through an unused hallway. There's a locked door that's hidden behind an old tapestry at the opposite end. Then we go down a narrow path leading to the clearing. The captain of the guard revealed that this place was maintained to accommodate meetings with the occasional visitor whose presence may be considered 'unwelcome' by some members of the High Council. Although no one admits that these private meetings take place, they are sometimes a necessity to maintain a mutually beneficial peace among the races.

"The groundskeeper explained that most commerce and travelers to the castle commonly use the north gate. But in certain areas around the castle walls, the thorn bushes and thistles had been deliberately left to grow wild as a natural barrier

26

against invaders or assassins. They're cleverly hidden behind flowering shrubs and hedges, so most visitors to the castle never realize that they're there. But a casual walk around the perimeter could turn into a very painful experience if someone wandered into a clearing without noting the exact location of the entrance. There's no chance that anyone will accidentally stumble upon us while we're trying to unlock the book's secrets. The less people that know about us attempting to open this book, the better.

"The captain of the guard has assigned one of his most trusted men to unlock the side door and stand watch for an hour. If we haven't returned by then, he'll bolt the door from the inside, go call for a squad of guards and come looking for us."

The walk to the clearing took a few minutes, and Shirell was in no great hurry. Cooper was one of the few people that she could let down her guard and speak openly with, and she was pleased to have the opportunity to do so. Since accepting the role of orcanus, nearly every conversation that she had was required to be formal and important.

When she met with the leaders of the different peoples of the land, tradition and protocol had to be observed. The young novices to the guild treated her with awe and hung on her every word, but they maintained a certain respectful distance, and Horus's personality was far too erratic for casual conversation. She often found herself wishing that she had someone that could just sit down and chat with besides Pinkie. The little snicker was a good listener, but any conversation with him was one-sided. She couldn't remember the last time that she had laughed or joked with anyone.

"I notice that you're not carrying the dragon staff," said Cooper. "Are you having trouble using it? Sometimes it takes a while for a talisman to acclimate to a new user. Heaven knows what damage Marcus may have done to it."

"No, I'm not having any problems with it, though I am still testing its limits. I just find it a little clunky to carry around when I'm here at the castle. I keep knocking things over with it. I do have the amberstone that Susan gave me, and I'm a bit more comfortable using that. I know that the staff is the symbol of my position, and I did take it with me when I met with King Marinus."

"How was the meeting with the king?" asked Cooper.

"Oh...the usual. I thanked him for his generosity in providing and maintaining the hall. I promised to keep him abreast of anything that might be a threat or concern, including anything that we discover today. His valet kept the audience short. King Marinus's health seemed to have deteriorated noticeably since the last time I was here. He was very anxious to see Susan, though. He perked up considerably when I mentioned that the two of you were here."

"Yes, he is very taken with Susan. He's even polite to me when she's here. Ashley told us at lunch that he's had a few bad spells. He is over one hundred years old. Even elves don't live forever. Ashley could become queen sometime soon. How are the two of you getting along?"

"Our official relationship as princess to orcanus is excellent. She's been generous, courteous, and always reasonable. She'll make a good queen. I believe that she's already dealing with many of the day to day responsibilities.

"But our relationship as woman to woman is still a bit...strained. I have to admit that some of that is my fault. I spent years hating her and blaming her for my mother's death. Some days it's a real struggle to keep that old anger from creeping back into my thoughts. We both adore Susan and Bodkin, but I

28

think Ashley's a little jealous of me where you're concerned. Not as a rival for your affection, but I think she believes that, if not for me, you could be persuaded to become the orcanus and come live at the castle. You do, of course, know that she'd take you as her consort in a heartbeat."

"Yes, I know," answered Cooper with a smile. "We seem to be everyone's favorite topic to gossip about. We've talked about it many times. I admit that I do have some old feelings for the princess, but I have no real desire to marry again. Besides, I like being the guardian. This world is wonderful, amazing, and sometimes incredibly dangerous, but the human world is my home. Susan and her mother Elana, Mina, and Cookie, they're all my family. I could never leave them behind. And I love the quiet of my workshop. I find working with my hands to be very soothing and therapeutic. There aren't very many individuals that pass through the portal these days, but most of them that do use it are old acquaintances. They stop for a short time and keep me abreast of any important news. I'm very comfortable there."

"I think I understand, and I envy you. I remember the solitude of my little cabin at the edge of the Dark Woods. I do miss those late nights sitting in Quisp's pub, listening to him tell of all the local events. He really was an excellent storyteller."

"Yes, he certainly was. I think of him often."

"And he always had that wonderful chocolate."

"Oh, yes. Susan brought some along for you. Don't let her forget to give it to you."

"Oh, I certainly won't forget that."

They turned at a slight bend in the trail, and the trees parted in front of them. The glade was almost round and about fifty yards from one end to the other. Cooper crossed to the center and removed the book from the backpack. He carefully laid it on the soft grass and moved back twenty yards.

Cooper held his staff and Shirell brought out the amberstone from beneath her tunic. Both were glowing blue, prepared for any surprises, as Cooper opened the small leather-bound journal that he had recovered from Marcus's possessions and slowly began to read the incantation that Marcus had promised would neutralize the books defenses.

As Cooper read the first few words, a faint glow began to emanate from the book, and they could feel the vibrations through the grass of the clearing. As he continued, the light became increasingly brighter, and the shaking became more violent. A cold wind suddenly swirled through the center of the clearing, buffeting the leaves on the trees. The instant that the last word was read, the book's cover violently flew open as if caught by the wind, and the light was immediately sucked back into the book by a swirling vortex emanating from within its pages. In a flash, the light vanished, and the book lay still.

A full five minutes passed as the two watched the book carefully before attempting to approach it. Up close, it looked very much like any other old book, except the pages were blank. Nothing but old parchment, slightly yellowed at the edges, completely devoid of any writing or symbols. There was no trace of the violent reaction that opening the book had unleashed. It appeared to be exactly as Marcus had described it. The book only contained a handful of pages, and initially they flipped through them quickly to be sure that none of them possessed any text or markings. Then they went back and slowly inspected each page carefully and thoroughly. They held it up to the light, delicately ran their fingers over the old parchment, and finally probed it with magic. They could find no trace of runes or writing of any kind. Not the slightest imprint from pen or stylus, nothing but empty pages.

"I certainly don't trust Marcus," commented Cooper. "But it appears that everything he told us was accurate. There just isn't anything to be found on any of these pages."

"Yes, I'm very suspicious of Marcus giving us any information so easily," Shirell agreed. "There must be something that we're missing, but I don't think that we're going to find it here. As much as I hate the idea, I'm afraid that we're going to have to go back and try to talk to him again. He'll likely be even less cooperative now that you've beaten him at chess. I have no doubt that he'll gloat over the fact that we didn't find anything and had to come back to him again."

"It was a calculated risk. If we're lucky, his anger and his ego will work to our advantage and he'll be just arrogant enough to let something slip."

"I hope you're right. Either way, we need to start back. It's been almost an hour and the guards will come looking for us soon."

"You're right, we better get moving." Cooper closed the book and carefully returned it to the backpack. "We'll have to lock this back in the archive room until we can talk to Marcus again."

The side door opened immediately upon their first knock. The guard was a seasoned veteran of the Gremlin Wars and remembered Cooper from long ago.

"It's good that you returned when you did, Guardian. I was just about to gather some men and come looking for you."

"No need for that, old friend. Our trip was rather fruitless. Thank you for waiting here."

"It was my duty, Sir. While you were out there, word came

of a dragon approaching from the north. I thought that you would want to know."

"Prax is here? Oh, that could be the best news of the day. He may be able to tell us something helpful about our book. C'mon, Shirell, it's time that the last of the dragons met the new orcanus."

Cooper started down the hallway at a lively clip, leaving Shirell scrambling to keep up with his long-legged stride.

Chapter 5

After returning the book to its vault in the basement, Cooper and Shirell exited the castle only to be caught up in a wave of curious onlookers heading for the north gate. There was great excitement. The opportunity to see a live dragon in the flesh didn't happen often. The story of Prax's imprisonment had been widely told, but few had had the chance to see him the last time he was at the castle. Many of the younger elves had heard the ancient tales of dragons but had never seen one. Those old enough to remember the Gremlin Wars were anxious to see the mighty Prax who had won the final battle that ended the war.

Prax swooped in low over the trees and landed gently in the open area outside the north gate. From his vantage point at the rear of the crowd, Cooper marveled once again at the fact that anything as large as Prax could move so gracefully.

The sunlight glistened off his scales, and the crowd was frozen in place as they stared in awe at the magnificent creature. Finally, curiosity got the better of a small girl near the front of the crowd, and she took a step forward. Her mother instinctively reached to pull her back when Prax spoke.

"Please, let the child approach," he said. The dragon turned his massive head toward the girl. He spoke in a voice that was calm and soothing, not what one would expect from a creature so large. "Come forward, little one, and touch my scales, stroke my wings if you wish. You have nothing to fear from me."

The crowd watched, spellbound, as the girl walked up to Prax with the fearlessness that only a child possesses and touched him on the snout.

"Would you be kind enough to reach under my chin and scratch the small scales of my neck?"

The girl giggled as she did what she was asked.

Prax made a sound that was almost like a cat purring. "Oh, that feels wonderful. What is your name, child?"

"Miri," answered the girl.

"Thank you, Miri. Will you do something else for me? Go back to your mother and tell the people in the crowd that they may come forward if they wish, but please be careful of my tail as sometimes it twitches on its own and I can't always see if anyone is near."

Miri nodded, then ran back to her mother and repeated, word for word, what Prax had told her to say. She was grinning from ear to ear as she took her mother's hand and led the crowd toward the dragon.

Shirell was about to start forward with the crowd when Cooper touched her arm. He directed her to an old stump near the edge of the field.

"Come and sit down," said Cooper, as he pulled two small pieces of fruit from his pocket and handed one to Shirell. "Let the crowd have a few minutes. Marcus and the Boc book aren't going anywhere, and I believe Prax is enjoying the attention."

Twenty minutes later, as many of the curious were beginning to disperse and return to their daily routines, Cooper rose and started forward. Those that remained began to move away out of respect as the guardian and the orcanus were recognized. Little Miri was climbing on Prax's shoulder.

When Miri's mother saw Shirell wearing the insignia of

the orcanus, she quickly tried to collect the child. Prax, who had been aware of Cooper and Shirell's presence the whole time, spoke to the girl's mother.

"Stay just a moment, woman, I wish to speak to young Miri before you go."

The young mother lifted Miri down from her perch and brought her forward to face Prax.

"Miri, I have something for you, but I need my friend Cooper to help me get it." The dragon directed his attention to the approaching Cooper. "Guardian, I have a loose tooth. Second from the left, on the bottom. Could you pluck it out and give it to young Miri for me?"

Prax opened his huge jaws. Cooper, Shirell and a handful of others from the crowd could have stood upright in his cavernous mouth. With a bit of wiggling, Cooper was able to remove the loose tooth as instructed. After wiping it clean with his hand, Cooper gently handed it to the child.

"Use both hands and hold it carefully from underneath so it doesn't drop."

"Ooo...A tooth," said Miri, with a huge smile. She turned to her mother. "Look mama, a dragon's tooth!"

The girl's mother curtsied low. "My lord Prax, you are far too generous."

"Nonsense, woman, it's just an old tooth. Miri, do you know who Princess Ashley is?"

The child nodded. "Yes, she's very beautiful."

"Yes, she is. I'll tell you a secret. She's in love with our friend Cooper here."

Cooper's face flushed red as Miri oohed and grinned up at him, but he said nothing.

"Now, I fear that I've embarrassed the guardian, but we are old friends, so I'm sure that he'll forgive me. Now, I need you to do something special with that tooth. Have you seen the necklace that the princess wears for special occasions, the one with the white pendant in the center?"

"Uh-huh, it's pretty."

"It was made for her by a friend of mine. A gnome artisan named Bartus. He is very skilled and will be traveling here soon to sell some of his work. When he comes, I want your mother to give him this tooth, and he will make for you a pendant like the one that belongs to the princess. He'll make it a little different than the princess's so that it will be special just for you. Then everyone who sees it will know that you are my new friend."

"I would like that. Thank you." Miri did a little curtsy as her mother had earlier.

"You're welcome, Miri." Prax turned his attention to the young mother and spoke quietly to her. "When Bartus arrives here, seek him out, give him the tooth and have him make the child a pendant as I've instructed. He will know what I want and will only need a small portion of the tooth to do that. Tell him to give you fair price for the remainder of the tooth. He is a shrewd businessman and will make a sizable profit from what remains. But he can sometimes be too shrewd for his own good, so be sure to remind him that if he does not give you it's proper value, I will learn of it and he will be sorry for his actions. Now, you should probably take Miri home. I think that she's had enough excitement for one day."

"I will do everything exactly as you've asked. Thank you, Lord Prax. You are too kind. Thank you again," said the young woman as she scooped up the girl who was hugging the tooth like it was her favorite doll and carried her homeward.

"You are an old scoundrel, Prax," said Cooper, as the young woman headed for the castle gates. "Starting rumors about me and the princess. And, of course, you said it loud enough for all to hear."

"Those rumors have been around for many years, my friend," Prax answered with a devilish grin.

"And they don't need your help to keep them alive. But you're right, I will forgive you because giving the girl your tooth was an extremely generous thing to do, old friend."

"Bah...it's nothing but an old tooth. It would have fallen out soon and been lost."

"We both know better than that. Years ago, dragon teeth became valuable for their ivory, but the supply has been exhausted since the end of the war. Now that you are the only one of your kind left, dragon ivory has become priceless. That tooth is worth a small fortune. And you, of course, knew that."

"So I did," answered Prax, with a chuckle. "Wealth is of no use to me, but I do still keep abreast of what goes on in this land. Young Miri's father died in an accident a few months ago. The money they receive for that tooth will allow her mother to support her comfortably until she is a young woman. Could you suggest a better use for an old tooth?"

"I cannot. You are kind and wise, my friend," said Cooper, as he turned toward Shirell. "Let me introduce..."

"The new orcanus, of course. Prax Dragonus, at your service, m'lady. Your name is Shirell. Our friend Cooper is getting up in years, and perhaps he has forgotten that we've met before. I was present when your mother and the elf, Quisp, were laid to rest."

Cooper scowled at the dragon, but did not respond.

"I could never forget that," said Shirell. "You have my sincerest thanks. You showed them both great honor, and I did not have the opportunity to thank you at that time."

"There was no need, m'lady. It was my privilege. Only barbarians do not honor their dead. I did mention that very little goes on in this land that I don't hear of. When I learned that you had an interesting artifact that I may be able to help you with, I returned from my search for more of my kind to offer my assistance."

"Have you had any success in your search?" asked Cooper.

"None so far, but I have not abandoned hope just yet," answered Prax. "But, please, tell me of your artifact."

For the next twenty minutes, Cooper carefully relayed all that had happened since the discovery of the book: Lady Coramina's violent attack of nausea, their own initial examination of the book and subsequent meeting with Marcus, Marcus's revelation that the book was of Boc origin and that he possessed the key to unlocking the book, and finally their opening of the book to find nothing but blank pages, exactly as Marcus had described.

Prax listened attentively, his eyes never blinking, until Cooper finished detailing all their experiences with the book. Then he spoke. "I fear that my ability to help you is limited. I remember the Boc. They were not friendly toward my kind, but neither were they unfriendly. We shared a mutual dislike of gremlins, but they kept their distance, as they did with most others. When they vanished, I found it odd that there seemed to be no trace of them, but beyond that, I paid them little heed. I confess that I know very little about runes and the symbols used in writing. Much of my knowledge comes from centuries of observing the races. But I do recall someone who may be able to help you. One who thrives on information. His name is Crall."

"Crall? The Lurker of Ramses Marsh? I haven't heard that name since before the war. Does he still exist?"

"I'm not certain that he can die," said Prax, with a nod. "He was ancient when I was a mere hatchling. But he does still live. Of that, I am certain."

"Wait a minute. A lurker?" interrupted Shirell. "When I was a child, my mother told me frightening stories about the lurker. But when I got old enough to question the stories, she admitted that they were all made up just to scare children into listening to their parents."

Prax cocked his head and looked at her curiously. "Oh, the lurker is quite real, though he doesn't actually kidnap badly behaved children and cook them in a large stew pot. Usually, he just eats their brains and leaves what's left of them by the side of the road."

"Prax is kidding," interrupted Cooper as Prax flashed a devious grin. "Crall doesn't eat children, or anyone else. No one actually knows what he eats, or much else about him except that he really is a lurker. When I trained with the Guild, they knew of his existence, but little else. I'll admit, I thought that he must have died decades ago, and I had completely forgotten about him. But Prax, Crall was always known to speak in riddles. Can he be relied on to tell us the truth?"

"His information is often confusing, but always accurate. Getting any information from him is the difficult part. And he will always demand payment."

"So the stories have said. I'm not sure what we could offer him in payment, but if he has knowledge of the Boc, it could be worth our time. I doubt that Marcus is going to willingly offer us any more help than he already has, but if the lurker can give us something useful, we may be able use that information to coerce Marcus into revealing what he's hiding. I'm sure that just the idea of us talking to Crall will serve to anger Marcus. It'll take a good portion of a day's ride on horseback to reach the marsh. If you think that it's worth our trouble, Shirell, I'll have the princess make arrangements."

"By all means, I'd like to meet this Crall. If he is a source of hidden knowledge, his help may be invaluable. At the moment, we know Marcus is a dead end, so we have nowhere else to proceed. If Crall can offer us even a glimmer of information, it'll be a starting point. And even if he can't help us much now, there may be times in the future when I will have need of his knowledge."

"Be careful what you wish for, Orcanus," warned Prax. "Crall is not one to be taken lightly. Making a deal with a lurker may cost you far more than you bargained for."

"Thank you, Prax," Shirell answered. "I did not mean to dismiss him so casually. I'll try to remember your warning and chose my words carefully when we meet him, but we know that it's risky to trust Marcus, and I can't ignore the possibility that the book still holds some hidden danger. I think that we have little choice but to go see the lurker."

Cooper nodded in agreement. "It's settled then. I'll talk to Ashley."

Chapter 6

The journey to Ramses Marsh was planned for the next day. Cooper's original idea was for him and Shirell to go alone. Ashley's duties and the king's health required the princess's presence at the castle. But the instant Susan and Bodkin were told about the trek to speak with the lurker, they demanded to come along. Cooper tried to convince Susan that she was supposed to be on a quiet vacation and that they should remain behind and enjoy the hospitality at the castle, but she wouldn't hear of it. After enduring a twenty-minute onslaught from the two girls, he finally relented and agreed to allow them to accompany him.

It was mid-afternoon before the princess was able to seek out Cooper. She found him sitting alone on a small bench in the corner of the courtyard, idly nibbling on a piece of fruit while quietly watching the preparation of the supplies and horses. When he saw her approaching, he motioned for her to sit down next to him.

She handed him a small drawstring pouch. "I brought you a bag of silver to offer as payment to the lurker."

"Thank you. I'm not sure if Crall has any use for money, but it's best to take it along. I'll see that it's returned to you if he doesn't accept it."

Ashley had already been told of the girls' insistence on

being included in Cooper's trek to the marsh.

"Susan and Bodkin are both smart girls, and there's very little chance of any danger where you're going. They really shouldn't be any trouble."

"Oh, I know that. It's the main reason that I finally agreed to let them come. I just thought that it would be faster if Shirell and I went alone. Were you as persistent as those two when you were a teenager?" he asked.

"I think that I was probably worse," answered Ashley, with a mischievous grin. "I was a princess, in case you've forgotten. There were a few rude people who dared to suggest that I was a bit headstrong back then. I had them thrown in the dungeon, of course."

"Well, of course. I'm certain that you were completely justified."

"Father didn't think so. He had them all released."

Ashley placed her hand over Cooper's as they shared a laugh. He remembered a time when Ashley was not so quick to make jokes at her own expense.

"You could come with us. The girls are already coming, and you won't slow us down."

"You do know that you're never going to win me over offering to spend time with me when you know I can't come. I wish I could, but with my father's health as it is, I have to remain here. Chancellor Adronis tries to seize control of the High Council every time my father has a bad spell. He already has half of them in his back pocket. If something happens to Father and I'm not here, I'm sure that he'll try to have himself declared king in my absence."

"Could he get away with that? The chancellor's not a part of the royal family."

"Not by blood, but he was married to my Aunt Zaneth, so

42

he'll try to make the claim that he's in the line of succession, and most of the council members are too spineless to stand up to him on their own. His ambition knows no limits. That's one of the reasons that Zaneth finally left him."

"Yes, can't say I blamed her. I remember meeting him once or twice. Didn't like him much. Too slick, even for a politician. I could easily picture him patting you on the shoulder an instant before sticking a long knife between your ribs."

"You're absolutely right to think that, and if you should meet him again while you're here, be careful what you say. He has his spies watching everything."

"I was sure that I saw someone following me earlier."

"You did. Korin reported to me that you were being watched. Adronis isn't the only one with spies."

"But why would he care about me? Until recently, I was banished, and I don't even live in this world."

"Isn't it obvious? You were a hero of the Gremlin Wars. You're respected among magic users. You were married to one princess and you're friendly with another. Everyone knows our history together. In his mind, that puts you in front of him in the line of succession."

"Yes, I can see where someone with his ambition would think that. I'm beginning to remember why I don't like politics, but I did always like your aunt. They certainly were a mismatched pair. Where did she go?"

"North, she lives by herself in a small cabin on the outskirts of a tiny farming village. She's become a bit of a recluse. I try contacting her from time to time to invite her to some gathering or special event, but she never responds."

The princess's smile turned serious. "I should go check on Father before dinner, but before I go, there is one other thing that I do need to ask you about."

"I promise you that I'm not interested in Shirell, if that's what you're worried about."

"Oh, I know that. This is something far more important. It concerns the eye of Bangor Khan," Ashley said quietly. "The eye's been lost for many years."

"Yes, that's right," answered Cooper with a nod.

"Yet, even now, Marcus is absolutely convinced that you know where it is. Why does my uncle think that you, of all people, have it?"

Cooper sighed "Because somehow he has discovered that I'm the person who made it disappear. He may just be guessing, but he's pretty firm in his belief that I have it. Almost as if someone told him. Years ago, Eldred gave it to me for safe keeping. I've been hiding it in the human world for years. We agreed that was the safest place for it. It was actually your sister Anna's idea. She felt that it was her duty as princess to protect your world. It's essentially harmless in my world where no one practices magic, but it's just too dangerous an object to remain here where it could be used to unlock the Barrier. Even the castle vault isn't secure enough to protect it. If Marcus managed to break into the vault and steal the dragon staff, the eye certainly would have been next. We felt that if no one believes that it still exists, then no one has any reason to look for it. Even old Horus thinks that it was lost."

"And you didn't trust me enough to tell me?" Mild irritation crept into Ashley's voice.

"Of course I trust you, but Eldred swore me to secrecy before he disappeared. We didn't even tell your father, the king. It was absolutely essential that no one in this world knew the fate of the eye. If you knew, there was always a slim chance that someone could force it out of you. Elana is the only other living soul who knows that I have it and, for her own safety, I've never told her where it is. I don't know how Marcus could have found out that it still exists or that I have it. I originally thought that when he went through the Gnome Door and ransacked my workshop, he was trying to steal my amberstone, but now I'm sure that he was looking for the eye.

"Eldred went to great lengths to maintain the secret of the eye's location. He never would have written anything down, so the only other option is that he was somehow forced to tell someone. Could he have been captured and tortured to reveal his secrets? Or perhaps tricked into telling someone? I just can't believe that that's possible. No one could get that or any other information from him against his will. He was just too strong to be forced and too smart to be fooled. The problem is that we've never been able to discover what happened to him. I have a few more questions for the lurker than just those concerning our mysterious book."

"Do you think he knows Eldred's fate?"

"If anyone in this world knows, it would be Crall. Whether he'll tell us or not...?" Cooper shrugged as he left the question hanging.

Chapter 7

Al-Ron banged his fist on the table in frustration. He had poured over the volume before him a thousand times. The Codex Stygia, the mystic book that contained glimpses of magical secrets, tantalized him with its elusiveness. It offered up tidbits of information if one just had the patience to unscramble them. After twenty years, he was certain that he had only uncovered a fraction of what the book contained.

As the last of the Boc, heir to the dark magic and its mysteries, and the only remaining descendant of the original shadow mages, this book should have been his. The Codex Stygia was one of the artifacts entrusted to the Boc for safekeeping many years ago. The old Guild Hall, along with its library, had been destroyed years ago, so books of magic were very rare, and this particular volume was the only one of its kind. That made it valuable. So valuable that, years ago, one of his clan had broken his blood oath, stolen the book from its hiding place, and sold it. Al-Ron had been forced to spend many years searching for it. He had been incredibly fortunate and finally reacquired it. The book had come into his possession indirectly, compliments of a petty thief named Carel. Without Carel's intervention, the book would have almost certainly wound up locked away in the vaults of Kestriana.

Carel was a simple street urchin who had no idea of the

book's true value or content. He had stolen it simply because he had overheard the book's most recent owner, a traveling merchant who had consumed too much ale, confessing to the barman at the pub that he had recently acquired an ancient book of magic and was hoping to sell it for a considerable profit at Kestriana, the castle of the elf king. A good thief always keeps his ears open for an opportunity, and clearly the merchant deserved to have the book taken away from him due to his carelessness and loose tongue.

Carel figured that he could make use of the profits from the sale of the book just as well as the merchant, and the man had already been kind enough to suggest where he might find a potential buyer. With a bit of luck, someone at the castle might offer him a good price. At the very least, he had hoped to get enough money to cover some of his outstanding tab at the pub before they cut him off and refused to allow him in the door. In the last few years, Carel had come to enjoy the creature comforts of a hearty meal, a warm bed, and a full tankard of ale. Sadly, innkeepers were not known for their charity and insisted on being paid.

Carel was a good thief. Taking the book from a drunken merchant was child's play, but sadly, planning and forethought were not always Carel's strongest points. Once he had stolen the book, he quickly came to the realization that the merchant might report the theft and that his face was known to most of the guards at the castle. Should he try selling the book openly, it was very likely that one of them might become suspicious and call over the captain of the guard, who would undoubtedly ask some rather difficult questions about where a simple street rat like him had acquired this unusual and extremely rare volume.

The captain was not someone to be trifled with. You don't get to be captain of the guard by being gullible. His reputation was not one of forgiveness and understanding. He could see through a lie just by looking at you, and if he wanted to know the truth, he would certainly "persuade" you to tell it. Carel constantly lamented the fact that everywhere he went, he was forced to deal with "unkind" people and their lack of trust in him.

Perhaps a safer course of action would be to accept a smaller return for his efforts and avoid the risk. So, he put feelers out among some of his more discreet connections. Surely, someone local would be interested in such a rare commodity without asking any bothersome questions. Word quickly reached Lord Adronis at Kestriana, who recognized the book's origins and took the necessary steps to acquire it and get it into Al-Ron's hands.

Al-Ron disliked dealing with Adronis, even if he was secretly a descendant of the Boc clan. He especially disliked being indebted to the man. Any favor from Adronis would need to be repaid tenfold. The devil himself was less demanding.

To most of the world, Adronis was the fiery councilor who, over the years had become the outspoken voice of the Elven High Council and who had swept the king's sister, Lady Zaneth, off her feet. But behind the facade, the man was a snake who would gladly sell out his own mother if it furthered his political ambitions.

Sadly, on the evening that Al-Ron received the book, Carel met with an untimely accident. Sneaking into the city of the elves always posed a certain amount of risk for Al-Ron. Though the Boc were one of the ancient clans of the elves, his green eyes and red hair were a sharp contrast to the blond, blue eyed features of most elves. Younger elves might be unfamiliar with the old clans, but if his face were seen by anyone old enough to remember the Gremlin War, he would instantly be recognized as one of the Boc, who most believed no longer existed. Coming here, in the very shadow of the castle Kestriana, especially to do some dirty little job like disposing of Carel, put him at great risk of exposure, but he didn't like leaving loose ends.

No point in taking the chance that Carel might make the same foolish mistake as the merchant. Tongues can loosen after one too many glasses of ale. He might mention the book's theft, or more importantly, who he sold it to, sometime when the wrong ears were listening. When Carel's body was found, it would be assumed that he got dead drunk, passed out, fell face first into a water-filled ditch, and drowned. There would be no marks or bruises on the body, nothing to indicate foul play.

Near the back of the castle, Al-Ron knew that he would find an inconspicuous door. A door normally used only by the servants. It would be unlocked, and the corridors and stairwells of the castle would be empty and silent. He was expected. Adronis's quarters were on the second floor. The chancellor was pacing back and forth like a cat watching the door as Al-Ron silently emerged from the hidden entrance behind the tapestry.

"The thief will trouble you no more."

Adronis spun on his heel, startled at Al-Ron's voice.

"No one will miss him," responded Adronis, quickly regaining his composure. "Well, perhaps the few tavern owners that he owed money to. Of course, they will all assume that he was just another vagabond who ran off to avoid paying his tab. How did you...?"

"Know about your little secret escape route?" answered Al-Ron. "I'm not as big a fool as our friend, Marcus. Besides, I wanted to be sure that you weren't waiting behind the door, hoping to stick a knife between my ribs as I entered."

"I find your lack of trust, shall we say, insulting."

"Save your outrage for others, Chancellor. The graveyards

are full of people who've trusted you."

"And you've just come from murdering a man who stumbled into more than he bargained for. We both know that you would not hesitate to do the same to me if you thought it was warranted. Both of us have blood on our hands."

"True, but I kill discretely and only when necessary. I'm not responsible for the needless death of thousands of innocents during the Gremlin War. I don't engage in wholesale slaughter just to further my ambitions."

"Watch your tongue, sorcerer!"

"Why?" sneered Al-Ron. "What will you do? Have me killed? No one knows where to find me, and I can count on one hand the people who know that I even exist. And you would have to admit to your association with a practitioner of dark magic, which has been strictly outlawed. Need I remind you that Bog, leader of the gremlins, holds a sealed message that will be hand delivered to the king of the elves if I do not contact him by the allotted time each month or if he should receive word of my demise?

"The letter is part of an agreement that I was, shall we say, required to make years ago. Bog believes that the letter contains my confession, stating that I tricked the gremlin leaders into a war that they couldn't win and that his people were not to blame for. Members of Bog's family have been kept imprisoned by the elves to ensure the lasting peace. He seeks their release, and the letter would help his cause. The only reason that he has not double crossed me and delivered it is that he fears me far more than he fears the elves.

"But we both know that he is mistaken. The letter in his possession actually details all of your treachery during the war. How you were the true architect of the Gremlin War, secretly working with Marcus, the self-proclaimed shadow mage, to

51

sabotage the elves defenses. It explains in great detail, how, if the war had gone the other way, if Marcus and the gremlins had succeeded in defeating your brother-in-law, King Marinus, that you had a plan in place to murder Marcus, leaving the gremlins leaderless, disorganized and ripe for the slaughter.

"Then, as a former captain of the forest wardens, you would rally the elves, lead the counter attack against the gremlins, backed by your secret corps of elite soldiers. Once you had butchered every gremlin, down to the last female and child, you would have yourself proclaimed hero of the elf nation and, ultimately, ascend to the throne.

"If I die, all that you've done will be revealed. You will be arrested, tried, and executed. To the elves, there is no higher crime than treason, as you well know. Your body will be hung on a stake for the birds to peck at. Even your marriage to the king's sister won't save you."

"Enough!" snarled Adronis. "You have reminded me of all of this many times in the past. I have not forgotten. As one of the Boc, you of all people should understand that the stain that is the gremlin race needs to be wiped from the land. Only when every last one of those foul creatures is dead, their corpses rotting in the sun, can the Boc be avenged for the murder of hundreds of our clan. The flaw in your plan is that Marinus must remain king and cannot die, though that could likely happen any day. An assassin or an unfortunate accident could, perhaps, befall him. Then I am directly in line to be king and your letter would be hand delivered to me, never to be read by another soul."

"Then you must hope that Marinus's good fortune fails him," said Al-Ron. "I'm certain that if his personal staff wasn't so dedicated, you would have tried poisoning him long ago."

Al-Ron picked up the book from the table and, in its place, dropped the bag of coins that Adronis had given the unfortunate thief as payment.

"I've only come here to retrieve the book that was rightfully mine, return your gold, and assure you that the deed is done. It is goodnight, Chancellor."

Al-Ron slipped the volume inside his tunic, turned on his heel, and left the way he had come, thinking to himself that at some time in the future, he would need to rid himself of his association with Adronis. But for the moment, the chancellor was still useful.

Chapter 8

Twenty years later, Marinus was still king, Adronis was still scheming and Al-Ron had more important things to concern himself with than elven politics.

He had poured over the Codex Stygia endlessly until he knew every word by heart. But knowing the words and understanding their meaning were two very different things. It had taken him months to unravel some of the journal's quatrains, the cryptic four-line poems that made up the first half of the Codex.

Al-Ron had been patient and persistent, and his perseverance had eventually been rewarded. The risks he had taken to gain the book were proving to be justified. He had cracked bits and pieces of the code. Hidden in passages that could only have been penned by a madman, he had discovered things that were unheard of in any other text.

The book didn't contain actual spells, but information. Ways to strengthen his magic. Methods and talismans that doubled the effect of spells. Hidden weaknesses in certain magics and ways to render them ineffective. Although it was buried behind riddles and wrapped in the ravings of a lunatic, one of the secrets that he had managed to decipher was that of the dragon sleep, the regenerating hibernation that dragons could employ to aid them in recovering from devastating injuries. That bit of knowledge helped explain Prax's mysterious disappearance after defeating the lindworm and effectively ending the Gremlin War. It also gave him the clues necessary to have Marcus search for and imprison the sleeping dragon. The creature could have been destroyed and its threat to his power eliminated permanently if Marcus hadn't been such a coward.

Even more importantly, the quatrains had told him of the eye of Bangor Khan, an object steeped in legend and one of the things that Al-Ron desired more than anything else in the world. This incredibly powerful artifact could, when activated, neutralize all magic within its reach. With it in his possession, he could, if he so wished, tear down the Barrier and release a horde of demons on the world. Or hold the entire world to ransom by just threatening to open the Barrier. The powers attributed to the eye were widely known, and his patience had revealed some of the origins of the artifact, how it came to be, and clues as to how a new one could possibly be fashioned.

But the book couldn't tell him that one bit of information that he desperately wanted to know — the fate of the eye. Over the years, many had come to believe that the eye never really existed, but he knew that it had. The archives had confirmed it many times over. The most common story was that, like Eldred, it had been lost without a trace. Many assumed that Eldred had it in his possession when he vanished. Al-Ron knew that to also be wrong.

Marcus had repeatedly claimed that the eye still existed and that Cooper, the guardian of the Gnome Door, possessed it. In spite of his many assurances, Marcus had been woefully unsuccessful in retrieving it or even confirming its existence. Marcus used the title shadow mage and fancied himself to be one, but he was a pale imitation of the old order.

While his search for the eye continued, the other main

source of Al-Ron's frustration was his inability to discover any clues regarding the source of this book. Beyond the name Darkon Rhee, there was nothing. He had hoped that the book would finally give him some of the answers he desired, but it contained nothing regarding the author.

His search for Darkon Rhee had been going on for years He had studied everything ever written about the Guild of Conjurers and its members, tracing lineages back a number of generations. He had read every dusty old parchment, scribbled by ancient scribes, until his eyes started to cross. He knew all of them in great detail. If one of them had broken from the Guild and adopted a new name, or fathered a new blood line of conjurers, he would be able to determine who it was. But, in all his studies, that name Darkon Rhee was only mentioned in one other place, the Boc Passages, and there, only to say that Eldred feared him gaining all the secrets that he had collected. With Marcus's help, Al-Ron had secretly scoured all of the volumes and chronicles in the archives. He yearned to know everything he could about this elusive wizard and his magic.

Why did Eldred fear him, and did he still live? How could any wizard acquire knowledge enough to frighten Eldred, yet still manage to stay hidden and escape the notice of all the other magic wielders? Any unauthorized use of magic should have been immediately detected by the Guild. They had members whose sole purpose was to search for magic wielders outside the Guild.

Use of magic took a toll on its users, and the stronger the magic, the greater the toll. Did the magic drive him mad? It was hard to imagine that any sane person could have penned the Codex Stygia.

The final section of the Codex held no quatrains, but was written more in the style of a diary or journal. And for every entry that was lucid and rational, the next was raving and nearly incoherent. They focused exclusively on Eldred's puzzle box, the ultimate artifact, or so it claimed. Darkon Rhee was obsessed with stealing it away from Eldred. Possession of it was his all-consuming passion. How Darkon Rhee discovered the contents of the box was never revealed but, according to his journal entries, he believed that it held the key to both Eldred's power and immortality. And anyone opening the box could claim both.

Eldred clearly must have known of Darkon Rhee and made his own plans to thwart and neutralize the dark wizard. Before he disappeared, Eldred told the leaders of the Boc where to find the puzzle box and charged them with hiding both it and the captured Codex Stygia. The Boc swore a blood oath that, once hidden, they would guard that location. As the last of the Boc, Al-Ron already knew where the puzzle box was hidden. But Eldred had surrounded the box with magic so strong that Al-Ron could not break through.

Eldred was thought to be the most powerful wizard ever, and it was widely believed by everyone except Al-Ron that he had disappeared from all the lands without a trace. Eldred may have been the leader of the Guild, but he didn't share all of his secrets with them. Secrets like the presence of Darkon Rhee and that he intended to confront him. This mysterious conjurer would have had to be very powerful if he had managed to either destroy Eldred or imprison him in his own trap.

Al-Ron was convinced that the box held the key to Eldred's true fate. Did he seal himself in the box just to escape Darkon Rhee? Would he discover that the two wizards destroyed each other, leaving the box empty? Al-Ron's rage would be uncontrollable if he found that he had been cheated out of his prize and had been guarding an empty vessel all these years, though that would explain Rhee's disappearance. Eldred vanished just before the Gremlin Wars, and the Guild was destroyed shortly thereafter. Even the dragon, Prax, had disappeared from the lands. If Darkon Rhee did survive, there would have been no one left to oppose him after that, so it would seem unnecessary for him to continue to remain hidden.

The only other explanation was that Darkon Rhee had been severely injured in his confrontation with Eldred and had gone into hiding. If he had avoided the Guild for so long, there was little doubt that he could vanish again. If he could be found alive and sane, perhaps he could be turned into an ally. He obviously would have no love for the new Guild, and the enemy of my enemy could be my friend. Marcus was no longer of any use to Al-Ron. He had been helpful in his role as an insider to the elf castle, but help could be found in other places and, since being discovered and imprisoned, Marcus was little more than a liability now. Just another loose end that needed tying up. Sometime soon, Al-Ron would have to address that little problem as well.

But only by opening the puzzle box would Al-Ron find the answers he desired and, more importantly, the power and immortality that he craved.

Chapter 9

Cooper and the girls were just finishing breakfast when Korin approached and spoke quietly to Cooper.

"All your supplies have been loaded and secured, Guardian. I've arranged for the horses to be brought to the west gate when you are ready to depart."

"Thank you, Korin. We should not be long."

"Wouldn't it be faster to use the north gate, Grandfather?" asked Susan, as Korin turned to go.

"A simple precaution, Miss Susan," Korin responded before Cooper had a chance to answer. "Very few people know the purpose of your journey. We thought it safer to keep it that way. We have always had lingering suspicions that the shadow mage may have had confederates in the castle. So as far as anyone outside this small group knows, you are just going off for a few days of riding and enjoying the countryside. That story reinforces the idea that your presence here at Kestriana is just a friendly visit."

With that, Korin nodded and headed out the door, passing the orcanus as she entered the room.

"Good morning," said Shirell as Susan and Bodkin warmly embraced her. Both girls had taken to treating Shirell like their favorite aunt.

"We're so glad that you agreed to let us come along," said

Bodkin.

"Hey, don't I get any credit?" asked Cooper, pretending to be slighted.

"Yes, of course, Grandfather. Thank you," said Susan as she gave him a quick peck on the cheek. "Are we ready to go?"

"Almost. Shirell and I need to check on the book, and I'd like you two to go back to your rooms to see if there's anything you've forgotten. We'll meet you at the west gate in thirty minutes."

"Okay," both girl said in unison.

They had only taken two steps down the hall before Bodkin yelled "Race ya!" and took off at a run.

"Hey, no fair takin' a head start," yelled Susan as she dashed after her.

Cooper and Shirell turned and started down the hall in the opposite direction toward the archive room. One last check to be sure that the book was secure before leaving. They had agreed that the mystic book should stay behind, safely locked away until they returned.

"You have the sketches?" asked Shirell.

"Yes, Cora showed them to me last night and Korin personally oversaw them being loaded."

Rather than risk taking the book, one of Cora's assistants had hand drawn a set of sketches that meticulously reproduced the runes covering the face of the book. They had been carefully wrapped in oilskin to protect them and were currently secured in Cooper's backpack.

They found the archive room exactly as they had left it, and after taking a moment to check the lock, Cooper turned to leave.

"One minute, before we go," said Shirell. With a wave of her hand and three words spoken in a language that few besides

62

Cooper would recognize, a blue glow appeared around the doorway only to fade quickly as if absorbed by the stonework itself.

With a glance at Cooper, she said "That won't keep anyone out, but at least we'll know if anyone tries to get in."

"You've been working with Horus, I see," responded Cooper.

Only the princess and Lady Coramina came to see them off.

After a somewhat circuitous route to take them away from the castle and to the main road a few miles away, Cooper took the lead and set a steady pace that ate up the miles quickly without overexerting the takis, the two girls were riding. By mid-morning, they were nearly halfway to Finhaven, where they had planned to stop overnight. There was a light breeze coming from the mountains to the west and a few clouds to keep the sun from becoming too hot. It was a near perfect day for a ride. For a time, they almost forgot the reason why they were traveling.

An hour after they left Kestriana, Shirell rode up alongside Cooper.

"I'm unfamiliar with this town of Finhaven. Before we get there, is there anything special that I should know about it?"

"Finhaven is a little larger than most of local villages," Cooper answered. "Its situated at the edge of Everwood, the vast southern forest. Everwood borders one half of the southeastern corner of the elf kingdom. Along with the Equus, it separates the elven territories from the gnome lands to the east. The forest is said to extend to a vast ocean, three days ride to the south. Finhaven is the last outpost before entering the Endless Forest.

"Most of the inhabitants of Finhaven either farm or hunt the forest. A large deer herd inhabits the forest, and fresh venison is always in demand. A warden of the forest stays on hand to ensure that the hunters never thin the herd too much.

"There's a store and two inns; the Stone Hearth, where we'll be staying, is the larger and nicer of the two. They primarily serve the merchants who supply vegetables and meat to Kestriana and the surrounding villages. And from time to time, other brave souls travel through Everwood.

"Only one true road through Everwood exists. There were small side trails, but only the most experienced woodsmen or the very foolish traveler use them. The experienced usually returned, but there were parts of the forest where even the bravest of souls stay on the main road, especially after dark.

"Ramses Marsh lays on the northern edge of Everwood, with its back to the forest. It's fed by a slow moving tributary of the Equus. No one has ever bothered to map out just where the swamp ends and the forest begins as the edges expand and recede with the changing seasons.

"A small side road, little more than a trail, leads off the main road and into the marsh. No one fishes the marsh. Though the fish there are edible, they're foul and bitter to the taste. Most folks are discouraged from entering due to the venomous snakes, ape-like mudwumps and hidden pools of sinking sand that will swallow a man without a trace.

"There are a few brave trappers who risk the marsh to trap the slink. The slink is an otter-like cousin of the snicker that makes its home in the marsh. Its pelt is soft, warm, and highly prized. A skilled slink trapper can make a good living, but the risk is high, and more than one soul has left to go trapping one morning and never been seen again.

"Our innkeeper, a man named Fren, was a slink trapper in his youth. He made enough money off of the valuable pelts to purchase the inn, then he had the good sense to get out of the trapping business. In the swamp, you don't get many chances to be careless. There were no old slink trappers."

That evening, as they sat down to a hearty meal of roasted venison and local vegetables, Cooper and Shirell discussed plans for the next day.

"I've spoken to Fren," Cooper stated. "He recognized both of us immediately and understands our reasons for venturing into the marsh. We're not the first magic wielders to search out the lurker. In all his years of trapping in the marsh, Fren has never seen the lurker, and he is glad for that. He didn't know if any of the stories about the lurker were true, and he was quite content not to find out. He did point out that the marsh was no place for two young girls. When he was unable to convince Susan and Bodkin to remain at the Stone Hearth, he gave them a stern warning to stay on the path once they entered the marsh. There were places where the shifting sands came right up to the edge of the road and one step off the path could be disastrous.

"We can't take the horses into the marsh, and there's nowhere along the way to safely leave them," said Cooper. "We'll house them here at the Stone Hearth and proceed to the marsh on foot in the morning. I've looked at the stables. The horses will be well cared for, and Fren has assured me that if we don't return, he'll be sure to send word to the castle and have someone come and retrieve them.

"We all have hiking experience and, even though I expect to be back before nightfall, we'll each carry a small backpack with enough food and fresh water to last two days. We should all get a good night's sleep, and we'll head out after breakfast."

Chapter 10

The five mile hike to the marsh took a good part of the morning. Upon arriving at the edge of Ramses Marsh, they were all careful to follow Fren's advice and not venture off the trail. Some spots required them to walk single file, where others widened out and they could walk side by side.

At one of the wider spots, Bodkin moved up to walk alongside Cooper.

"Should we, perhaps, be armed, Guardian? There are many places here that would be perfect for the creature to ambush us from, if it wanted to."

"No," responded Cooper. "We have no reason to think that the lurker would be hostile. We've come only to talk to him, but legend says that if he doesn't wish to speak with us, we'll never find him. If we appear to be friendly, there's a much better chance that he'll be willing to talk with us."

"Your words...are wise."

Both Susan and Bodkin squealed as the voice spoke.

"Why do you...trespass here...Guardian?" The voice of the lurker was like none they had ever heard, halting and ragged as if the creature had run a great distance and was short of breath. When the creature spoke, he sounded as if he were deep within a cavern, his voice low and distant, echoing off ancient moss covered walls.

To their right, a shadow moved and disengaged itself from the gloom. If it had not spoken, they would have walked past within inches of the creature and never known of its presence. They quickly understood how the lurker had acquired his name and reputation.

Crall stood nearly seven feet tall and was skeletal, with arms that looked like rotting flesh stretched tightly over misshapen bones. The hands and lower arms, covered in boils and oozing sores, were the only parts visible behind the lurker's ragged garment that, at one time, must have been a cloak. Not even the slightest glimpse of a face was visible from deep within the hood.

Cooper stepped forward to face the monstrous apparition.

"We have come to speak with the one called Crall the Lurker. I am called Cooper and this is Shirell, Orcanus of the —"

"I know...who you are," the lurker interrupted. "Why have you...come into my domain? To seek knowledge...Guardian? Perhaps to ask...about the two young elf sisters...princesses, that accompany you?"

"But, we're not sisters or princesses," said Susan. "We came to —"

"Hush...child. I speak only...to your grandfather."

With Shirell gently tugging on her arm, Susan reluctantly took a step back and remained silent.

Without warning, the lurker suddenly turned and began to leave.

"Come...I have a dwelling...it's safer there...follow."

Despite his ragged appearance, Crall moved quickly. He was as silent as a ghost heading off through the gloom, never looking back to see if Cooper and the others were following.

It was difficult to judge distances in the swamp, but after only a few minutes, Crall stopped in front of what appeared to be a large moss-covered mound of decomposing vegetation. With a decaying hand, he pulled aside a curtain of vines to reveal a door.

"Enter...quickly...mudwumps around...stupid creatures...but very strong...they know...not to approach me...but they will smell you...and be drawn here." Crall looked toward Susan and Bodkin. "You know...of mudwumps." It was a statement, not a question.

"Yes, but how did you know?" Susan asked.

The creature made a sound that may have been a laugh and motioned them into the blackness beyond the door. With a wave of an emaciated hand, flameless torches came to life and lit the interior. The lurker was not without skills in magic. They found themselves inside a large single room that was surprisingly dry and clean. Near the center of the room, a large stump, cut off flat on top, appeared to serve as a table. Otherwise the room was empty.

"I have no...food or drink...to offer. What have you...found that would be...important enough for the Guardian...of the Gnome Door...and the orcanus of the Guild...to seek out one such as I?"

"A book," responded Cooper. "We believe that it was created by the Boc and infused with dark magic. We fear that the book is evil and could cause great harm if it fell into the wrong hands. The runes on the book's cover are Boc-Tan. The Boc vanished years ago, and there is no one left who can read the runes. The dragon, Prax, said that you are a seeker of knowledge and may have some understanding of the Boc."

"Prax sent you?...Foolish dragon...searching for his kin...I see his presence... stumbling about in the dreamscape...He searches in the...wrong places. I know something of...the Boc. Where is...this book?"

"We left it securely locked up at Kestriana, the castle of the elves," answered Shirell.

Crall's hood whipped around suddenly to face Shirell. There was a trace of menace in his voice. "I was not...speaking to...you, Orcanus." The creature returned his attention to Cooper. "Without the book...we have nothing...to discuss."

"She meant no offense, Crall," Cooper quickly responded. "What she says is true. The book itself is not here, but we had the runes on the cover carefully reproduced so that you could examine them."

"And what do you...offer as payment...for my help, Guardian? Surely the dragon...told you that I...would require something...in exchange for my knowledge."

"We have brought a bag of silver to pay for your services."

Once again, the strange sound that passed as laughter came from inside the creature's hood.

"There are few places in the...marsh that accept elven...silver coins, and I am...shall we say...unwelcome...in the village. They are useless...to me."

"Name your price and we will try to meet it," said Cooper.

"Be careful...what you promise, Guardian...The price may.......be more than you...bargained for. I know a little...of this book and...its blank pages. It is called...the Boc Passages. Show me your runes...and I will attempt to...read them. After I have...seen what you have brought...we will discuss payment."

Cooper laid out the drawings of the runes on the makeshift table. The young scribe had done an excellent job of precisely reproducing the runes and symbols covering the face of the book. Crall examined the drawings, tracing some of the symbols with a skeletal finger and occasionally uttering sounds that none of them had ever heard before. Finally he stood upright and turned toward Cooper.

"These runes do not...reveal much, but enough to know that...the Guild's work...sloppy, incomplete...arrogant fools that they were. Barely the brains...of a mere snicker...among the lot of them. Their translation skills...so pathetic, a wonder that they...succeeded in opening the books...without destroying themselves. Never discovered...their true purpose. Ignorant children, they were...believed the pages, all blank...offered nothing. The incantation...that they translated...was left there...to make fools of them. They needed to learn...learn to read runes properly...Then they would know...know what happened to the Boc...know why the books...were left behind. You must...return with the book."

"I will bring you the book," said Cooper, with a nod.

"That is not all...Guardian." A boney finger pointed to one of the runes. "Here...it tells of a talisman. A ring...of hammered silver, holding a black stone...where colors swirl. It will reveal...what is hidden...on the pages within. Retrieve the talisman...and bring it here...along with the book. That is...my price," croaked Crall.

Cooper glanced over at Shirell, who shrugged and shook her head.

"Neither of us has ever heard of this ring. I wouldn't know where to look for it. Do the runes tell where to find this ring?"

"The book...does not tell," wheezed Crall with a dismissive wave at the sketches. "But the Guild...kept many secrets...some of their secrets...are known to me. You'll find the ring...in the belly...of the serpent beneath the hall."

"The Guild Hall? But the Hall was destroyed. Prax killed the serpent, the lindworm. Its body was burned to ashes. I was there and witnessed the burning. No trace of any ring was ever found."

"I do not...speak of the lindworm. The serpent...remains.

71

When you go there. Touch nothing...but the ring...Beware the chamber...where the echo doesn't answer."

Shirell started to ask more about the Guild Hall. A gesture from Cooper stopped her. The lurker had turned his attention back to the drawings. His manner made it clear that he would not speak of the Hall again until he was ready. A boney finger pointed to a symbol in the bottom corner of the drawing.

"Careless muddle heads...overlooked the last, most important word. It is a word...that a Guardian should understand...if you are clever. In the Boc dialect...it is pronounced Crak."

"Crak?" repeated Cooper.

"It means...hole."

"Hole? Guardian? The Boc Passages. Portal! Of course!" Cooper's face lit up as Crall's cryptic message suddenly became clear. "That's where they went. Hole is another name for portal."

The Lurked uttered his guttural laugh.

"Clever Guardian...smarter than the Guild."

Shirell stared blankly at the two of them. "Hole? Portal? What does any of that mean? How is it important?"

"Don't you see? It all makes sense now!" Cooper was almost shouting in his excitement. "The title has a double meaning. It's not just literary passages. It's also a passage to other places. The book is a gateway. Like the Gnome Door. That's why one was found in each village. The entire Boc clan used the books to move to a new location, then booby-trapped them so they couldn't be followed. There must have been a second book at their destination. Their skills in magic must have been far greater than originally believed."

Cooper's mood quickly turned serious.

"Do you realize what that means, Shirell? Marcus has played us for fools. We knew that he was being too cooperative.

72

He wanted us to open the book. We've long suspected that Marcus had a confederate. If he was working with one of the Boc, we've just unlocked the door by opening the book. More than that, we've foolishly given them a pathway directly into the least guarded section of the castle by placing it back in the old archive room. That's undoubtedly how Marcus was able to leave the castle to be the shadow mage and then return without ever being seen. He must have had the book hidden in his quarters for years, then secreted it into the archives room before he faked his death. He didn't want it to be found among his things and examined too closely or possibly destroyed. He left himself a back door into the castle. We need to send word back to Kestriana and return as quickly as possible."

Crall rose from his position hunched over the sketches and pointed toward the door where they had entered. "Leave...the drawings. They belong to me now. I would study...them further until you return. Go fifty paces...turn right...stay on the path. It will...take you to the edge of...the marsh. Do not wander...left or right. Return with the book...and the ring...or do not return."

"But the ring and the serpent?" asked Cooper. "We don't understand. How can we bring it to you if we don't know where to look?"

"Ask the old fool...of a wizard...now go." With that, Crall picked up the sketches, turned his back on them, and began to shuffle towards a darkened corner at the opposite end of the room.

Shirell started after him, but Cooper put a hand on her arm.

"Don't bother. He's not going to tell us anymore. And we need to get back to the castle."

"But what does it all mean?"

"I don't know. He said to talk to the old wizard. We can only hope that he means Horus and that that crazy old man can shed some light on Crall's riddles."

Upon leaving Crall's shelter, they followed his directions and quickly found themselves back at the edge of the marsh near the road. They still had to hike back to town, and Cooper's frustration was obvious.

"If we had brought the horses, we could return to town quickly."

"But we didn't," answered Shirell. "The book has been at the castle for quite some time. We will just have to hope that if Marcus did have a collaborator, he doesn't know that the book has been opened, or that he will be unable to get beyond the locked archive room door, or perhaps that he has abandoned Marcus. If luck is with us, a few extra hours will not change anything."

"Yes, you're right, but it doesn't make me feel much better about it. I wish you had phones here."

"Phones?" Shirell stared at him blankly.

"Never mind, it would take too long to explain," said Cooper.

The hike back into town would take most of the afternoon, so they spent some of their time planning how to proceed. There was a network of messenger birds in most of these small towns, so word could be sent to Ashley at the castle warning her to guard the door to the archive room. Cooper would escort the two girls back to the castle and relay everything that they had learned to the princess while Shirell went on ahead to the Guild Hall to try and locate Horus, who sometimes wandered off for days at a time. Cooper would then circle back to the Guild Hall as soon as possible, and together they would try to unscramble the lurker's riddles.

Crall watched as Shirell and her companions rode away. The part of him that had once been called Brin sighed. The daughter that he had never known was now the orcanus, leader of the new order of magic-wielders. Somewhere in his jumbled mind, he knew that he should be proud of who she had become. He yearned to tell her who he was, that he was the one who had entered the dream world and helped her to survive the grueling ordeal of the kuri-aken, and then sent the she-wolf Shadow to guard and protect her until she was able to survive on her own. That he was also the one who had sent Marcus, the shadow mage, to her, knowing that he was evil, but understanding that her need for a teacher outweighed Marcus's flaws. It was a calculated risk that she would reject Marcus's view of the world. He was pleased that he had guessed correctly.

But the creature known as Crall that inhabited his body would not allow him to reveal who he had once been. Crall was a unique being, unable to exist on his own. He needed a host body to survive, even though his presence slowly destroyed the body, twisting it and steadily rotting it from within. As the most recent host, Brin still held some small influence, but, for all intents and purposes, Crall maintained control with an iron fist.

Only when the creature slept, from time to time, were Brin's thoughts his own. Sometimes the memories of the others who had come before him mingled in his mind and nearly drove him mad. Brin vividly remembered the terror of being confronted by this hideous creature, watching in frozen horror as it shed the husk of its last host and engulfed him and the helpless realization that there was nothing he could do to prevent his current fate. That was many years ago. He knew that eventually he would be discarded like the others when this body became too old and ravished by Crall's cancerous presence. The time would come when he could no longer sustain the creature. After that, only bits and pieces of his memories would remain, trapped in the mind of the next unfortunate that Crall inhabited.

Chapter 11

As the haze cleared, Al-Ron stepped cautiously into the old records room. The room was bare except for the small table with the Boc book laid out on it. The blue light surrounding him faded as he let out a deep breath and willed the muscles in his left hand to relax.

The impression, outlined on his palm, told him that he had been squeezing the talisman stone much harder than he liked to admit. His right hand had reflexively gone to the hilt of his long knife, and he allowed that to drop to his side. Using the passage without knowing the exact location of the book was a calculated risk. Although the book could show an image of its closest surroundings, it's range was only the area directly in front of the book. Anything or anyone more than a few feet away would be hidden from him.

The last thing that the dark elf wanted was to step out into a room full of guards. Fortunately for him, Cooper and Shirell had returned the book to its old location. Since all the other journals and manuscripts had already been relocated to the new library, the empty room in a little used part of the castle had seemed like the ideal place to store the book until a more permanent decision could be made as to what should be done with it.

The door was secured from the outside, but it was an old

and simple lock. A child could have opened it. A wave of the hand and a flicker of blue light was all that were needed there.

But there was something else, too. A ward, a simple spell to let someone know if the door had been opened. Invisible to the naked eye, but he recognized it instantly. It was one of old Horus's favorite spells. It was most certainly placed there by the orcanus, but she must have learned it from that crazy old wizard.

As the only surviving member of the old Guild, Al-Ron had studied Horus and was quite familiar with his techniques. Shirell was smarter than Marcus gave her credit for. Still, it required no longer to bypass the ward than it had taken to unlock the door.

It would be necessary to conceal himself as he traversed the halls to Marcus's quarters, but his cloaking spell should suffice in the darkened halls of the castle at night. Al-Ron preferred this spell. Unlike an invisibility spell that required absolute concentration and focus, the simple cloaking spell just caused others to become distracted and look away for a moment, allowing him to slip by unnoticed. It also required almost no energy at all, unlike the invisibility spell that left him drained and weary if he had to maintain it for long. Beyond the possibility of a few roaming guards, it was unlikely that anyone would be moving about in the depths of the castle at this late hour. Still, secrecy was of the utmost importance. He could not afford to be seen and, more importantly, cut off from his only escape route — the Boc book.

He silently cracked open the door and peered out into the corridor. Once again, his luck held and the hall was empty. No guards had been posted. Not really surprising, considering that no one actually knew the book's true purpose and only a handful of people were even aware of its existence. Under most circumstances, a locked door deep in the bowels of the castle would certainly have seemed like adequate precaution. Now all that was necessary was for him to navigate the two flights up and three corridors over to Marcus's rooms.

Al-Ron glided down the hallway like a ghost, barely disturbing the dust in the corners. Silence was of paramount concern. The long hallways tended to echo and, with their pointed ears, elf hearing was twice as sharp as that of humans. He quickly reached the base of the stairwell and was up the first flight in an instant.

The second flight presented a small problem. A guard was milling about aimlessly on the landing. The cloaking spell did not seem to be affecting the man. Some individuals exhibited a stronger resistance to the influence of magic. Al-Ron had no reservations about killing the man, but a dead guard just down the hall from Marcus's quarters would raise some suspicions.

Currently, the elves believed that, as the shadow mage, Marcus had always worked alone. That was an idea that Al-Ron wanted them to continue believing. But a dead body outside Marcus's rooms would almost certainly alert them to the idea that Marcus had at least one confederate in some of his schemes. Both Cooper and the new orcanus were not to be underestimated. They would both instantly realize that that person not only presented a new threat, but must already have some hidden form of access to the castle. He did not want his existence to be known about. Not yet.

While he debated with himself over what to do, the problem solved itself. The man turned abruptly and started up to the next level. Perhaps his spell was working after all. One other guard posted by the door was dozing in a chair. With a simple spell to ensure that the man did not wake up and a spark of blue light to unlock the door, he achieved his goal.

The dark elf slipped into the room, making no more

sound than a shadow. Marcus stood with his back to him, peering over the chessboard where a game seemed to be in progress. Al-Ron couldn't help smiling to himself as Marcus visibly jumped at the sound of his voice.

"Good evening, Marcus. You don't appear to have an opponent for your game."

The former shadow mage recovered quickly. "Yes...yes, I often play both sides of the game, using two entirely different strategies. A simple mental exercise that helps to relieve the never ending boredom of being imprisoned here. Now that you're here, we can leave and I shouldn't need to occupy my time with such trivial things."

"Playing both sides of the game? Sounds like you're moving into politics, Marcus. Before we go, let's talk for a few moments. The castle is asleep. There's no great hurry."

"If you wish," Marcus answered reluctantly.

"I'm afraid that I'm somewhat disappointed in you, Marcus. Against my best advice, after you discovered the whereabouts of the dragon Prax and had him imprisoned, you neglected to destroy him outright. Looking back at it now, that seems to have been rather poor judgment."

"I don't agree. I felt that it was the best choice at that time. Prax is the largest and most powerful of all the dragons. Even while asleep, he was still extremely dangerous."

"Precisely the reason that he should have been destroyed while recovering from his injuries utilizing the dragon sleep."

"I have only your word regarding this whole mysterious dragon sleep process," Marcus snapped back at him. "It is not mentioned anywhere, in even the oldest of the archives, and you will not reveal the source of this knowledge. If your information was wrong, I certainly would not have survived a direct confrontation with Prax."

"I'm sorry, but at the moment, I am unable to reveal my source of information," said Al-Ron, trying to quiet Marcus's outburst. "You are, of course, correct in your belief that during normal circumstances, he would have awakened instantly and any attack on him in such close quarters would have been suicide. But as I explained to you at the time, even the mighty Prax is helpless when under the spell of the dragon sleep. That is exactly the reason that you were able to bind him so easily. Now that he is free, he will most certainly come looking for those who imprisoned him. Namely, you, and that may eventually lead him to me."

"He never should have been found!" snapped Marcus, his voice rising. "He was trapped under a net of binding spells beneath a mountain of stone. The entrance to the cave was tiny and hidden. I even placed the Golem twins at the entrance. I took every precaution. Even you didn't know that Prax could still communicate through the dream world. Your secret source of information apparently didn't tell you that. And Cooper was in exile. No one could have ever guessed that he would return and bring along a granddaughter who had the ability to perform red magic."

"Yes, everything that you've said is true. Nevertheless, all of those things could have been prevented if you had just followed my suggestion and killed the creature when you had the chance. But, what's done is done and we shall have to address that problem when the time comes. You did also promise me that you could acquire the eye of Bangor Khan, and you've failed to do that."

"We know that Cooper has the eye. You said so yourself. I'm certain that he's hiding it in his world!"

"So you've said repeatedly. But even after passing through the portal and searching his workshop in the human world, you were still unable to retrieve it. I then made arrangements to get you into the vault so you could steal the dragon staff. No easy task, I would remind you, and there is still a chance that someone may make the connection that only members of the High Council have access to the vault. You assured me that no one could stand before you if you held the staff, yet here you are, a prisoner in your own quarters, and the staff now belongs to your former student, the new orcanus."

"Treacherous little witch," snarled Marcus. "I took her from nothing and made her what she is."

"I would remind you who her father was. Brin was Eldred's illegitimate offspring. Had he not disappeared, he probably would have one day become leader of the Guild. There was strong magic in the girl long before you found her. Even without your help, she would have discovered her abilities. It may have taken her a bit longer, but it would have happened just the same."

"I still trained her how to hone those skills, and she repays me by turning on me. I would have dispatched her just as easily as that annoying elf, Quisp, if not for the princess's interference."

"Sadly, there does always seem to be some excuse for you failing to accomplish your tasks."

"There were circumstances beyond my control," said Marcus. He was becoming progressively more agitated with the direction of the conversation, and he quickly tried to change the subject. "We should leave here and return to the Keep in the Dark Woods. There, together, we can plan how to destroy them all. There will be no more failures!"

"Oh, of that, I'm certain," said the dark elf quietly. "Come along then and we'll go."

As Marcus rose from his chair, Al-Ron deftly stepped up from behind and placed his hands on Marcus's temples.

Suddenly a demon appeared directly in front of Marcus. A misshapen monster covered with greenish gray scales and spikes protruding from his back at odd angles. Spittle dripped from a mouth sporting cruel six inch long teeth.

The creature viciously slashed at Marcus's midsection with a clawed hand. Marcus had no time to react before he felt the searing pain of razor sharp talons tearing into his flesh. He tried to scream, but no sound came from his lips. He looked down in horror, expecting to see his abdomen torn wide open, but there was nothing. The pain had been excruciating, but there was no sign of injury and, just that quickly, the demon was gone.

In its place were insects, hundreds of them, large and black, with stingers and pincers, all racing towards him from every corner of the room. He kicked and swatted at them as they scrambled up his legs. He could feel every sting, every bite. He was repulsed as he felt each tiny creature crawling up inside his clothing and across his skin. He flailed about wildly, falling to the floor, trying to rid himself of the tiny pests. Then, as quickly as they had appeared, they were gone and, again, he was unharmed.

When he tried to rise and catch his breath, he found himself surrounded by nightshade dogs. The vicious canines bit into him and tore flesh from his arms and legs. He attempted to cry out in pain, but again, nothing but silence came out.

Al-Ron slowly closed and locked the door behind him. As he was leaving, he glanced over at Marcus, huddled in the corner, frantically kicking at the army of imaginary rats that he now believed were gnawing off his toes. The guard was still asleep in the chair as he passed him in the hallway. His route was clear, and he was back in the archive room in less than two minutes.

He locked the door from the inside, being sure to leave no trace of his visit, then stepped into the portal opened by the book, and was gone from the castle.

As Al-Ron stepped out of the portal and back into his sanctuary, he had one more small task to complete before retiring. The jet black crow perched over the door looked at him curiously, as if it anticipated that its services would be needed.

"I have a job for you, Tor," Al-Ron said to the bird as he gathered writing materials from a small cabinet.

Chancellor Adronis woke the instant the bird alighted on his windowsill. Many years had passed since he had been a captain of the forest wardens, but his senses were still sharp and keen. He was instantly on his feet and quietly coaxed the crow onto his hand to remove the message tied to its leg. The message was short: "Marcus is no longer a concern." The letter wasn't signed, but he already knew who it had come from. The black bird had visited him many times before. He dropped the paper into a small brass bowl and lit one of its corners with a candle. Then with a slight smile, he returned to his bed and slept peacefully the remainder of the night.

In the morning, the servant that normally brought Marcus's breakfast immediately summoned the warden. Marcus was not in his usual spot at the chess board. Together, they found him curled in a ball in a corner of his closet, eyes glazed over and unable to speak. Healers were called. They were able to sedate him with herbs, but all attempts to reach him were unsuccessful. The monsters in his head were gone now, but after a night of believing that he was being attacked and savaged by a never ending array of the most vicious creatures imaginable, his reason had snapped. He had become the mindless invalid that he had spent so many years pretending to be.

Chapter 12

Wysp did not like this place at all. She had never been this deep into the Dark Woods before. There was bad magic here. She could feel it. She wanted to just blink out of here. Back to where the elves lived. She liked the elves, especially the princess and that young girl, Bodkin. They were nice and kind to her. She sometimes carried messages for them, crossing into the human world where the Cooper and Susan lived. Some of the other sprites had laughed at her, saying that she had allowed herself to become a mere servant to the elves. But she knew that the elves were her friends and she could trust them. She would go and visit them after she left this evil place.

But the other sprites and fairies were her friends too. Why had so many of them disappeared. Where had they all gone? Sprites loved to play games and hide from each other, that was the nature of fairies, but this was different. They always left clues when it was a game, but there were none. She knew all the best hiding places, even the special ones that no one else knew. She was the best hide and seek player of all the sprites. The Dark Forest was the only place left where she hadn't looked. Why would they come here? Every fairy knew that this was a bad place. What could have lured them here? She could feel the traces of fairy magic left by their passing, bread crumbs left behind to lead them back home and she had followed them this far. But now the trail led even deeper into the forest. Every fiber of her being screamed for her to turn around and run for home, but she couldn't give up now. Her friends were lost, and she was sure that something was wrong. She had to find them, so mustering every ounce of determination she had, she went on.

It was midday, but the ever-present gloom of the forest made it look like twilight. The traces of magic led her to a stand of gnarled old oaks. She passed through as quickly as she could, trying not to look at the ancient trees that were twisted into grotesque shapes that nature had never intended, and came upon a clearing. In the center, standing alone, was an imposing sight — a huge dark tree.

Something about the tree reminded her of the Golden Willow, but it was horribly altered somehow. The coarse bark was so dark that, in the dim light, it appeared almost black. The branches were contorted and bent with large knuckles. Misshapen burls dotted the trunk like warts or boils from some plague victim's skin. Initially, she recoiled from the appearance of the tree, but she found that it both repelled and attracted her at the same time. She was drawn towards it like a moth to flame, and the closer she came, the stronger the draw.

Her instincts told her that something was wrong. She fought the attraction, but as she started to pull away, something familiar caught her eye. Resting in the split created by a large branch and the trunk of the tree, she saw Lute's staff.

Years ago, she and Lute had been lovers. Fairy relationships were far different than those of humans or elves. They came and went like the seasons. They had both had many lovers since then, and even though she hadn't seen him in over a year, Lute was always her favorite and she still loved him. Something terrible must have happened to him. Lute would never abandon his staff. Unlike humans or elves, fairies didn't need staffs or talismans to do magic, but Lute's staff was like a part of him. He would feel naked without it. She had to retrieve it and see if it offered some clue to his whereabouts.

Wysp approached the tree cautiously. Lute was fast and strong, and despite their small size, fairy magic was still nothing to be trifled with. Anything able to overpower him would have to be very quick as it was nearly impossible to sneak up on a fairy, even for another fairy. Wysp landed next to the staff, her eyes darting from side to side, alert for any movement. She gingerly picked up the staff. It was definitely Lute's. She had seen it a thousand times, occasionally stealing it herself while he slept and hiding it to force Lute to come and find her when she wanted to tease him. As far as she could tell, it was undamaged and offered no real clues to his fate. With staff in hand, she was anxious to get as far away from this unsettling tree as possible.

To her horror, she found that she couldn't fly away. Her feet were stuck fast to the tree, trapped in a gooey liquid that was hidden in the shadows of the branches. If she was restrained or couldn't fly, she couldn't blink and transport herself away. She used the staff to try and pry herself loose, but hard as she tried, she couldn't break free. The noxious smell emanating from the branch was noticeable when she landed. Now, the more she struggled, the stronger the odor became as her struggles caused the ooze to release a vapor. Her vision began to blur, and she felt lightheaded. Wysp clutched Lute's staff and desperately tried to hold herself up as her knees began to buckle and she quickly succumbed to the mist induced sleep.

Chapter 13

When Cooper arrived at the entrance to the Guild Hall, Shirell was there to meet him.

"Horus's quarters are this way," said Shirell as she led him down the hall to the right. "He's just returned an hour ago, and I haven't had a chance to speak with him yet. It took me a day and a half to locate and get word to him. My message said only that it was urgent for him to return immediately. He doesn't know anything about the book. When word came that you were on your way, I felt that it would be best if I waited and we spoke to him together."

"Let's hope that he can offer us something useful. He may be our last chance to discover the secret of this book. Marcus can no longer help us."

"Why? What's happened?"

"His mind is gone, and he's not faking this time. Something, or maybe someone, got into his room. Korin met me at the castle gates with the news, and I went to see Marcus myself. He's completely snapped. He spends half his time huddled in a corner, raving about horrible creatures trying to eat him. The rest of his time, he just stares blankly at his chess board."

"That's horrible, even for Marcus. When we return to the castle, I'll check the wards that I placed around the archive room door. It'll tell us if someone came through there." Shirell turned a corner and knocked on the first door on the right. "This is Horus's room."

As the old wizard ushered them into his rooms, Cooper looked around with a bemused smile. Horus's quarters looked like a whirlwind had recently passed through them. Old books and manuscripts were piled at least three high on every flat surface, some of them weighed down by strange looking objects, many of which Cooper couldn't identify.

The old wizard often appeared somewhat absent minded, and his hands fumbled nervously with a small mechanical contraption while he listened. Shirell relayed all that had transpired regarding the mysterious book and their subsequent visit to the lurker.

When Shirell finished, the old wizard rose and began to wander aimlessly across the room, scratching at his few remaining wisps of white hair.

"You actually spoke to the lurker? And he sent you to talk to me? Amazing. I can scarcely believe it. How does he even know who I am? I've never even been within ten miles of that marsh. You say that he told you to ask me about the serpent under the Hall? Oh my, I haven't heard that phrase in years. Back in the days of the Guild, we all believed that it was just a myth. Of course, many of us thought that the lurker was just a myth, too. Now where did I lay that book? Oh, I really must get organized one day."

He crossed to the far side of the room and, after rummaging through some of the clutter and clumsily sending three different piles of assorted objects clattering to the floor, he picked up a small volume. "Let me think, now. How did that legend go? Oh, I know It's here somewhere. Can't remember what page it was on. My memory is just not what it used to be."

Bony fingers leafed through the book, finally settling on a

page.

"Yes, here it is. Apparently, Eldred discovered a network of natural caves and tunnels that turned and twisted like a snake. He then commissioned the Hall to be built directly over the caves and had a secret entrance dug under the basement of the Hall, hence the name the serpent under the Hall. Eldred just loved giving things mysterious sounding titles. It's said that deep in the caves, he created a vault. Eldred spent countless nights scouring through old manuscripts, searching for legends and rumors about powerful and dangerous artifacts created by the old wizards, long before there was a Guild. Then when he thought he had some idea where he might find one, he would go on a trek and search the countryside. If he was able to find an artifact, this vault was where he stored the object upon his return. Eldred protected the vault with powerful wards and spells. It all sounds very noble on the surface, but I think that the whole idea was a bit of self-preservation brought on by paranoia, actually. If he locked up all the dangerous objects, no one could use them against him."

Horus shook his head as he interrupted himself. "But these were all just stories. Countless rumors existed about Eldred, many of them started by Eldred himself to confuse his enemies. It was also said that the serpent under the Hall and it's hidden vault was just a ruse to get his enemies to reveal themselves. Anyone who came snooping around for the vault, he knew to be suspicious of. After his disappearance, the lower levels of the hall were thoroughly searched, both physically and with magic. No trace of an entrance was ever found. Then the hall was destroyed in the Gremlin Wars."

"What about the builders? There would have been an architect who designed the Hall," asked Cooper. "They must have had plans to work from. Some records or diagrams that might give us a starting point."

"All lost. A suspicious fire at the builder's home. And the architect vanished around the time that the finishing touches were being completed. He was never heard from again. Rumor was that Eldred sent him down into the caves and made sure that he never returned. Eldred could be completely ruthless."

Cooper sighed. "Well, the lurker claims that these caves still exist and the only way that we can get his help is to find them and retrieve this ring that he demands. It seems that we have little choice but to go to the ruins of the Hall, search for the entrance, and hope that we have better luck than the members of the Guild."

"Oh, there is one other thing here, Guardian," said Horus as he turned the last page. "This suggests that the original entrance to the cave was never sealed, but left as a sort of back door into the vault, a way for Eldred to come and go without the other members of the Guild knowing what he was up to. It should still exist somewhere in the woods near the ruins of the Hall, but it's a much more dangerous path to take. You must pass through a number of cursed chambers to get to the vault from that direction. And the entrance is, of course, hidden."

"Does that book give us some idea how to find it?"

Horus traced the words on the last page with his finger. "Well, it's very cryptic, but it does list some landmarks to look for. It's been a long time. You'll have to hope that they still exist and haven't been overgrown or lost."

"It seems like that's our only choice if we want Crall's help," said Cooper. He glanced over at Shirell who had maintained an anxious silence for the last few minutes. "Unless you have an alternate idea."

Shirell looked back at him warily. "No, it's just that I was trapped under the rubble of that Hall and nearly died there. I still sometimes wake up in the middle of the night, terrified that I'm going to be crushed if I move just an inch in the wrong direction. I am not anxious to return to anywhere within five miles of that place, but it's what we need to do. Horus, will you come with us? That book and your knowledge of the hall may prove very valuable."

"Oh, I'm getting much too old for adventures," said the old wizard as he shook his head and paced across the room, nervously wringing his hands. "But curiosity has always been a weakness of mine. Oh, I hate hard decisions. If there's even a possibility that Eldred's vault really exists, the chance to study and examine artifacts not seen for decades. The opportunity to hold in my hand, objects that are only spoken of in some of these old texts you see around you. Why I could spend a lifetime in such a pursuit. If you wish it, m'lady, I will accompany you."

"Thank you, Horus. We'll leave in the morning."

The afternoon sky was just turning pink as Cooper, Shirell, and Horus rode into the small settlement of Doon. The old wizard proved to be rather spry for his age, and they were able to make good time. Even so, the sun was slowly settling behind the tops of the tall pines to the west as they arrived. It would be dark in less than an hour.

Doon was the only settlement for miles around, bordered by farms in one direction and forest in the other. It was also situated a mile and a half from the ruins of the old Guild Hall.

They had been advised by Korin to discreetly seek out a man named Lon. Lon owned the tavern near the center of town and had lived his entire life there. He would be able to provide them with rooms where they could stay the night, and maybe he could also offer some helpful information.

Korin had stressed that it would be wise for them to maintain as low a profile as possible. There were still quite a few residents of the town who remembered the horror of the Hall's destruction and the war that followed, folks who didn't trust magic or those that used it. Many believed that disturbing the abandoned ruins might just stir up old evils that were best left alone. The presence of three such prominent magic-wielders would not be a welcome sight to some of the locals.

At the tavern, the young girl serving ale behind the bar looked the three travelers over with dark, piercing eyes that seemed like they could burn a hole right through them.

"I'm looking for a man named Lon," Cooper said.

The girl said nothing, finished serving the two young men at the far end of the bar, then motioned for the three to follow her. She led them to a door, partially hidden in the corner, that opened into a small back room, secluded from the noisy tavern atmosphere of the great room. She left them there, returning ten minutes later with a hearty meal of pork and savory vegetables cooked in a thick broth and accompanied by freshly baked bread, then she vanished.

It was almost an hour after the girl left when Lon appeared in the doorway. He was a big man with large, rough hands. Attached to the back of the inn was a large pen, and Lon had the look of a man who spent a fair amount of his time working with the hogs.

After a simple greeting, Lon took a chair from its place leaning against the wall, turned it around, seated himself facing the three, and launched into conversation as if they were all old friends.

"Korin sent word that you were coming," Lon stated. "The serving girl is Lana, my adopted daughter. She doesn't speak much. I told her to watch for you. Was the stew to your liking? It

96

is my wife's recipe and a favorite here."

"It was excellent," responded Cooper. "As fine as anything served at Kestriana."

"Thank you, I shall pass your praise on to my wife. She'll be pleased. Been a long time since we had an orcanus stay here, m'lady," said Lon, nodding to Shirell. "My family has run this inn for five generations. There was a time when there were many regular visitors to the old Guild Hall. Important people, even members of the High Council and royal family.

"Then the Gremlin War came. I was just a lad when the Hall was destroyed. My father had us all hide in the woods. You could feel the ground shaking like an earthquake while that monster smashed the hall with all those poor members of the Guild trapped inside. I'll never forget that terrible day."

"None of us ever will, Lon," said Cooper, quietly.

"And to have Cooper, the guardian, staying under my roof. It is indeed an honor, Sir. We've heard many stories of your bravery, Sir."

"Stories tend to get embellished with each telling. Don't believe everything you hear, Lon."

"I am an innkeeper, it's my job to listen to folks. We hear so many tales. But if I may be so bold, Sir, did you really marry the princess and take her away to your world?"

Cooper nodded his assent. "That was a long time ago. We had many happy years, but she's gone now. Taken by the ravishes of a terrible illness."

Lon lowered his head. "My deepest sympathies, Sir. But you didn't come here to listen to me prattle on. How may I help such distinguished guests?"

"As far as most folks need to know, our journey here is just so that the new orcanus can see the old ruins firsthand and pay her respects."

"That would, indeed, be a noble gesture. But your tone suggests that there is more to it than that, Guardian." Lon flashed a wicked smile. "I grew up around magic-users. If I was to guess, I'd say that there's something in those old ruins that you're looking for."

"You're a shrewd fellow, Lon."

"As I said, Sir, I'm an innkeeper. I hear things every day. My livelihood depends on my ability to be discrete. Nothing said at this table will go beyond the confines of this room, Sir. Of that, I can assure you. But if you wish to enter the ruins, you'll need to be very careful. Many folks around here consider the old Hall a tomb, not just for the Guild members, but for all the poor souls that worked there as servants and staff. A lot of local people lost loved ones that day. Some would consider going into those ruins no different than desecrating a grave site."

"We're not so much interested in going into the ruins as much as under the ruins."

"Not the old caverns, Sir?" Lon asked, sitting up straight in his chair.

"You know about them?" asked Shirell.

"The caves have been there for centuries, and everyone around here knows of them. They only became cursed when Eldred built the hall above them. After the war, a few treasure seeking scoundrels tried to find the old entrance, hoping to steal whatever valuables Eldred and the Guild may have left behind. Grave robbing scum, they were. Most of them never found the entrance. But a few of the craftier ones bribed a local ne'er-do-well to show them where to look, and they were able to find it. Of those that entered, very few returned. The ones that did manage to escape the caves all raved like maniacs, and none lasted more than a few days. All died by their own hands, and no tears were shed for any of them. The local man was run out of town and, eventually, word got out. Even the boldest thieves decided that the risk was far greater than any possible reward. None have tried to find the entrance for many years. Folks around here give that area a wide berth."

"Can you take us to the entrance?" asked Cooper.

"I can get you close, though I would warn you against it. As I've said, the entrance is sealed and hidden. You may not be able to find it, and if you do, it is still extremely dangerous, even for magic-wielders."

"It's what we must do."

"My conscience requires me to advise you once again to reconsider this trek." Lon looked across the table with a sigh. "But I can see that your minds are made up, and you will not follow that counsel. So, then I must get you there safely. Once there, your fates will be in your own hands. How soon do you wish to go?"

"Tonight," answered Cooper. "Best to get it over with as soon as possible, and there's no moon tonight."

"As you wish. You've had a long day traveling. It would be best if you got some rest for a few hours. I'll come back at eleven. Be ready to leave then."

With that, Lon rose from his chair, returned it to its place against the wall, and left. A short time later, Lana appeared to collect the serving dishes and escort them to rooms where they could change and sleep. Once they were settled, she returned, bringing them dark cloaks with hoods. The girl never spoke, just hung the cloaks on pegs near the door and left.

Chapter 14

As promised, promptly at eleven, Lon knocked quietly on their doors. He carried a small pack containing torches. All three were dressed in the cloaks and prepared to go.

For a big man, Lon moved silently as he guided them down a back staircase and into the night. Four shadows moving in the dark. Within minutes, they were beyond the confines of the settlement and en route to the ruins.

Once clear of the buildings, Lon led them unerringly through the trees, though none of the three could distinguish any sort of path in the darkness. There was no moon, and they couldn't risk using the torches as long as they were within a half mile of town. Once their eyes adjusted to the dark, they could see just enough to keep from getting separated.

It was impossible for Cooper to judge distances in the blackness, but after what seemed like a mile, they came out of the trees onto a grassy rolling hillside. Without any moonlight to overpower them, a million stars of all sizes lit up the night sky in a dazzling array. After another ten minutes of walking, Lon stopped and pointed to a small knoll. The outline of crumbled walls and shattered masonry was silhouetted against the night sky.

"That is the spot where the entrance is said to be. It's also where those that tried to enter before were found. There is no need for me to continue any closer. I feel no shame at admitting my fear of this place. I will return to the safety of the trees and wait one hour. If you have not returned by then, I will go home and return in the morning." Lon handed the pack to Cooper. "I have brought torches for you, and I pray that you fare better than those who have tried before you. Godspeed."

With that, Lon turned and quietly strode off, back the way they came.

Shirell watched Lon's retreating figure until he faded into the mist near the trees, then she turned to the old wizard. "What clues does your book offer that might help us find the entrance, Horus?"

"Well, there is a passage here, mistress. I was studying it earlier, but I don't fully understand it."

"Could you read it for us?"

"Certainly, mistress," answered the old wizard as he fumbled with both the book and his glasses simultaneously. "Yes, here it is:

Look to the heavens to undo the seal
The serpent withdraws when the light becomes real.
Follow the snicker, the wolf, stag and hare
Starlight will drive the beast into his lair."

Horus shook his head as he looked up from the book.

"That's all it says, but it's a bit of a riddle. Part of it is rather easy to guess. These four animals are quite familiar to folks like sailors and wardens of the forest. They're constellations in the night sky. It says to look to the heavens, and each of these constellations is known for its guiding star. The snicker to the east, the hare to the west. The eye of the wolf points due south and the heart of the stag is the north star. But they all point in different directions. You can't follow four paths at once. And how can light become 'real?' I'm afraid that I'm not very good at riddles."

Cooper, who had been standing silently a few feet away, spoke up.

"What was the order of those animals again?"

"Oh, let me see," said Horus, as he ran his finger down the page.

"Here it is, snicker, wolf, stag and hare."

"Good, they'll need to be in the correct order."

Shirell and Horus both watched curiously as Cooper walked a short distance into the clear then raised his staff and pointed it east, directly at the bright star in the center of the constellation known as Bunn, the snicker. Light from the star instantly formed a path as it arced across the sky and alighted on the tip of the staff.

Cooper moved his staff deftly, capturing the starlight and forming it into the shape of a rune. As he worked, the light appeared to take on substance and become solid. Cooper wove the light into a shape, the elven script for snicker, that hung suspended in the air.

He then turned and repeated his actions with starlight captured from the other guiding stars, carefully writing each one in the proper sequence. When he finished and all four runes floated in the air, surrounding him in a circle of light, he lifted his staff up and struck the ground sharply.

The runes began to circle Cooper, quickly gaining speed and swirling faster and faster until they blurred into a ring of solid light. Then without warning, the ring suddenly flew toward the hillside, changing into an irregular oval shape as it outlined a cave entrance that had not been visible a moment earlier.

"There is our doorway," announced Cooper. "All the traps set at the entrance should be rendered harmless by the light. But we need to remember the words of the rhyme: 'The serpent withdraws to the center of his lair.' Eldred didn't name these caves the serpent without a good reason. There will still be dangerous spells as we get nearer to the vault. We must not allow ourselves to get careless. The light will fade quickly. We need to go." With that, Cooper started toward the cave entrance.

Shirell whispered in Horus's ear as they quickly followed.

"Have you ever seen someone write with starlight before?"

"No, m'lady," answered Horus. "Years ago, I witnessed Guild members doing amazing feats of magic, but I didn't even know that such a thing was possible."

"Nor did I. I'm beginning to think that our friend Cooper learned a lot more from old Eldred than he admits to. When this trek is over, remind me to have him teach me how to do that before he goes home to his world."

Just inside the cave entrance, the tunnel walls opened up into a space fifty yards across. Cooper stopped and removed three torches from the backpack that Lon had given him.

"I remember Eldred mentioning the vault once, but I didn't realize that this is where he hid it. It should be located at the other end of the main tunnel, but the path won't be straight. And there may be side chambers off the tunnel. Remember the lurker's warnings to touch nothing but the ring, and beware the echo that doesn't answer."

"Do you have any idea what that means?" asked Shirell.

"None at all," responded Cooper.

As expected, the tunnel was dark as pitch and slightly damp, and though it turned and twisted, it was not too difficult to navigate. Then they came to the split.

"Any thoughts on which path?" asked Shirell.

"The light from the torches only penetrates a few feet, but both tunnels look identical," responded Cooper. "You're the orcanus. It's your choice."

"Horus?"

"I would go left, m'lady, only because most folks are right-handed and would automatically go right. If I was going to set a trap to keep people out, I would expect most of them to go that way."

"A good observation, Horus. Let's hope that Eldred used the same logic and, whether you're right or wrong, we should have an equal chance either way. Left it is."

Shirell held up her torch and started down the left-hand corridor with Horus following and Cooper bringing up the rear. The passageway continued straight for a few hundred yards before turning sharp to the right and opening into a large chamber. The three entered slowly as the torchlight only cut through the outer edges of the gloom.

Ten yards into the room, Cooper held up his hand, signaling them to stop.

"Listen!"

"I don't hear anything," whispered Shirell after a moment.

"Exactly, not even our own footsteps," said Cooper. He whistled softly and got no response except eerie silence.

All three stood frozen for an instant.

Then it came like a tsunami.

The wind howled through the room, shrieking like a banshee and extinguishing the torches. The suddenness and sheer force of the blast forced Cooper to stumble sideways a dozen steps before he was able to regain his footing. He re-lit the torch and discovered that he was now alone in the great room.

Both Shirell and Horus were gone. He quickly scanned the room with the torch, but there was no sign of either of them. Not a trace. Not even a footprint in the dust on the floor.

Cooper circled the room, discovering a doorway off to the right. None of them had noticed it when they entered the room.

The torch sputtered and flickered, sending shadows dancing across the walls as he cautiously stepped through the doorway. The gloom resisted the invasion of light, receding only slightly as he cautiously proceeded into the newly found chamber. His staff glowed blue in anticipation of something unpleasant lurking in the dark, though its glow was no more effective against the gloom than the light of the torch. A shape in the corner drew him across the room and as he got closer, it moved.

"Shirell?" he whispered. "Are you hurt?"

His staff flared brightly, and he held the torch up high to see what huddled in the corner. The sight before him left him stunned.

Curled in a ball, battered and bloodied, was John.

John, who more than thirty years ago, had crossed over with him into this land from the human world. The same John who had been his partner when they made barrels for the elf brothers at the Dragon's Breath pub. And the same John who had been lost when the princess carelessly led them into an ambush of marauding gremlins.

They had been a good pair together. John was smart as a whip, but small and thin. A sharp contrast to Cooper who was tall and more athletic. They both had a taste for adventure. When given the opportunity to train with the elf wardens, they jumped at it. Cooper was the natural athlete. John struggled with the physical demands of the training, though he excelled at the magic. He was being considered for an apprenticeship with the Hall of Conjurers, quite an accomplishment for an outsider, when he went out on that fateful patrol.

It was to be his last patrol with the other trainees, and he trusted Cooper to keep him safe. But the princess was leading the patrol, and in her haste to get back to the castle, she made a foolish amateur mistake. She led them directly into an ambush. Cooper and Ashley were separated from the others in the initial attack and barely survived. John and the other elves were not so lucky. The gremlins butchered the inexperienced elves. John's body was never found.

Gremlins were known for their brutality. If John had been taken alive, his fate would have been far worse than if he had been killed outright. For years, Cooper had blamed himself for John's death.

Cooper stared in disbelief. How could John be here? It had to be an illusion. Even if he had somehow survived the attack by the gremlins, how could anyone still be alive after decades of torture and captivity? How could he have wound up here? These tunnels had been sealed for years. There were no gremlins here to keep him alive, even if just for the fun of tormenting him.

The wretched creature in the corner looked up at Cooper with his one good eye.

"John? But how...?" was all Cooper could say.

"My friend, Cooper...you did this," wheezed John. "Left me to die. All you cared about was your precious princess."

"No, John," stuttered Cooper. "I tried to protect you. We were separated, cut off. We searched for you for days."

"Only after you abandoned me to save her," John spat at him.

Cooper's mind was numb. A thousand times over, he had accused himself of the exact same thing. After the gremlin attack, he had carried the princess to safety, leaving John behind.

In the fever of the moment, he had abandoned his closest friend. Time after time, he had tried to convince himself that all three of them, Cooper, the princess and John, would have died if he had not carried the princess back to the castle. He had barely survived his own wounds, but all his explanations fell short of relieving him of the crushing guilt. He knew that he could never truly forgive himself. Cooper felt himself fall to his knees as a black wave of despair washed over him.

Chapter 15

"Cooper...COOPER!"

A stinging slap to the side of his face forced Cooper to open his eyes. He found himself staring into the weathered old face of Horus.

"Oh, thank the gods...I thought I had lost you. C'mon, on your feet, son. We need to find Shirell."

"But...what?" Cooper tried to rise and found his legs to be weak and unsteady.

"Shake it off, boy," said Horus, dragging him by the arm. "That girl's in mortal danger if we don't find her soon."

Between the cobwebs in his head and Horus's urging, Cooper stopped trying to make sense of what had happened and just followed the old wizard as quickly as his shaky legs would allow.

They found Shirell huddled in a corner, arms wrapped around her knees, eyes staring off blankly. She offered no resistance as they lifted her to her feet and half carried her from the room. Horus insisted on going well down the tunnel before stopping and setting Shirell gently on the floor.

"Talk to her, son," Horus told Cooper. "She knows your voice."

"Shirell...Shirell, can you hear me?" asked Cooper, as he rubbed her hands between his.

"Her hands are like ice," he whispered to Horus.

Cooper gently shook her shoulders, but her eyes remained glassy.

Horus leaned over and looked directly into her eyes.

"Stupid girl. Marcus was obviously right about you," he said to her in a voice dripping with contempt. "He said that you weren't ready to be orcanus. Probably never will be. Why, you're barely more than a child."

Cooper stared in disbelief as the old wizard mercilessly berated the unresponsive Shirell.

"You should just go back to the woods and live with the wolves. They won't notice that your skills are only second rate. Eldred had more magic in his little pinky finger than you. Why, you're barely worth enough to be a serving wench."

Shirell's eyes blinked twice, then they flashed in anger.

"Why, you miserable old coot. How dare you! I will turn you into a mouse and give you to my snicker as a plaything."

The aged wizard cackled like an old hen. "Ha! There's my girl. Forgive me, m'lady, but you were slipping away, and I have no wish to take over your position."

"Why, you wily old buzzard," said Cooper with a smile. "You're not half as crazy as you pretend to be."

Horus gave them a devilish grin before turning serious.

"Can you tell us what you saw, Shirell?"

"My mother," answered Shirell after a moment. Cooper was still rubbing her hands and could feel them begin shaking as she spoke.

"It was horrible. She was hanging on a stake, beaten and tortured, barely alive. She told me that everything was my fault. After my father disappeared years ago, she knew that the same thing would happen to me. She couldn't bear losing both of us. She had to follow me. She said that if I hadn't left her, this never would have happened to her. It was all so real."

Shirell buried her head in Cooper's shoulder and sobbed.

"There is a spell protecting that room," said Horus quietly. "I've heard of this sort of spell, but had long ago forgotten about it until I experienced it. It burrows into the darkest recesses of your mind and makes you live out your worst nightmare, your biggest regret. The guilt and self-blame become so overwhelming that you lose yourself. The lucky ones run off screaming and recover in time. The unlucky can be lost forever, prisoners in their own minds. These spells were banned by the Guild."

After a moment, Shirell looked up from Cooper's shoulder.

"Horus, how were you able to resist? What did you see?"

A look of intense sadness passed over the old man's face before he answered.

"I saw the Guild. All of them. Every single one of my old friends and colleagues. All together. Dozens of them that all died when the Guild Hall was destroyed. Only I survived because I was off picking mushrooms that morning. Mushrooms! My life was spared because of stupid old mushrooms. All my friends gone in an instant, horribly crushed under tons of stone and debris. I've lived with that for years. I was able to survive today because I see their faces every night. Every time I lay down to sleep, I see them. They're with me always, smiling and waiting patiently for me to come and join them. But today, when they were angry, accusing me, cursing me and blaming me for their fate, I knew it was a trick. Perhaps they really were there, helping me today. I don't know, I just knew that what I was seeing was wrong."

"Why would Eldred place a spell around the vault that was so horrible that the members of his own Guild had banned its use?"

"There can only be one reason," responded Horus.

"Because the contents of that room are even worse than the spell. Because there is an object in that room that is so cursed that they never want anyone to enter or even know of its existence. I believe that room must contain the monkey's paw."

"The monkey's paw? But that's just an old fable," said Cooper. "And it's not even a story from this world."

"Like many of your legends, the story is based on an object from this world," said Horus. "It is one of the most cursed artifacts ever created by dark magic. There were whispers that Eldred had gone into your world and recovered it, but no one in the Guild wanted to believe that it resided in a vault just below our feet."

"Will one of you two please explain to me just what exactly is a monkey's paw?" said Shirell.

"According to the legend," began Cooper, "it is the preserved paw of a monkey that's been infused with the darkest of magic and has the power to grant you one wish. Any wish. Well, who could resist that? Absolutely anything you could possibly wish for, it will grant.

"But it's always at a horrible cost. If you wish for wealth, you will likely receive it as compensation for the loss of your dearest loved ones. Ask for that loved one to be brought back to you, they'll return as a rotting corpse. If you should try to trick it and wish for something simple, like a quiet life, you will gain it as the only survivor of a devastating holocaust or trapped on an island after a terrible shipwreck. Anything anyone wishes for will cause death and destruction on a terrible scale. There is no safe wish with the monkey's paw."

"And it cannot be destroyed. Many have tried," added Horus. "That's why it must be kept locked in a room, protected by a spell that is so horrible that it makes you want to run away screaming."

Cooper stood and offered Shirell his hand.

"There's nothing we can do about the monkey's paw except try to forget that it exists. If you're feeling better, we should get what we came for and get away from here as quickly as possible."

"There's still a few cobwebs in my head," answered Shirell as she got to her feet, "but I think I'll be fine once we get away from that room."

"I still need to retrieve the ring," said Cooper as he tore small pieces of cloth from the inside of his cloak and plugged his ears with them. "That room we were in was just the antechamber for the vault. We've already broken the protective spell and, with my ears blocked, I should be able to enter in relative safety. I'm taking Horus along to wait outside the vault in case I'm wrong. You should be safe here."

"No, I'm coming with you, and don't argue with me. I'm the orcanus. It's my responsibility. My head's clear and we know what to expect. Let's go and get this over with. Besides, Susan and the princess will never forgive me if I allow you to get hurt."

"All right, I can see that I'd be wasting my time pointing out that you're safer here, so plug your ears and stay close."

Cautiously, with the torches re-lit, they returned to the chamber. Directly opposite the entrance, an ominous doorway beckoned them. All three breathed a sigh of relief as they crossed the anteroom and Cooper was proven correct. No further attack came.

The torches drove the gloom back as they entered. Arranged in a semi-circle, a dozen pedestals each three feet high occupied the room. Most contained some artifact under glass. Two of them sparkled — jeweled objects that reflected the torchlight back at them. The three pedestals on the end were empty. On the center stand resided a shriveled hand covered in short black fur — the monkey's paw. Horus had been right.

"Remember the lurker's warning," whispered Cooper, his voice muffled by the cloth in their ears. "'Touch nothing but the ring.' I think we would be very wise to follow that advice."

Both Shirell and Horus nodded their agreement.

On the fourth pedestal to the right of center rested a ring of hammered silver. Cooper crossed quickly to the stand and gingerly removed the glass cover. No one moved, anticipating some response. When none came, Cooper retrieved the ring, placed it in a small pouch, and tucked it carefully inside his tunic before replacing the glass cover.

"Time to go," he said.

Even Horus's steps were lively as they began their return to the mouth of the cave. None of them wished to spend any more time in the tunnels than needed.

They heard the sound behind them just as they saw the starlit sky on the other side of the cave entrance. They broke into a run as the sound grew louder, steadily gaining on them as they got nearer to the exit.

Cooper's long stride and Shirell's youth carried them to the mouth of the cave quickly, but Horus was lagging behind. He was still fifty yards back and struggling to keep up. Whatever was chasing them would catch him before he could get clear of the tunnel.

Suddenly, in a jumble of robes and old bones, Horus tripped and went down. The invisible threat behind them would be on him in an instant.

"Stay down!" yelled Shirell as she dropped to one knee and hurled a fireball of blue magic over the fallen wizard and down the tunnel.

The concussion swept Shirell off her feet and flung her onto the grass. Somehow Cooper managed to keep his footing and was racing down the tunnel before the dust had a chance to settle. He had Horus over one shoulder and was back out on the hillside by the time Shirell had struggled back to her feet.

"Is he hurt?" asked Shirell as she dashed over to where Cooper knelt beside Horus.

"You singed his hair a bit," answered Cooper with a grin. "But besides a few bruises, I think that he should be fine in a moment."

Almost on cue, Horus shook his head and opened his eyes.

"Oh, m'lady. I did say that I was getting far too old for adventures."

"Are you all right? Can you stand?"

"Well, I don't think anything's broken. If young Cooper here will help me up, I'll know better."

"What was that?" asked Shirell, turning her attention to Cooper. "I didn't actually see anything chasing us. Why didn't it attack us when we were in the vault?"

"One last little surprise from Eldred. I can only guess that it was placed near the entrance to stop anything from being removed from the vault. It didn't become active until we tried to leave with one of the objects."

A rustle in the grass brought all three about suddenly. Lon stood ten feet away, watching them.

"I saw a bright flash and approached carefully, fearing that I would find the three of you either dead or off your heads. I believe that you are the first since Eldred to escape the tunnels unharmed."

"Thank you for returning, Lon," Cooper responded. "If

115

you could lead us back to your inn, I think we could all use a cup of your wife's stew and a few hours of sleep."

"Excellent," said Lon, giving Cooper a hearty slap on the shoulder. "My wife will be pleased."

Chapter 16

Two days after returning from the village of Doon, Cooper and Shirell rode out once again toward Ramses Marsh for another visit with the lurker. The silver ring and the Boc book, wrapped separately in oilcloth for the subsequent hike into the marsh, resided in a small backpack, secured to Cooper's saddle.

"Tell me about the old Guild," said Shirell, after an hour's ride.

"What would you like to know?" asked Cooper.

"Anything you can remember. I've been working with Lady Coramina, trying to restore as much of the Guild's history as possible, but she says that there's only general information in her records. She has almost nothing on individuals. On his best days, old Horus's memory is sketchy. He's told me the same story three times, and each time he tells it, he claims that it was a different member of the Guild. All of the Guild's original records were lost in the lindworm's attack that destroyed the hall, so every scrap of information that you can provide is valuable."

"Well, I'll try to be a little more accurate than my old friend, Horus," chuckled Cooper. "Will you be able to remember what I tell you without writing it down?"

"My memory's pretty good. I'll remember the important parts. And then maybe sometime you could sit down with

Coramina, fill in any details that I miss, and see if I got it right."

"I'll plan on that for the next time I visit. I'm not sure where to start, though."

"When we went to see Marcus, he mentioned someone named Poole. Why don't you tell me about him?"

"Poole?" answered Cooper with a wide grin. "I forgot that Marcus spoke of him. Poole was quite the colorful character, and he was probably Horus's best friend. Among other things, they were drinking buddies, although Poole could drink Horus, and just about anyone else, under the table any night of the week. I'll admit that I shared a few pints with him.

"One time, Poole tried to create a mug that magically refilled itself, but he could never get that to work. With Horus's help, he did finally succeed in making a mug that transferred most of the contents from one mug to another when they touched. He was a sly old bird. He would sneak his mug into the pub, propose a toast to the king's health or something else that everyone would gladly toast to, tap his empty mug against someone's full mug, and then quickly turn away before that person noticed that their cup was now almost empty. It didn't take too long until he was banned from every pub and tavern within twenty miles. Finally, after enough complaints, Eldred confiscated the mug, destroyed it and threatened to expel Poole from the Guild if he ever tried to make another one.

"Beyond the drinking, he was brilliant. He was the Guild historian. You could have filled an entire bookshelf with just half of what he knew. He had an incredible memory, but he was very lax about writing things down. If he did write anything down, no one ever found it. Coramina could have spent a month with him and barely scratched the surface of his knowledge.

"Actually, Poole is the reason that I suspected the book was from the Boc the first time I saw it. We were at the pub one night, after they let him back in, and he was telling me about this script that he was trying to unscramble. He loved puzzles and he liked to be mysterious, so he would only give me hints about what he was working on, but I suspected from a few things that he said that it involved the Boc. When I saw the book in the archive room, I knew that it had to be what he was talking about."

"Wait, if he knew about the Boc and their books, why didn't Coramina have any record of it in the archives?"

"I can think of two reasons. Members of the Guild were killed trying to open the first few books. The Guild was pretty secretive about their failures. Second, Coramina's predecessor was the father of Macilon, the king's valet. He was a dull and pompous snob who looked down his nose at anyone who drank. He treated Poole with scorn, and there was probably a fair amount of jealousy, too. Poole was ten times as knowledgeable as that pretentious old fool, and he knew it. Poole hated the man and would have rather poked himself in the eye with a sharp stick than tell him anything."

"So Poole was killed in the destruction of the hall?"

"We believed that he was, but no one's ever dug into the rubble looking for bodies. After the war, as our new friend Lon pointed out to us just two days ago, the ruins of the Hall were treated like a sacred tomb. Once, Horus claimed that Poole wasn't there that day, but he was never seen or heard from again. And as you've pointed out, Horus's memory can be unreliable, so we had to assume that Poole was inside when it was destroyed."

"How many were in the Guild Hall when it fell?" asked Shirell.

"About fifty," responded Cooper. "As best we could count, there was twenty full-fledged members of the Guild, a dozen apprentices, and around twenty locals who cooked or worked

119

there in some other job."

"I was trapped at the far end of the west wing," Shirell said with a shudder. "I'm sorry. I don't think I want to talk about this anymore."

"I understand. When we get back to Kestriana, we'll send for Horus. Between the two of us, we should be able to help Coramina fill in some of her Guild history."

Chapter 17

By midday, they had arrived in Finhaven, stabled the horses, and hiked the last few miles to the marsh. A hundred yards in from the main road, it seemed like they had entered a whole different world. The air was thick and pungent, and there were sounds made by creatures that neither one of them wanted to meet.

As before, the lurker appeared shortly after they entered the swamp. Silent as a ghost, Crall suddenly materialized on the path before them.

"Come," he said and started away, never looking to see if Cooper and Shirell were following. Once again, he led them into his shelter that, even to Cooper's trained eye, was indistinguishable from the surrounding vegetation.

"I am pleased...that you survived...Eldred's traps, Guardian," wheezed Crall. He motioned toward the flat stump that occupied the center of the room and appeared to serve as a table. "Place the...book there and bring me...the ring. Let us see what...this book can tell us."

Cooper carefully unwrapped the book, set it in the indicated spot, and placed the ring in the emaciated hand of the lurker.

With the silver ring hanging crookedly on a misshapen finger, Crall extended his skeletal hand over the book, muttered a few words from a language that was long dead, and turned the first page. A misty image began to appear before them. As they watched, shapes slowly emerged, revealing the interior of a ruined cottage. Mottled sunlight filtered down through gaping holes in the roof. Across the room, partially blocked by coarse vines that sported cruel looking thorns, was a slender window opening.

"This is...where one...of the books rests," wheezed Crall.

"Is there any way to tell where that is?" asked Shirell.

"It must one of the old Boc settlements," answered Cooper. "I can't say exactly where, but I recognize the architecture. Their villages were situated all along the borders of gremlin lands. The tall narrow windows are a classic characteristic of their dwellings. It made their homes easier to defend against the constant threat of roving bands of gremlins. After the Boc vanished, the other elves searched for them, but no one was ever sure if they had found all the smaller settlements. This is most likely one of their abandoned villages that was never found. Clearly, no one's been there for years. I don't think we'll find anything useful here."

The image dissolved as Crall closed his hand. Once the vision had completely dissipated, the lurker turned the next page with a boney finger and extended his hand again, but this time, no image would appear. Crall closed his fist and moved his hand away. After a moment, he tried again with the same result.

"This book...no longer...exists," he said.

"Marcus said that the first few books that were found exploded in large fireballs when attempts were made to force them open," responded Cooper. "That page must correspond to one of the books that was destroyed. Many of the remaining ones were also lost when the Guild Hall fell. The book held by Marcus's confederate may very well be the only other one still intact. Please try the next page, Crall."

The lurker turned the page, and then another with similar results. Four more pages produced nothing.

On the eighth page, trees seemed to appear in the swirling mist. But as the image focused, it became clear that this was not any forest that they were familiar with. The trees were stunted and small, surrounded by thorny weeds. Misshapen branches shot off in all directions, and what leaves there were looked yellow and blighted.

As the image cleared, they could see movement. A creature prowled between the twisted trees. From snout to tail, it was over fifteen feet long. Its hide was varying shades of greens and browns. Its feet sported talons that could effortlessly rend flesh and when it moved. Its head swung back and forth deliberately, as if searching for prey. The creature paused momentarily, looking directly at them, as if it was somehow aware of the book's magic and that someone was watching. Then, slowly, it turned and moved away.

"Shades, what was that?" asked Shirell, in a whisper.

"It is called...a scree...It is one of the...demon creatures....that destroyed the shadow mages."

"But that means...." Shirell began as a chill ran up her spine.

"That there is a book somewhere behind the Barrier," finished Cooper. "This book that we have has suddenly become far more dangerous than we originally thought. With it, you wouldn't need to destroy the Barrier. You could just open a pathway and release all the nightmare creatures imprisoned there. We need to find that last missing book. Crall, please go on."

Crall closed his hand, and the image dissipated like smoke. The next two pages produced nothing.

As Crall held his hand over the next page, colors swirled

and, once again, blurred objects appeared in the mist. This book still existed. Shelves on the walls lined with colored glass bottles of various chemicals and herbs revealed what appeared to be a laboratory. A window opening on the opposite wall gave a glimpse of moss-covered stone walls and parapets outside that were badly in need of repair.

"It looks very old," said Cooper. "But I don't know of any abandoned castles. I wish we could see more of the surrounding landscape. Something to give us an idea of where this place is."

"It is...a keep," wheezed the lurker. "I know of...this place. It lies...deep in...the Dark Woods."

"But, how —" began Shirell.

Crall interrupted Shirell's question with a frightening growl.

"Do not...question how I know, Orcanus...I have lived many lives...and I have...been to this place."

"The Dark Woods are vast and dangerous," Cooper said. "Half the elven army could spend weeks searching for this place and not find it. Can you give us a more precise location, Crall?"

"There are...no maps of...the Dark Woods...and no one knows...how far they extend."

"But you say that you've been there."

"I do not...lie. The forest has...long ago...reclaimed what were once roads...to this place...But, there is...a passage...I know of...that will take you there. Through the...Ice Caves."

"That makes sense," said Cooper. "That's where we had our first encounter with Marcus. He must have been using the caves to travel back and forth. After faking his demise, he would no longer have had access to the book that was in the archive room."

"As the shadow mage, he showed me some of the passages in the caves and how to avoid getting lost in the labyrinth," said

124

Shirell. "I shouldn't be surprised that some of them lead elsewhere and that he kept that information from me."

"The Ice Caves lead...many places. Some places where...you should never go."

"Can you tell us which tunnels can take us to this keep?" asked Cooper.

"Take the first...three branches to the right...then the next three...on the left...You will find...an oaken door. It opens into...a small cabin. The keep is...a mile north from there."

"I wonder, will the cottage still be standing?" said Cooper. "As with the roads, the forest quickly reclaims anything left unused."

"This cottage...will still stand. No vines...can pull it down. They cannot grow...in the soil...that surrounds it. Even the insects....know that to burrow...into its beams...means instant death. They are poison."

Cooper glanced at Shirell. "Remember the archive room? There were no insects there. No spiderwebs or black flies buzzing near the windows."

"They are...creatures of the earth. They sense evil...Humans and elves...have lost that ability. You must go...to the keep...and retrieve this book. Bring it back here...to me...and no man nor elf...will ever see it again."

"You're being very helpful, Crall," observed Cooper. "And no riddles. Why the sudden change of heart, and why should we trust you?"

"My fear of the book...equals your own. I have....some history...with the scree...the creature that we saw earlier. I have...encountered it before. Much of my...appearance is due...to this creature. It has tasted...my flesh...and desires more. If it were to escape...from behind the Barrier, its first instinct....would be to hunt me down...and tear me...limb from limb. Finish the job...it once started. It will not...stop until it has achieved that end...and there is...nowhere to hide from it. It can smell...me from half...a world away. I am old, but I am neither...immortal or indestructible. I have no wish...to perish in...such a manner. And after the...creature finishes with me...it will destroy...every living thing in its path. It is...in both our interests...to help each other."

"Then you will need my consent," said Shirell. "And don't you dare snarl at me, you ancient sack of bones. As reigning orcanus, I have final say over the fate of all objects of magic. I do have some obligation to consult with the king of the elves, or in his place, Princess Ashley, before making any binding agreement, but mine is the final word. So, if they agree, we will be willing to return the book to you for safekeeping, but only for a price."

The lurker made a sound resembling a growl. "What is...your price, Orcanus?"

"There may come a time when I will have need of your knowledge. I don't know when that might be, but when I need it, you will share any information you have with me freely. No riddles or games, just the truth."

"Agreed," wheezed Crall. "But only once, so chose...your question carefully, Witch."

"Well, before we make too many agreements about the book's fate, we need to return to Kestriana and consult with the princess. Then we must make our way through the passage in the Ice Caves, find this keep, retrieve the other book, and return with it, hopefully, without having to battle Marcus's confederate or get eaten by something in the Dark Woods. So, if you two are done negotiating, we should be leaving."

Crall held up an emaciated hand and pointed toward the book. "There is...one last page, Guardian...You may find it...important. The script is quite...different from the runes...that make up the rest of the book. Perhaps it was added much later. It

126

states the terms of an agreement...struck between Eldred...and the whole of the Boc clan. It is signed...in what looks like blood...by both Eldred and...Boron, leader of the Boc long ago. Eldred helped them...escape from the emerging elf kingdom...and keep their way of life...by creating the books...that spirited them away...and prevented them from being followed."

Crall was forced to pause for a moment as a coughing fit shook his skeletal frame.

"In return for his aid...they agreed that, someday...after they were settled in a new location...Eldred would...send word to them...tell them where to find an artifact. They must create for it...a new hiding place. Just a small puzzle box...but encased in a web of magic to prevent it ever being opened...The ring, such as this one," Crall gestured to the hammered silver talisman on his bony finger, "would allow them to handle and transport it...Eldred was dying, the magic...taking its toll, slowly destroying him...from the inside. The box would contain his essence. All his power...and secrets....any member of the Boc...current and all future generations to come...would be duty bound...by a blood oath...to guard that puzzle box...and never reveal its location. They were charged...not with protecting the box...but rather protecting the entire world...from the contents of the box. Eldred warns....that no one could possess...such power and...not be corrupted. Darkon Rhee...must never be allowed...to possess what was...contained in the box. When the time came...Eldred intended to close himself...inside the puzzle box...where, once it was sealed...he would remain...confined for all time. It was the only...way to prevent Darkon Rhee...from gaining the power Eldred held."

Both Shirell and Cooper stared silently at the lurker as he finished speaking.

"I can scarcely believe it," Cooper said in a whisper. "We

finally know Eldred's fate. But who is Darkon Rhee? I knew many of the Guild members before the war. There were none by that name nor rumors of any renegade magic wielders."

"Even I, have never heard...the name before, Guardian." wheezed Crall, once again pausing to cough violently. "But Eldred...would not charge the Boc...with such a task lightly. If the book you seek...is held by one of the Boc...they may possess this puzzle box...or know of its hiding place. Should you encounter it...do not be tempted...by the promise of Eldred's power. Heed my warning...Do not open the box...Eldred never left things to chance. There will be other safeguards...It is a trap." Crall straightened up as much as his twisted form would allow. "You have a long journey...to complete the task...you have undertaken...You should go now. Take great care...I...wish you luck, Guardian."

Chapter 18

Crall watched out of a small, hidden window until Cooper and Shirell were out of sight, then he shuffled through the concealed doorway into the other portion of his dwelling that had remained virtually hidden from his guests. The entrance blended so perfectly with the wall that even he occasionally had difficulty finding it. He visibly shivered when he thought of the scree. Few things frightened the lurker, but the scree was one of them. Even though his wounds were decades old, they still caused him pain and had never fully healed, having been wrought by claws infused with dark magic. He had lied to Cooper, and that small portion of him that had once been human felt a twinge of remorse. Cooper was a good man, and Crall had only met a few of them in all his lives.

Crall knew all too well who Darkon Rhee was. Darkon Rhee had set the scree upon him. Decades ago, Eldred had lured Crall out of his self-imposed exile and persuaded him to aid in the construction of the Barrier. It was too large an undertaking for any one magic wielder, even one as powerful as Eldred. And Crall was unique in that he could work with both light and dark magic. Together they had woven the spells that created the outer ring of the Barrier, the one formed of white magic.

Then Eldred left to drive the demons toward the Barrier. Darkon Rhee appeared soon after that, and the far more difficult job of forming the inner ring of dark magic began. Crall had not heard of Rhee or met him before that day, but Eldred had sent him, so Crall accepted that he would be up to the task.

When the ring was nearly complete and only a small opening remained, an army of dragons recruited by Eldred drove the demons and creatures of evil through the doorway. It took the combined strength of twenty of Prax's kin to force the scree through the opening. Darkon Rhee's task was to surround the monster with constantly changing illusions, confusing it and holding it at bay while Crall sealed the inner ring. Once the monster was inside the Barrier and contained, Crall began to work. Crall's spell had to be absolutely seamless. Anything less and the creatures would eventually find and break through any crack or weakness in the wall. When Crall finished and the Barrier was sealed, Darkon Rhee needed only to continue to restrain the creature long enough for the two of them to reach the portal provided by one of the books Eldred had created for the Boc.

Crall worked feverishly to seal the inner ring. The creature could only be held for a short time, and he had to be sure that the wall was smooth as glass and blemish free. When he was satisfied that his work was perfect, he turned toward his escape route. But he was struck down from behind before he could move. Through the haze in his head, he heard Darkon Rhee laughing.

"You've done an excellent job, Crall, but now that you're finished, I'll be releasing the scree. The portal's only a few hundred yards away. We'll need to hurry before the creature attacks us. We can make it if we run. Of course, I don't have to outrun the scree. I only have to outrun you."

With one vicious final kick to the side of Crall's head, Darkon Rhee sprinted toward the open portal.

Desperately trying to shake the cobwebs from his head, Crall struggled to his feet and stumbled toward the portal. He had to get to that book and escape.

Fifty yards from his goal, the scree hit him with the fury of a tiger, bowling him over and tearing a huge chunk of flesh from his thigh. Rolling and throwing magic in every direction to try to protect himself, Crall tried to rise, but the injured leg wouldn't support him.

Again and again, the scree crashed into him like a battering ram, finally able to vent its blind fury at being imprisoned on someone. The monster's talons battered him back and forth like a rag doll. Crall lay on the ground, nearly helpless, as the monster mauled him, occasionally stopping just long enough to tear off indiscriminate chunks of flesh and shriek out its rage.

In one final, desperate move, Crall shoved his fist into the snapping jaws of the beast. Praying that it would be enough, he released every ounce of magic he could call upon in a blast that would have decapitated most creatures.

The scree was thrown backwards, stunned and partially blinded. Fortunately for Crall, their struggles had brought them within a few yards of the portal.

Blinking the blood from his eyes, Crall half crawled, half dragged himself through the portal, collapsing on the other side after slamming the book closed, ensuring that the creature couldn't follow.

Darkon Rhee had already gone, assuming that the scree had finished Crall and, being a mindless beast, would go off in search of other prey.

In one last act of self-preservation before passing out, Crall muttered a spell that encased him in a tightly woven web of magic. The cocoon protected him and hid him while sealing his wounds and allowing him to sleep for a week while his body attempted to heal itself.

Months later, after his body had recovered as much as it ever would, Crall searched for Darkon Rhee to exact his revenge, but the dark wizard had vanished without a trace.

Chapter 19

"**A**bsolutely not!" said Cooper.

"I'm afraid that I have to agree with your grandfather, Susan," added Shirell.

"But, Grandfather —"

"No buts, it's too dangerous. Your mother would skin me alive if I let you come with us. I guarantee you that she'll already have some pretty choice words for me because I'm going."

Susan turned to the princess.

"Please, Aunt Ashley. Bodkin and I've been involved with this since we arrived. We've even met Crall. You can't shut us out now."

"I'm sorry, Susan, but your grandfather's right," responded Ashley. "There was very little risk going to see the lurker, but this is completely different. Now, there's a very good chance that they may meet whoever was working with the shadow mage, and we have no idea how powerful they may be. Both your grandfather and Shirell are experienced magic wielders. Even Horus is staying behind. We're sorry, but the answer has to be no. I promise, I'll make it up to you. I'll make some time in my schedule while they're gone. We'll go riding together."

"Oh, this is so unfair," said Susan, throwing up her hands. "Besides, you don't even like horses," she snapped at the princess as she stomped out the door.

"She'll be fine," said Ashley. "She's just angry and frustrated. She sees the adventure, but not the dangers. I remember that feeling. Almost got me killed a few times."

"I know," responded Cooper, shaking his head. "She is so much like her mother that it frightens me sometimes."

Bodkin was adjusting the tension on her bowstring when Susan stormed into the room they shared and threw herself on the bed.

"I just can't believe that they won't let us go with them. Oh, I'm so angry at all of them. My grandfather, Shirell, even Aunt Ashley's ganging up on us. How can you be so calm?"

"Oh, I don't know," answered Bodkin. "Elven patience? My training as a warden? Or maybe because I already know where they're going."

"What? You sneaky little elf. You were eavesdropping on them, weren't you? You do know that the Shirell will cut off your pointy little ears if she catches you spying on her."

"Well, I can't help it if some voices carry."

"So, c'mon, don't keep me in suspense. Tell me where they're going to find this other magic book."

"Through the Ice Caves. There's a passage that leads into the Dark Woods. We could slip out the west gate, ride to the cave entrance ahead of them, stay just out of sight, and then follow them in after they enter. Crall told them to go three times to the right, then three lefts to an oak door. We can't really get lost, and once we're there, they'll have to let us come along the rest of the way."

"Grandfather will be furious."

"I know, but he would never leave us alone in the Dark

134

Woods or dare to send us back into the Ice Caves on our own."

"We will have to be very careful that they don't catch us following them, at least until we get through the caves."

"Agreed. So, are you in or not?"

"I'm in. We'll have to act like we're still really mad at them, though. If we don't, they'll suspect that we're up to something."

Early the next morning, Susan went to see Cooper.

"I'm sorry that we argued yesterday, Grandfather, but since you won't let us come with you, Bodkin and I have decided to ride out to visit Pen. I do still think that you're being terribly unfair not letting us come along."

"We went through all this yesterday, Susan," answered Cooper with a sigh. "Please, let's not argue before I have to leave. I'm glad that you've found something pleasant to do until I get back. I'm sure that Pen will welcome the company. And I promise I'll be careful."

"You better be. And keep Shirell safe," said Susan, giving Cooper her sternest look. "She's one of my best friends."

"I will. I also promise that I'll come find you as soon as we return and fill you in on everything that happened. Give my best to Pen."

Susan left her grandfather's room and quickly descended to the stables at the rear of the castle. Bodkin was already there, getting the takis ready. Both girls knew that they had less than an hour before Cooper and Shirell were scheduled to leave. They needed to get to the west gate and be away from Kestriana before that happened. And they would need a little extra time to circle around and still maintain their head start. Fortunately, Cooper had no reason to race to the Ice Caves, so if they hurried, everything should go according to plan.

Bodkin was waiting outside the stables when Susan arrived. In her hands, she held the reins of the same two takis that they had ridden on the day Susan and Cooper arrived. Strapped to the pony's flanks were two backpacks filled with supplies.

"I told the stable master that we'd be a few days, so no one will worry if we don't come back by nightfall. How did it go with your grandfather?"

"Good, but I feel terrible lying to him. I don't like deceiving him. He'll be angry when he finds out that we followed him, but the idea of sitting around the castle waiting, while he and Shirell attempt to retrieve a magical artifact from a spooky old keep in the middle of the Dark Woods. It's just not fair that they leave us behind. I told him that we're going to visit your brother. We should get started if we want to stay ahead of them. C'mon, I'll feel better once we're on our way."

"We're all set. Let's go."

The guards at the west gate were accustomed to seeing the two girls riding out in the morning and just gave them a friendly wave as they went by. They kept the takis at a lively trot for the first few miles until they were well away from Kestriana.

"What are we going to do with the takis once we get to the Ice Caves?" asked Susan. "We can't just abandon them."

"We're in luck," answered Bodkin. "A mile from the cave entrance, there's a secluded valley where a herd of wild takis live. It's well known to the wardens of the forest. We can just take off their bridles and they'll join in with the herd. There's plenty of food and water nearby. They're well trained. When we come back, they'll respond to a whistle and come. Your grandfather and Shirell will most likely do the same thing with their horses."

"But, won't they recognize our takis if they leave their horses there at the same place?"

"No, they share the valley, but the wild ponies shy away

from the full-size horses. The taki herd will keep its distance and our two will blend in. They should never get close enough for your grandfather to pick them out."

By late morning, the two girls had arrived at the valley of the wild takis, released their mounts, stored the bridles in a hollowed out oak that was easy to locate on their return, and hiked the last mile to the entrance of the Ice Caves. On a small ridge overlooking the entrance, they settled down to wait behind some bushes that were tall enough to provide good cover.

The morning had just passed into afternoon when Cooper and Shirell appeared near the cave entrance. Having left their horses in the same valley as the girls did, they were now on foot. Susan and Bodkin watched quietly from their hiding place, then gave them a ten minute head start before following them into the caves.

Just before entering, Bodkin stopped Susan.

"We don't know how far our voices may carry in these caves so we probably shouldn't speak once we're inside. Remember the directions. Three to the right, then three to the left to an oaken door. And remember what Quisp told us the last time we were here — we don't stare at the crystals on the walls, they'll confuse and disorient us."

Susan nodded. She hadn't forgotten.

Once inside, they followed the main corridor to the first split. Though they were faint, footprints in the dust confirmed that Cooper and Shirell went to the right. Not expecting to be followed, they were making no attempt to hide their tracks. Following them was turning out to be easier than Susan had expected.

Three turns to the right, then three to the left. The last

tunnel ended abruptly at an oaken door. Bodkin cracked the door slightly and peered out, hoping not to run face to face into Cooper and Shirell.

Exactly as Crall had told them, the door opened into a small cottage. Shirell and Cooper had already gone and the single room hut was empty. Bodkin and Susan quickly slipped past the door, which swung open silently and smoothly despite its appearance. They went quickly through the cottage and were outside in an instant.

"Their tracks lead this way," said Bodkin, pointing north and silently thanking the old warden who had taught her how to read the signs of a trail.

Once they were away from the cottage, Bodkin's job became much easier. Although severely overgrown, an ancient path was easily discernible. They followed quickly for a half mile when the trees suddenly parted, and they almost walked right out into the open.

Chapter 20

Spread out before them stood the remnants of a long abandoned village —a central square surrounded by houses and huts in an uneven circle. The road opened up directly into the main square of the town, and at the far end of the square, facing the opposite direction, stood Cooper and Shirell.

Before Susan had time to think about it, Bodkin had grabbed her arm and dragged her out of sight behind the nearest set of ruins. At one time, it was probably someone's home, but now it was little more than three collapsing walls and a pile of rubble that may have once been a roof.

"What are they doing?" whispered Susan as Bodkin peered around the edge of the wall.

"They look like they're just resting for a moment and getting their bearings. I can see traces of the path in front of them. They should move on in a moment. Let's circle around behind the ruined houses. If they don't leave, we might be able to get close enough to hear what they're saying."

Susan nodded her agreement, and the two girls began working their way around the perimeter of the old village, peeking between the ruins from time to time to check on Susan's grandfather. As expected, Cooper and Shirell resumed their trek and disappeared into the forest at the edge of the clearing.

Susan watched them depart from behind one of the few

buildings that still seemed almost intact.

"They're moving on. We should give them a few minutes head start."

"All right, we can wait here."

A rectangular area behind one of the ramshackle huts caught Susan's eye.

"Look, this must have been someone's garden. You can see that it was cared for once. I wonder what became of the people that lived here."

"Maybe we're better off not knowing. The Dark Woods isn't known for being a nice place."

A splash of color drew Susan to a small pile of rocks.

"Look, you have snapdragons here. I never would have expected to find them in this dreary old forest."

"Snapdragons?"

"The flowers. We call them snapdragons. They look a little like the snout of a dragon. If you squeeze the back of the flower, it opens and closes like a mouth. They've always been one of my favorites."

"I've never seen flowers like that before." Bodkin said, leaning over for a closer look. "They are a nice color. Show me how they work."

Susan plucked one of the flowers from the group and held it up for Bodkin to smell. The instant Bodkin got within six inches of the bloom, it sprayed a pollen-like powder directly into her face. In a heartbeat, Bodkin's eyes rolled up as her knees gave way and she collapsed.

"Oh my God, Bodkin!" shouted Susan as she hurled the offending flower away and attempted to catch the falling elf girl. She managed to keep Bodkin from falling face first into the dust, but just barely.

Susan silently cursed her own foolishness as she untangled

140

herself from the limp Bodkin. How could she have been so stupid? How many times had her grandfather told her that things in this world were not always what they seemed. She shook Bodkin and carefully brushed the dust from her face, being careful not to breathe any herself. All her attempts to wake her friend were proving ineffective. In one last desperate attempt, she tried using her small amberstone to summon some magic, but she really didn't know any healing spells. The magic fizzled and dissipated ineffectively.

There was only one choice. She had to get Cooper. He was just ahead on the trail. Her grandfather would be furious with her, not only for following them but also for lying to him, but she would have to face that fury if she had any hope of waking the unconscious elf girl. She dragged Bodkin inside the one hut that still had most of its roof and prayed that she would be safe for the few moments she needed to go and get help.

"Bodkin, I'm so sorry. If you can hear me, I have to go and get my grandfather. I'll be right back. I promise."

After propping Bodkin's head up with her backpack, Susan dashed for the trail at the edge of the clearing, shouting for her grandfather as she ran.

Cooper was looking ahead, trying to catch a glimpse of the keep when Shirell placed a hand on his arm.

"Listen," she said. "I'm sure I heard a voice."

Both of them stood perfectly still and listened.

Faintly, the sound muffled by the thick vegetation, they heard it.

"Grandfather! Shirell! Please wait!"

"That's Susan!" exclaimed Shirell. "What in the world is she doing here?"

"Isn't it obvious?" answered Cooper, with a scowl. "They followed us. I'm sure Bodkin must be with her. I am going to lock that girl in her room for a week when we get back to Kestriana. C'mon, we need to go back and find them before they get lost in these woods."

Hurrying back down the trail at a trot, it took only two minutes before they saw Susan coming through the trees.

Susan saw Shirell and Cooper at the same instant that they saw her.

"Bodkin's hurt, I need your help. I had to leave her back in the deserted village," she said before either adult had the chance to say anything.

Anger was clear from his expression, but Cooper held his tongue as both adults quickened their pace. Though it was impossible to run through the thick underbrush, they hurried back toward the ruined village as quickly as the forest would allow.

"This way, over there, she's in the one with the roof," said Susan, as they broke into the clearing and turned toward the hut where she had left Bodkin.

Cooper's long legs allowed him to reach the doorway a few steps ahead of Susan and Shirell.

"She's not here," exclaimed Cooper, standing in the doorway.

Susan and Shirell reached the doorway a few seconds later. Cooper was right. The cottage was empty.

"No, she has to be here," cried Susan, in between breaths.

"Are you sure that this is the right hut?" asked Shirell.

"Yes, it's the only one with a roof. I'm sure that this is the one. She couldn't have just gotten up and wandered off. I was only gone for the few minutes it took to catch up to you. Oh, Grandfather, I'm so sorry. This is all my fault. We have to find her."

Shirell stepped between Susan and Cooper, the look in her eyes telling him to remain silent, and put her arms around the girl.

"We'll find her, Susan. Cooper, use some of those tracking skills the elves taught you years ago and see if you can tell us anything."

After a quick examination of the room, he stated, "Well, fortunately, they're a lot of dust on the floor. Here's Susan's boot prints where she dragged Bodkin in here."

"Yes, that's exactly where she was when I left."

"There's another set of footprints over here that look like they were made by some sort of sandals. But near the door, everything's wiped away, like something big came through here. I think someone came and carried her away, maybe dragged her out on a blanket. There's no signs of blood or any sort of a scuffle. It's strange, though, that the marks just stop outside the door, like they just flew away. Stay here. I'm going to take a more thorough look around this village."

Cooper moved toward the ruins of the other buildings and began to scan the surrounding area when he heard Shirell cry out.

Blue fire lit up Cooper's staff as he ran back to where he'd left Shirell and Susan. He found them standing over the blackened remains of a creature that very much resembled an ant, the only difference being that it was as big as his foot.

"That thing stung me just above the top of my boot," said Shirell. "We didn't even see where it came from, it just appeared out of nowhere. It hurts like hell, and now my foot's starting to go numb."

Seconds later, a chittering sound was accompanied by dozens of the giant ants materializing from behind every rock

143

and bush and moving steadily towards the three.

Cooper burned the ones closest to Shirell and Susan, hoping to frighten the rest of them off, but they just continued to advance.

"Shirell, can you still walk?" asked Cooper as they slowly backed away from the creatures to avoid being surrounded.

"I won't win any races and I may hobble a bit, but I think I can run if I have to."

"Then head for the trail to the keep. Hopefully, the forest will slow them down. We'll be overrun if we stay out here in the open. Go!"

Cooper laid down a semi-circle of blue fire six feet tall as hundreds of the ant creatures suddenly erupted from every hiding place imaginable. Acrid smoke filled the air as dozens of the insects burned, but the instant the flames died, others crawled over the charred remains of their comrades and pursued the three humans. While Cooper protected the rear, Shirell burned a path in front of them, searing not only the insects, but also the vegetation that covered the trail ahead.

With Susan's help, Shirell half ran/half hobbled out of the ruined village with Cooper covering their escape.

A hundred yards down the trail, the throbbing in her leg became too much. Shirell could run no further. She had to turn and make a stand against the pursuing insects. The dragon staff flared with blue fire as she planted it in the ground and spun to face her attackers, only to find that there were none.

The ant creatures had stopped at the edge of the clearing and were already beginning to return to the hiding places from which they had come.

The three travelers watched in disbelief as the huge insects vanished almost as quickly as they had appeared.

"Grandfather, why did they stop?" asked Susan.

"My best guess is that they must have similar instincts to the ants that we're used to. They're just protecting their territory. Their nest or hive must be close by. Once we're out of the village, we're no longer a threat to them and they can return to their normal routine. We've probably already been forgotten." Cooper took Shirell by the arm and guided her toward a large rock. "Here, let me have a look at that leg."

Cooper pulled off Shirell's boot to reveal a red welt, three inches in diameter. Gentle probing of the surrounding muscle caused Shirell to grimace. After a quick examination, Cooper announced, "Well, the good news is that it doesn't look much different from a standard bee sting, just bigger and more potent. I believe that I can neutralize the venom, and you should be getting some feeling back in in that leg in a very short time. But a half dozen of those stings would probably paralyze a person, and any more than that would be almost certain to cause your heart to stop. Let's hope that there aren't any more nests close by."

"I'm so sorry, Shirell. I'm glad that you're going to be okay. I know that we shouldn't have followed you, Grandfather, but what about Bodkin?" asked Susan, the concern clearly in her voice.

Shirell chimed in before Cooper had the chance to respond.

"We have to assume that whoever took her knew about those creatures and removed her before she could be discovered. It seems like they were trying to help her which suggests that they may be friendly. If they meant her any harm, they could have just left her there for the insects. I can't imagine why anyone would want to live in this dreary place, but if someone does live here, they would need a safe place to stay and protect themselves. The most likely choice would be the keep, so it's likely that they would take her there. If Bodkin wakes up, she knows that that's where we were going and she'll try to make her way there, if she's able. We should continue on toward the keep. We can't go back into those ruins, so that seems like our best chance of finding her."

"And once we find her, perhaps the two of you can explain why you're here instead of back at Kestriana where you're supposed to be," added Cooper, with a scowl.

Chapter 21

Bodkin had been very careful not to move a muscle or give any hint that she was conscious even though she was now wide awake and had been listening intently for the last two full minutes. She knew that peering through slitted eyes was risky, but a quick glance was required to properly assess her surroundings. A quick peek confirmed her suspicions. She was lying on a bed of soft grasses and appeared to be in a makeshift shelter, not too different from one that she might make for herself if necessary. A young elf boy knelt ten feet away, carefully examining her bow. At least, she thought he was an elf. He had pointed ears, but his hair was bright red. Elves were blond. Even among the humans, red hair was unusual. She had never seen or even heard of a red-haired elf before.

His back was to her and he appeared to be alone. Faster than the boy could twitch, Bodkin was behind him, one hand covering his mouth, the other, pressing her knife delicately against his throat.

Keeping an iron grip on the boy, she slid her hand aside so he could speak, and in a hoarse whisper, she asked. "Where am I and how did I get here?"

"This is a very nice bow. Where did you get it?"

"Never mind the bow. Answer my question."

"You shouldn't do that. Kana won't like it," answered the

boy.

"I don't see anyone else here. I think you're bluffing," hissed Bodkin, still holding the knife to his throat. "Now, once again, where am I?"

"You really need to let me go. She's a little protective, and she's going to get very angry."

A low growl shook the tiny shelter and brought Bodkin around to find herself staring at a reptilian face that filled the entire entrance.

"Shades!" exclaimed Bodkin, shoving the boy aside and brandishing the knife at the creature in the doorway.

"I told you that she wouldn't like it. She won't hurt you if you'd please put down the knife. If you don't, she'll wreck my shelter trying to protect me, and I really don't want to have to rebuild it. I'll tell you anything you want to know if you just put the knife away and sit down slowly. Think about it. If I had wanted to hurt you or keep you prisoner, would I have left you keep your knife?"

"Okay, so you haven't tried to hurt me. That doesn't mean that I should trust you. It could just be a trick to gain my confidence."

"Shades, try and help someone and look what it gets you. You really are the suspicious type, aren't you? You've been here almost an hour. I could have killed you a dozen times over if I had wanted to."

Bodkin looked the boy up and down for a moment, trying to decide whether to believe him or not. His words had a ring of truth to them. He easily could have slit her throat with her own knife while she was sleeping off the effects of the flower pollen.

"All right, I guess you're telling the truth. So, what is that thing outside? Is she your pet? Can you control her? She looks almost like a dragon."

"How would you know what a dragon looks like? All the real dragons are gone."

"Prax still lives," Bodkin answered defiantly. "He was imprisoned under a mountain after the Gremlin War. My friend, Susan, the girl that was with me, released him. I've flown with him. Prax is my friend."

"The mighty Prax still lives?" scoffed the boy. "And he just happens to be your friend? He was trapped under a mountain and then rescued by some young girl, who also just happens to be your friend? And you've flown with him? You have to admit, that's a pretty incredible story. Now why should I believe that you're not just making it all up?"

"Because I don't lie. Believe whatever you wish, but everything that I've said is true. Now, you still haven't told me about your creature."

"She's not my creature, she's my friend. Her name is Kana and I'm Stiv. We help and take care of each other, but I don't control her. Around here, you need someone watching your back if you want to survive for very long. She's a wyvern, kinda halfway between a dragon and a serpent. She has wings but no legs."

"I've never heard of a wyvern. Where did she come from?"

"Her mother, Kai, was a dragon and brought her here to the dark forest to hide her when she was very young."

"Hide from who?"

"Well, I'm not really sure how much I can trust you, but I don't see any harm in telling you. From her father. If you do actually know of Prax, then you must also know about Kana's father. He was called the lindworm. Kai was horribly injured and slowly dying from the terrible things the lindworm did to her. She was forced to bear nightmarish creatures for the monster. Kana was her last offspring, but before the lindworm could discover and corrupt her, Kai hid Kana and pretended to be sick and dying. Angry that she was no longer of any use to him, the lindworm savaged her before leaving her for dead and going off to wreak havoc in the Gremlin Wars.

"As soon as the creature was gone, Kai took Kana and came here. The journey here took the last of Kai's strength, and she died shortly after they arrived. Kana had to learn how to survive on her own.

"I was out in the woods playing my flute one day, and she just appeared out of nowhere. Scared me half to death. She likes music, and she's smarter than most people. We discovered that we can sort of communicate telepathically. It's hard to explain how, but we just understand each other. She's saved my life on more than one occasion, and if not for her, you'd be dead right now."

Bodkin was reluctant to take her eyes off the boy, but a quick glance revealed that the wyvern had backed away slightly. She was still only a few feet from the entrance. Escape was impossible.

"What did you mean when you say that I'd be dead if not for your scaly friend?"

"She's not scaly. Her skin is very smooth, like leather. You don't remember anything, do you? That usually happens. You and the other girl went into the old village. Kana and I were watching from the edge of the woods. You don't see too many people here, so we just waited to see what you were going to do. Your friend saw the flowers and when you tried to smell them, they sprayed you. The powder from the plants put you to sleep, and your friend couldn't wake you. It usually takes about an hour for the effect of the flowers to wear off. I'm surprised that you don't have a headache."

"I do, now that you mention it."

"Well, she spent about five minutes trying to wake you,

even tried some sort of magic, but it didn't work. So she dragged you into one of the old huts and told you that she was going to get help, even though you couldn't hear her."

"That still doesn't tell me why I would be dead. You said that the powder only puts you to sleep for an hour."

"It does, but you'd be dead because of the gants."

"Gants?"

"Giant ants. I call them gants. They look like ordinary ants, but they're as big as your foot. And they sting. They can feel the vibrations from your footsteps on the ground. They're not very fast, but one of their scouts was already on his way to where you were before your friend left. They have a colony at the other end of the village. Anything that enters the village area is considered an intruder. You're usually safe to pass through quickly, but you don't want to stay there for long.

"Once the scout reports back to the hive, they'll come in droves. They're not really interested in killing you. They eat plants. They just want to drive you away to protect the hive. They'll go into a frenzy and attack anything that gets too close, even Kana. If you don't move away fast enough, they'll just keep stinging you until you're dead. Then they'll drag your body into the forest, away from their home. If Kana hadn't carried you back here, they would have stung you to death while you were asleep."

"Then I guess I owe you my life. Thank you for your help. Both of you. My name's Bodkin."

"Yes, we know. Your friend kept calling your name while she was trying to wake you."

"What about Susan?" asked Bodkin. "My friend that was with me. She'll think that I'm dead. We have to find her."

Bodkin tried to get up and move towards the entrance.

"Calm down," responded Stiv. "Once you were safe here, I left Kana to guard you and went back to the village. Your friend,

151

Susan, had already returned with the old man and the witch. They must have seen the footprints in the hut where we found you, but before I got there, the gants came and drove them away from the village. There was no trace of you once they were out of the village, so they assumed that you woke up and the gants drove you away, destroying any sign of which way you went in the process. Their trail led off in the direction of the forbidden castle. I could have followed them, but I knew that you would be waking up so I came back here to check on you."

"Forbidden castle? Is that what you call the keep? That's where Cooper and Shirell were going. Susan and I were following them. They would assume that that's where I would go to find them if I was able. Can you take me there?"

"I can, but you need to rest first. The dust from the flowers lingers and can make you dizzy for a few hours. The woods aren't a very safe place even when you're at your best. Kana and I will get you back to your friends soon."

"Nonsense, I'm fine now."

Bodkin rose and got halfway to the entrance of the shelter before her knees buckled. Stiv tried to catch her, and they both went down in a heap.

"Now will you believe me?" asked Stiv, rubbing the shoulder where Bodkin had ungracefully landed on him.

"All right, I'll rest. But wake me in an hour."

Chapter 22

Bodkin was on her feet the instant Stiv touched her arm an hour later.

"Not too fast, girl." Stiv warned her. "Those flowers mess up your balance. You think you're fine, and suddenly you're face down in a pile of weeds."

"I'll be fine." Bodkin assured him. "But I've been here far too long already. I need to catch up to my friends and let them know that I'm all right."

"Okay, we can leave right away if you want."

"What about your large friend outside?"

"Kana will follow at her own pace. She's big, but she's part serpent. She can fold her wings in close to her body and move through the forest much faster and quieter than you or I when she needs to. You don't need to worry about her. She'll always be close by."

"One other thing," said Bodkin. "Those flowers in the ruins. Is it possible to collect some of that pollen without getting sprayed or attacked by those ant creatures? That could be very useful sometime."

"We think alike. I have three small pouches of it here in my pack. Take two of them. I'll collect more later. Just don't let them spill."

Once outside the tiny shelter, Stiv immediately started off

through the trees. Bodkin hurried to keep up. Even though she insisted that she was fine for Stiv's benefit, the mild headache and faint buzzing in her head told her that the effect of the flowers had not completely worn off, but the fresh air outside was helping.

Stiv didn't appear to be following any sort of trail, and she was still unsure of how much she was willing to trust this strange elf boy with his giant friend.

"Are you sure that you know where you're going?" she asked.

"You said that your friends were going to the old castle," answered Stiv impatiently. "That's an evil place. The dark elf lives there sometimes. He comes and goes. He's not there all the time, the problem is that you can never be sure when he is there.

"For your friend's sake, you better hope that no one's home. Most of the forest animals know to keep their distance, but when one of them foolishly wanders into the courtyard, they don't come back out. Even the nightshade dogs avoid it, and they're not afraid of anything else around here.

"We don't want to just march up to the front door like visiting royalty. I know of a hidden entrance. The doorway is partially collapsed and it's a bit of a squeeze to get in, but the dark elf doesn't use that part of the castle."

"You've been inside?"

"Of course I've been inside. The last time I was there, I thought the place was empty so I went exploring, hoping to find a larder, maybe steal some food, but he was there. I was lucky. I heard him before he heard me, and I managed to get out without getting caught."

"Why were you stealing food? Don't you have a family, or a village somewhere?"

"You were in my village." answered Stiv with a scowl.

154

"Those ruins used to be my home. For many years, that was a simple little farming village. My family and a handful of others lived there. We were all that remained of the old Boc clan, except for the dark elf. The elders said that he was once part of our village. Then he moved into the keep and declared himself a shadow mage. Terrible sounds would come from within the walls. No one would go near it. Then, three years ago, people started disappearing. Every night, someone would vanish. It started on the outer edges of the village. Some of the elders thought that some large animal was coming out of the forest, a big cat or a bear, but there was never any sign of a struggle. Others believed that the dark elf had released something terrible with his magic. My parents were some of the first ones to go. I had my little shelter and I would often go off hunting with Kana for a few nights at a time. I didn't know that anything was wrong, but when I returned in the morning they were just gone. I couldn't tell anyone about Kana. They would have blamed her, and it would have caused a panic. The elders posted guards, but people still vanished. Search parties went out. Some found nothing, others never came back.

"On the last night, we discovered what it was. There was only ten of us left. It was the gants. They came after dark, stung people, then dozens of them would carry off the bodies. No one ever thought to look down at the ground. We had never seen them before. They came from behind rocks and out of holes in the ground. I panicked and ran. The others were surrounded. Kana heard the screams and came for me. We couldn't save them. Sometimes, in my dreams, I can still hear the cries as we flew away."

"I'm sorry," said Bodkin. "It must have been horrible."

"A week later, Kana and I discovered the hive from above. From the air, it looked like a regular anthill except much larger.

We found all the bodies a half mile from the village. The gants had just carried them away from the hive. There were too many to try and bury, so we burned them to keep the scavengers away. Now Kana and I are both orphans."

"What happened to the village? It looks like it's been deserted for a lot more than three years."

"You're right, it does. We get horrible storms here. They've been getting worse over the last few years. Terrible lightning and powerful swirling winds. With no one to repair them, the dwellings collapse quickly. I think it has to do with the dark magic surrounding the castle. The storms only come when someone's there. I said that the place was evil. Are you still sure that you want to go there?"

"That's where my friends were going. I have to go find them."

"Okay, don't say that I didn't warn you."

Chapter 23

A cold shiver ran up Cooper's spine as the upper parapets of the keep's towers appeared through the trees. The architecture was like something from a dream, or more accurately, a nightmare. It certainly didn't resemble anything Cooper had ever seen before. The central structure was round rather than the traditional rectangular design. The snatches of sunlight that filtered through the tree canopy reflected off the domed roof, revealing it to be a pale-yellow glass-like material. Jagged openings showed where time and the elements had taken their toll on the structure. At one time, three towers had spiraled upward in a triangular pattern along the outer perimeter, strategically placed to allow easy observation of the surrounding landscape. Only two of the towers remained standing. The third tower appeared to have been struck by lightning and blasted apart, scattering stones from the upper half in a radius of fifty yards.

"How long has this place been here?" whispered Shirell.

"Just looking at the design, I'm certain that it wasn't built by gnome architects," answered Cooper. "It must have been built very long ago, probably by the Galtians. They were an ancient race, but almost nothing is known about them beyond their name."

The crumbling masonry of the towers was blanketed with

a layer of black moss that seemed to ingest any small bits of sunlight that managed to land on it. The entire structure radiated an aura of doom and foreboding. Twisted brambles replete with two-inch-long thorns surrounded much of the last hundred yards adjacent to the ancient walls, and a cold fog hugged the ground. To their right, an aged stone wall that at one time must have outlined a courtyard lay crumbled and broken.

Rather than risk the possibility that someone, or something, may be in residence and keeping watch over the main entrance, Cooper silently directed them toward a sizeable gap in the dilapidated wall, hoping to find a less conspicuous route into the ancient structure. The larger pieces of crumpled wall should allow them to get close while still providing them with some degree of cover.

"We'll circle around the end of the wall," said Cooper, pointing off to his right. "Hopefully, we can find an entrance on the far side."

Silently, they skirted the remnants of the wall until they came to the base of the tower at the northern end. Under a half-hidden arch blackened from years of harsh weather hung an ancient oaken door partially open on rusted and shattered hinges. Inside, broken steps led both upward into the tower and down into pitch blackness.

"Up or down?" whispered Cooper to Shirell.

"Up, the tower is easier to defend if necessary, and you can see if anyone approaches. It's where I would stay if I lived here, and the image that the lurker showed us had windows. You lead, and I'll take the rear with Susan in between us where we can protect her if we need to. Keep our eyes and ears open. We don't want something coming up behind us with no escape route. Let's get in, find the book as quickly as we can, and get out."

"Agreed."

The stairs circled the outer walls of the tower, ascending into blackness as they climbed. After two revolutions, a small landing presented itself. Cooper stopped abruptly as the flickering light of his small torch fell on the far edge of the platform. The stairs had long ago crumbled and fallen away. They could go no further.

"It appears that we have no choice. We'll have to venture down into the depths of the lower levels. Let's hope that no one's home," Cooper said ominously as they began to retrace their steps.

Cooper led the way down the steps. The stairs spiraled just the same as above, and once again he was forced to light a torch. The blackness was absolute, like the inside of a cave. By the time they reached the bottom, the air was thick and musty, with a faint odor of sulfur.

They stood in a small room facing a single doorway opposite the stairs.

"It doesn't look like anyone's been down here for years," whispered Shirell.

"Let's just hope that no one's here today," Cooper responded as he carefully started out through the doorway and into the hallway outside.

The hallway stretched off into the darkness, and the three had no choice but to follow it. Not a single turn or doorway appeared in the Stygian darkness. It was impossible to judge distances, but the corridor seemed endless. Finally, Cooper's torch began to sputter and die. As the light dimmed, they were able to see a faint glow far down the corridor.

As they approached, the feeble light slowly increased until the passageway opened into an enormous gallery. Immense columns rose upward toward a ceiling that was shrouded in shadows. Mottled sunlight filtered in through the strange yellowish material they had seen from outside that served as both roof and windows far above. Unrecognizable debris littered the floor, and small clouds of dust arose with every step taken. Directly in the center of the gallery, an unmistakable silhouette appeared through the gloom.

Shirell whispered to Cooper, "I thought all the dragons were lost."

"So did I. He must have been here for years if Prax doesn't know about him. It looks like someone's been using him for a watchdog. This one isn't nearly as large or powerful as Prax, but it's still plenty big enough to be dangerous. We seem to be in luck. He appears to be asleep...or dead. If he's just sleeping, let's try to keep it that way."

All eyes were focused on the motionless dragon as Cooper led them around the outer perimeter of the room. Shirell's casual brush with a large cobweb brought a shower of dust down onto the three.

"Grandfather, I..." Susan's voice trailed off as her knees buckled and she slowly sank to the floor. Cooper turned to catch her, but his arms felt weighted down and sluggish. Out of the corner of his eye, he saw Shirell sprawled in an awkward position on the ground. As the dark shadows began to close in around him, a large shape moved out from behind a column and approached.

Chapter 24

Stiv was being generous when he described the entrance as partially collapsed.

"Are you insane?" asked Bodkin as she stared in disbelief. "How can we get inside from here? Half the wall is crumbled, the other half is on the verge of falling down, and you expect me to crawl through there? We'll be crushed before we get ten feet."

"I said it was a little tight. I've been in and out a few times. C'mon, it's no fun if there isn't a little risk involved. Follow me and step where I step. Unless you're afraid of getting dirty."

"All right, lead on," responded Bodkin. She shook her head and told herself for the twentieth time that this was where she needed to go to find her friends.

Stiv turned sideways as he slipped through the remains of the doorway and into an antechamber, carefully picking his way through the rubble. He squeezed between two huge stones that looked like they were ready to topple over and crush anyone unfortunate enough to be in their vicinity. At the far side of the room, they were forced to scramble over a pile of broken timbers that had once supported a section of ceiling. Finally, they entered a hallway that led off into the darkness in both directions.

"Which way?" whispered Bodkin.

"This way," said Stiv, pointing off to his left. "I don't know what we'll find there, but I've been down the other way, and there's nothing but empty rooms and a dead end. The one time that I started to explore this direction, I heard something coming and had to get out quick."

"You heard "something" coming?"

"It didn't sound like anything human."

"Let's hope that we have better luck today," said Bodkin.

She and Stiv moved silently down the hall, listening carefully, aware that even the slightest sound might give away their presence.

Bodkin froze and held up a hand to stop Stiv when she heard the whisper: "dancer."

Stiv looked at her questioningly.

"Dancer," repeated the voice.

"Did you hear that?" she asked.

"I didn't hear anything," Stiv answered in a hoarse whisper.

"Someone said 'dancer.' It was faint, but I heard it clearly. Listen carefully."

They stood, statue still, for two minutes before the voice spoke again.

"Please, dancer."

"There, it sounds like they're asking for help from someone called Dancer."

Bodkin stared at Stiv, who just shook his head.

"I swear I didn't hear a thing. Maybe only you can hear it."

"It came from this direction. C'mon," Bodkin started down the hall.

"Bodkin, wait. This place is evil. It could easily be a trap."

"No, I don't think so. There was something familiar about that voice. I know that I can trust it. I don't know why, but I'm sure that it's someone who needs our help. We have to find them."

"All right, but we can't afford to get careless. We won't be much help to anyone if we get captured by the dark elf. Lead on, and let's see if we can find your mysterious voice."

Fifty yards further on, the corridor split. Bodkin stopped and listened for a few seconds before taking the branch on the left. After three more turns and a few hundred yards, the hallway ended at an enormous iron-bound door.

"Whoever it is, they're on the other side of this door," stated Bodkin as she cautiously tried the door. It didn't budge. "It's locked, but there's no keyhole. There must be a hidden latch."

"If there is, we could search for hours and not find it. The dark elf is a wizard. It's more likely that he locked it with magic, like that Gnome Door that your friends came through. If you speak the right words, it'll open. Can that mysterious voice give us any clues on how to open it?"

Bodkin shook her head. "I don't know but I'll try to ask." She leaned in close to the door and whispered, "We're here. There's no key. Do you know how we can open the door?"

"Ko-marra," answered the voice.

"Ko-marra?" repeated Bodkin.

Stiv looked at her, puzzled. "Ko-marra? What does that mean?"

"I don't know. I know what the Ko-marra is. It's a ceremonial dance. It's always done at the Festival of the Solstice."

"Okay, I remember it now. I had forgotten the name, but my people used to do it when I was young. How does that help us?"

"It's the key," Bodkin said. "Look at the floor. The ko-marra is a very precise dance with intricate steps. The stones seem to be laid out in a pattern. If you dance the ko-marra on the stones, step on them in just the right sequence, maybe it'll unlock the door.""

"Well, the voice kept calling for someone called 'Dancer,' but why would anyone use a dance as a key?"

"In a crazy way, it sort of makes sense if you think about it. I remember Cooper saying that the Boc were almost fanatical about preserving their traditions. You can't forget something if you need to use it every day. No one but an elf would know the dance, and who would ever think to try dance to unlock the door? Most people would be looking for a hidden latch or trying a special word. It's worth a try. The dance begins from a circle, drawn in the center of the floor. There's a big round flagstone here in front of the door. If we're right, that should be the starting point."

"I think you need to do this," said Stiv, shaking his head. "I dance with all the grace of an old milking cow. I remember the melodies that they used to play for the festivals. I can play the tune if that will help, but we'll have to do it very quietly. These halls echo, and we don't know where the dark elf might be."

Bodkin handed Stiv her staff and stepped onto the round stone. She stood silently for a moment, then took a deep breath.

"It's been a long time. I hope I can remember this correctly," she whispered.

Stiv began to quietly play on his flute. Bodkin closed her eyes, focusing on the rhythm of the music, then stepped delicately to the right. Two steps forward and turn left. One step back and a jump to the left. Another step to the right. Then a spin and slide two paces further right. The final move of the sequence was a double twirl in midair and a delicate landing with both feet together. Intensity showed on Bodkin's face as she leaped, spun, and came down with both feet on one small flagstone. They both heard an audible click. A few seconds later, the door swung silently open.

Chapter 25

Both Bodkin and Stiv gasped as they cautiously entered the room. Once their eyes adjusted to the semi-darkness, they stared in stunned silence at what they saw before them. The dusty gray stone walls were lined floor to ceiling with shelves cut from old oaken planks, and on each shelf, dozens of misshapen globes of transparent blue amber, each one containing a fairy. Pixies, sprites, nymphs, they were all there, imprisoned in the stone-like resin. Embedded in the ceiling, a large crystal threw shadows around the room as light pulsed from it.

Eldritch fire danced from one end of the crystal to the other as thin tendrils of blue vapor snaked upwards from the captives in the globes to the glowing stone. Ethereal wisps of magic were being drawn from each sphere. And on the wall, facing them, trapped in her own sphere, was Wysp.

"Shades, there must be hundreds of them," gasped Bodkin as her eyes scanned the room in disbelief. "Wysp! It was you. You were the one calling out to me. I knew the voice was familiar. Oh, Wysp, how did you come to be here?"

Stiv caught Bodkin's arm as she was about to start across the room.

"Careful! Someone's been here recently. Look at the floor."

The dust on the floor was crisscrossed with footprints,

some of which were not human. With weapons drawn, they quickly surveyed the room to be certain that no one was lurking in the shadows, waiting to surprise them. When they were certain that the room was empty, they returned their attention to Wysp.

"The dark elf must have some way of capturing them and bringing them here," said Stiv. "Look at that crystal! Their magic is being slowly drained off and stolen from them. The dark elf must be trying to concentrate their magic for something terrible. We have to try to release them and stop whatever it is he's planning."

Before Bodkin could respond, she was overwhelmed by a chorus of a hundred tiny voices crying out inside her head.

"Dancer, help us!" Bodkin could hear the words echoing in her head.

"Dancer...Set us free...Help us...Dancer...Please, free us Dancer."

Bodkin put her hands over her ears trying to quiet the voices.

"Stop! We want to help but we're not trained in magic"

"Dancer...You have the power...Set us free!"

"Please, stop! There's too many of you in my head," pleaded Bodkin, as she pressed her hands against her temples, trying to muffle the dozens of voices all talking at once inside her head.

"I can't hear them," said Stiv. "What are they saying? How can I help?"

"Two years ago, the fairies let me dance with them at the Glade of the Golden Willow. It's a magic place, and they hardly ever invite anyone to dance with them. That must be why they're calling me dancer, but I don't have any special power. I don't know what can I do? All I have is this tiny sliver of amberstone.

166

It's not strong enough to free anyone."

"You danced with us...In the glade by the Willow...You are one with us...Dancer...Use the magic!"

Bodkin held out her pendant with its tiny splinter of amberstone. It was glowing brighter than she had ever seen before. As she watched, some of the globes began to vibrate as the tiny wisps of blue that were being drawn upwards changed direction and now began to snake across the room and merge with her crystal.

"Use the power...Dancer...Free us!"

Looking around, Bodkin saw one of the blue amber spheres stop quivering. It had gone dark and cold. The fairy inside had given up her last trace of magic to try to save her companions. To Bodkin's right, another went dark. Then a third.

"They're killing themselves to help you, Bodkin! You have to try!"

Bodkin focused her full attention on the jewel in the ceiling. She didn't know what would happen, but she knew that she couldn't let the fairies die while she stood by helplessly and watched.

A small beam of blue light flowed from her hand to the jewel in the ceiling. She tried to force it to grow stronger, to do something, anything that might help the captured fairies, but the jewel just seemed to just absorb the light with no ill effect. If anything, she was just speeding up the process, draining the magic faster. More and more wisps from the fairies flowed toward her, coalescing into a small stream of blue smoke, all filtering through her talisman and making the beam brighter and stronger. The jewel began to vibrate. Another crystal containing a fairy went dark. Then another.

"No! I won't let them die!" screamed Bodkin.

As her words echoed off the walls, the light from her

pendant began to change. Slowly, blue became purple and then bright red. For a few seconds, the jewel overhead shook so violently under the onslaught of the red magic that Bodkin thought that it might explode. Then a black spot appeared in the center of the jewel and spider webbed outward, snuffing out the jewel's glow as it expanded. As the dark spot reached the outer edges, the jewel began to crumble until it was nothing more than a small pile of black dust in the center of floor.

Bodkin collapsed onto the floor, spent from the exertion. Stiv knelt next to her, holding her up.

"Look at the globes!" he exclaimed.

As they watched, the blue amber spheres holding the fairies began to melt like wax held too close to the fire. One by one, the fairies were released from their prisons and the air quickly became filled with tiny wings as they surrounded Bodkin in their joy.

"Thank you, Dancer...Freed us...Dancer." A thousand words of thanks echoed in her head all at once, but this time she didn't try to cover her ears or shut the voices out. She held out both hands for the fairies to alight on, and tears of joy ran freely down her cheeks.

"Thank you. Thank you all for your help," said Bodkin through the tears. "You must leave this terrible place so your magic can't be used for evil anymore. Some are too weak to fly. Help them. Carry them far away from here. I'll never forget any of you, but you must go before we are discovered. Hurry!"

"Never forget, Dancer...Dancer saved us...Goodbye, Dancer," the tiny voices whispered in her head as, one by one, the fairies began to blink out of the room until only two remained.

"You must go too, Wysp"

"No, Lute and I will stay!" answered the sprite, crossing

her tiny arms across her chest. Lute planted his staff on the shelf that he was standing on to confirm his agreement.

"All right, I can't force you to leave. But we need to get away from here quickly before someone comes to see what's happened. And we need to find our friends."

"Follow," said Wysp as she and Lute flew into the corridor.

Chapter 26

Cooper tried to remember where he was, but the noise from the jackhammers was making it hard to concentrate. Slowly, he came to the realization that the pounding was in his head, not outside. When he tried to open his eyes, the pain slammed him like a fist. Through slitted eyes, he attempted to glimpse his surroundings.

He found himself shackled to a wall. Shirell was on his right and Susan on his left. Both appeared to be breathing normally, but beyond that, neither one was awake or moving. At the far end of the room, a mudwump carrying a large sack lumbered toward the doorway. And across from them, in plain sight, on a small table, the object of their search – the Boc book – and laying next to it, the Codex Stygia.

Carefully, he tested the strength of the shackles. They were old but still very solid. A few whispered words of magic confirmed his suspicions that they had been treated to resist magic. He could easily have overpowered the magic dampening spell on the shackles if he had his staff, but both his and Shirell's staff stood off to the side, propped up in the corner. There was nothing he could do but wait for the owner of the castle to show himself.

Shirell woke ten minutes later, and Susan a moment afterward.

"Oh, my head," whispered the orcanus. "Any ideas on what happened and how we got here?"

"Something knocked us out before we had a chance to react," answered Cooper. "Then that mudwump must have carried us here. Our host has yet to appear."

It was a full hour later before Al-Ron strode into the room, followed closely by a large black crow that perched on a small outcropping on the wall directly across from the prisoners.

"Feeling better?" asked the dark elf. "The headaches should be fading by now. I waited so that you wouldn't be distracted while we chat."

"Who are you, and why are we being held prisoner here?" demanded Cooper.

"You were trespassing. Even an orcanus and a guardian don't have the authority to invade someone's home. I do have a right to protect myself. And, in answer to your first question, I am Al-Ron, last of the Boc, and the only true shadow mage."

"We've met another," said Shirell.

"Marcus?" scoffed Al-Ron. "A pale imitation using a borrowed title that he had no claim to. He was mildly useful for a time. That is no longer the case, although it is because of him that I know who both of you are. You must be Shirell, former student of his and self-proclaimed orcanus of the new order of magic wielders."

The dark elf walked past Shirell and stopped directly in front of Susan. He looked her over slowly, as if trying to decide what to make of her.

"Leave her alone," snapped Shirell. "She can't harm you. She's my niece and in training to be a forest warden. She was supposed to stay behind and care for the horses, but she

172

disobeyed and followed us. She thought it would be an adventure."

Al-Ron placed a finger under Susan's chin and raised her head, chuckling.

"Well, it seems that you've gotten more than you bargained for, haven't you?"

With a dismissive wave toward Cooper, he continued. "And you must be Cooper, guardian of the Gnome Door, hero of the Gremlin Wars, son-in-law to Marinus, king of the Elves, and, most importantly, student of the wizard, Eldred. Marcus seemed to think that you were important enough for Eldred to give you the eye of Bangor Khan. Was he correct about that?"

"How did you know that we were here?" asked Cooper, trying to redirect the focus of the conversation. "Your dragon didn't seem to be a very good watchdog."

"Yes, I'm sure that a child could slip past poor old Spot. My 'watchdog' no longer has any desire to warn me about intruders. The truth, which I find quite amusing, is that I actually didn't know that you were here and that the two most powerful magic wielders in the land walked right into the simplest of traps," answered Al-Ron with a grin. "The cobwebs in the lower gallery are covered in a powder extracted from a local plant. It renders one unconscious for an hour or so. No real magic involved. You were fortunate, though, that you didn't wake the dragon. He is blind and in constant pain. His only relief is sleep. He hates me and just about anyone else who comes near him. He tolerates the mudwump who brings him food, but otherwise he is unapproachable. Spot was the focus of one of Darkon Rhee's last experiments before he vanished. The dragon's participation in the experiment was not voluntary. Sadly, Rhee was unsuccessful in his efforts to create a new eye. Now then, Guardian, you never did answer my question. Do you know where the eye is?"

"The location of the eye vanished along with Eldred," said Cooper. "And the secrets to its creation died with Bangor Khan."

The pendant Al-Ron wore around his neck glowed brightly as he waved his hand at Cooper, who jerked violently as if hit by an electric shock.

"Marcus tended to be a fool in most things, but where the eye is concerned, I think that he was telling the truth. I believe that you do possess it or, at the very least, know where it is. I have the ability to shred every nerve in your body. It is a very painful process. I can start slowly. The pain will increase steadily until your mind snaps. Of course, you will tell me what I want to know long before that happens. Or you could just save yourself all that pain and trouble and tell me the whereabouts of the eye."

Once again, Cooper twisted convulsively from Al-Ron's assault.

"I grow tired of asking, Guardian!"

Between ragged breaths, Cooper gasped. "Stop, you've made your point. I'll tell you where the eye is, but you won't like it."

"Cooper, no, you can't!" cried Shirell.

"I don't know how Marcus ever found out, but he was right. Eldred gave me the eye for safekeeping. He knew that anyone possessing it in this world would be unstoppable. The only solution was to hide it somewhere where no one could ever find it."

"You're stalling, Guardian. Where is it?" demanded Al-Ron.

"It is gone from this land completely. I took it through the Gnome door, traveled to the other side of my world, and threw it into a volcano."

Al-Ron's face was livid as he screamed at Cooper. "You did

what!? I'll kill the orcanus right before your eyes and then slowly tear your body apart, one limb at a time, if you try to lie to me!"

A slight smile crossed Cooper's face.

"It's the truth, so I'll repeat it for you. I said that I threw it into a volcano. A mountain of fire. You should know what that is. There are a few of them in the far north, beyond the gremlin lands. We knew that the eye was indestructible, so we put it somewhere where it can never be reached. I can tell you exactly where it is, but it's surrounded by a lake of molten rock. No amount of magic from either my world or yours can reach it. Neither you nor anyone else will ever be able to use it to destroy the Barrier."

A twisted smile came across Al-Ron's face.

"Use the eye to destroy the Barrier? Do you think I'm a fool?" he sneered at Cooper. "Marcus was mad in his desire to have revenge on his brother. I do not suffer from his delusions. Why would any sane person want to destroy the very world that they live in? Who wants to rule a world that's been devastated by demons and populated by nightmare creatures? You've grossly misjudged my intentions, Guardian. I don't seek destruction. I seek power!"

With a wave of Al-Ron's hand, an alcove directly behind him lit up. Perched atop a pedestal in the center was Eldred's puzzle box. The entrance to the alcove shimmered and blurred like the surface of a lake after a stone has been thrown in. A curtain of magic blocked entry. Affixed to the ceiling, directly in front of the opening, a large crystal glowed and projected a beam of blue magic at the obstruction filling the doorway. The Barrier flickered and wavered before the onslaught, but it held.

"I want a world where all bow down before me!" shouted the dark elf. "A world where the name of the Boc brings respect and where kings, lords, and even the mighty dragon Prax kneel

175

before me. Where I alone rule and will continue to rule forever. I need only open Eldred's puzzle box, and all his power and knowledge will be added to the magic that I already possess. Plus, immortality! I will rule forever. None will be able to challenge me. I will be a GOD!

"The eye would have allowed me to breach the wall protecting the puzzle box quickly. If what you say is true, then the eye is truly beyond reach, but I am not defeated that easily. I already have the means in place to achieve my ends without the eye. Rhee may have failed in his attempt to reproduce the eye of Bangor Khan, but he was able to fashion something almost as good — a pair of crystals that drain the essence of magic from those who wield it, and then allow me to direct it where I wish.

"Has the absence of fairies come to the attention of the Guild?" asked Al-Ron, turning his attention toward Shirell. "They are elusive creatures, so perhaps you haven't noticed that I've set up a little trap and captured hundreds of them. Thanks to Darkon Rhee's crystals, I've been able to siphon off their magic and focus it on the wall surrounding the puzzle box. I've managed to substantially weaken it, but it's just not enough to break through. When the power drained from the two of you is added, the wall will yield."

"And what if we refuse to cooperate?" asked Cooper.

"You have no choice!" sneered Al-Ron. "When the mudwump returns, it will take you to the lower level where the fairies are. Even now, the creature is on his way to prepare your cells. Without a talisman to focus your magic, the shackles will be enough to hold you. Once there, that crystal will drain your magic and send it here to its counterpart. I feel that I must thank the two of you for coming. With your help, I no longer need the eye, and I shall soon be master of this world."

"Your coronation may be delayed," said Cooper. "Look

behind you."

Al-Ron spun around just in time to witness the beam from the crystal slowly fading until it vanished altogether. Without the magic to power it, the crystal began to fracture and crumble to dust.

"No! No! It cannot be!" screamed Al-Ron.

"Tor," he shrieked at the crow, "go and check on the fairies. Quickly!"

178

Chapter 27

Wysp and Lute led the two young elves through the darkened hallways until they reached a stairwell.

"Dark elf in tower," said Wysp. "Go quietly."

They ascended the stairs as silently as ghosts, arriving at a landing at the top. A hallway that circled the outer wall of the tower led off to the right. They had only taken two steps when Lute whispered a warning.

"Hide quickly, mudwump coming."

Bodkin and Stiv darted into a shadowed doorway partway down the corridor.

"It must be going to check on the fairies," whispered Bodkin. "But he's not hurrying, so they may not know what's happened yet. Once they discover that the fairies are gone, they'll know that someone's here and come looking for us. Lute, Wysp, come here. I have an idea that should buy us a few extra minutes to find our friends."

Bodkin quickly rummaged through her pack and produced one of the bags of pollen that Stiv had given her earlier.

"Lute, I need you to distract the mudwump. Buzz around his head, but be careful. They're not as slow or stupid as they look. Then Wysp, I want you to drop this powder on his head to put him to sleep."

"I've tried that stuff on mudwumps from the marsh near

my old village," said Stiv. "They're tough. It should work, but only for a few minutes. We'll have to hurry."

"Do you two think you can do it?" asked Bodkin.

"Easy job," answered Lute. "Lute much too fast, mudwump never catch him. Fairies have score to settle with mudwump."

Wysp nodded her agreement, reaching for the bag of pollen.

The two fairies flew down the hallway in the direction of the creature, concealing themselves in the shadows near the ceiling.

The mudwump shuffled around the bend and started down the corridor in their direction. Lute buzzed past it from behind, lightly tapping the creature on the ear with his staff as he passed. The mudwump paused, looked up, and rubbed his ear, a confused expression on his face. Lute quickly circled in low behind him and tapped him on the back of his heel, instantly darting away before he could be seen. As the puzzled creature looked down, Wysp descended on him from above, dumping the bag of powder over his head. A glazed look came over the brute's face as it slowly dropped to its knees, then fell face first to the floor.

Bodkin hesitated a moment before poking her head out to make sure that the beast was down and out. Before Stiv could follow her, she darted back in, shoving him back into the shadowed doorway.

"What's wrong?" whispered Stiv. "Is it still awake?

"No, it's out, but it's blocking the hallway. We can't get past it without waking it up."

"Shades! So, what do we do now? It'll only be asleep for a few minutes."

Before Bodkin had a chance to answer, a black streak came

hurtling down the corridor and flew right over top of the beast and down the stairs.

A moment later, the bird returned, landing on the shoulder of the prone mudwump and squawking loudly in its ear. The bird's verbal onslaught roused the brute and, as Stiv and Bodkin watched from their hiding spot, it slowly got to its feet and shuffled back the way it had come, the crow screeching in its ear the whole time.

Al-Ron was pacing furiously back and forth as the black bird flew into the room, alighting on a beam near him.

"Tor, what's happened? Tell me!"

"Crystal broken. Fairies gone. Mudwump asleep," squawked the crow in a sing-song voice as the still groggy mudwump lurched through the doorway.

Al-Ron flew into a blind rage. He hurled a bolt of blue at the hapless swamp creature, striking it square in the chest. The mudwump was sent flying backwards through the opening to land in a crumpled heap in the corridor.

"Who could have...you did this!" the dark elf screeched at Cooper. "You brought someone else with you. I'll find them, and when I do, it will take them weeks to die. How did they destroy my crystal? Tell me!"

Cooper twitched helplessly, like a puppet on a string, as Al-Ron threw bolt after bolt of blue light at him.

"Grandfather!" screamed Susan. "Stop! You're killing him! He doesn't know anything about your crystal. We didn't even know it existed before we came here."

The dark elf froze.

"What did you say?" He turned and strode over toward Susan. "You called him grandfather. My dear Orcanus, you lied to me. This girl isn't your niece at all. How foolish of me not to recognize her. This young lady is Susan, great-granddaughter of the king and the one who was able to free the mighty dragon, Prax, because of her ability to utilize the elusive red magic."

"Leave her alone, Al-Ron," said Shirell. "She's just a girl. Do whatever you like to me, but let her go."

"Oh, I wouldn't dream of harming her, Orcanus. As you say, she's just a girl. A girl with the ability to neutralize the protective curtain keeping me from Eldred's box. I need her help. Of course, if she doesn't wish to help me, I may be forced to dissect her grandfather's internal organs very slowly and painfully. After that, I would have to turn my attention to you."

"I'll do whatever you ask," answered Susan. "Just stop hurting my grandfather."

"Think about what you're doing, Susan," pleaded Shirell.

"I have thought about it. Let him have his stupid box. I won't let him kill you or Grandfather if I can stop it." Susan faced the dark elf. "What do you need me to do?"

"A simple task, really. Just use the red magic to make an opening so that I can enter the alcove there and retrieve the puzzle box."

"I'll need my amberstone. It's in my backpack."

With a wave, Susan's shackles clicked open.

"Your bag is there on the table. No tricks, or your grandfather will suffer."

"I understand. I don't know if I'll be able to do this. I haven't practiced using red magic very much, and I don't know how strong the magic protecting that box is."

"I'm sure you'll manage knowing that your grandfather's fate is in your hands."

After a moment of rummaging through her backpack, Susan brought forth the small, round amberstone given to her by the Spirit of the Golden Willow. Intensity showed on her face as the stone lit up with a blue light that slowly transformed to purple and then to red. The light encompassed the entrance to the alcove, and a small opening appeared in the center. Beads of sweat rolled down Susan's forehead as she forced the opening to expand. Once the hole was large enough to enter, she motioned for Al-Ron. He stepped through the gap and, using the hand protected by the silver ring, picked up the box and returned to the larger room.

As Al-Ron left the confines of the alcove, the protective shell began to disperse, and Susan allowed the red magic to fade.

Chapter 28

Al-Ron placed the box on the table and said a few words in an ancient language that Susan had never heard before. As the last remnants of the alcove's protective shield dissipated, the box began to vibrate. The sides delicately rotated clockwise a half turn, the top rolled forward to replace the front, and the box separated into two sections on a diagonal from corner to corner. The runes on the sides blurred as the pieces spun rapidly before joining again to reconstitute the box which then expanded to twice it's normal size. Finally, four triangular sections on the top slowly opened to reveal the interior of the box. In spite of their bonds, both Cooper and Shirell strained to see what was contained within. Greenish smoke surged from the box, almost obliterating it from view. From the center of the cloud, a gray figure began to materialize.

"Eldred," whispered Cooper as the visage of the wraith slowly became recognizable.

"Who has called me forth?" asked the spirit in a voice that sounded like a distant echo.

"I am Al-Ron of the Boc, and it was I who summoned you."

The shade of Eldred looked at the dark elf with hollow eyes.

"What is it that you wish of me, Al-Ron of the Boc?"

"I have read the both the Boc passages and the Codex Stygia. They promise power and immortality to anyone who can open the box. I have unlocked the puzzle box and released you from its prison. Give these things to me!"

"The Codex Stygia was penned by Darkon Rhee, a being of pure evil. The Boc Passages were written as a warning to the Boc and all who may come after them. Are you certain that this is what you desire?"

"Yes! The power is mine! The Passages say that you cannot refuse my claim!"

"The Boc Passages do not lie. I must honor your request."

Cooper struggled at his bonds.

"Al-Ron, stop! You mustn't do this. Crall warned us that this can bring nothing but disaster."

"Silence!" Al-Ron shrieked at Cooper. "The lurker warned *you* not to do this, not *me*. And he lies! He is an ancient and jealous creature who believes that no one else is worthy of immortality. Once I have the power, I shall go to his marsh and repay him for his arrogance. I will make him dance for my amusement."

The spirit of Eldred's expression never changed as he said, "The warnings of a lurker should not be taken lightly. Are you certain that immortality is your wish?"

"Yes, I am certain! There is no doubt in my mind!"

"Then say it! Speak it aloud!" commanded the spirit.

"I, Al-Ron, last of the Boc, wish for power and immortality. I have done the impossible and opened the puzzle box. Give me what is rightfully mine, spirit!"

The mists surrounding the shade swirled and billowed, filling the entire room as the wraith moved forward to hover directly in front of the dark elf.

"Then take my hand," the spirit quietly answered as he

186

extended an ethereal hand.

Al-Ron took a step forward and reached up for the hand of the shade. The look of triumph on his face instantly turned to one of fear as their hands touched.

Instantly, the spirit of the dark elf was drawn from his body and raised up to stand next to the wraith. The blank-eyed shell of the dark elf remained upright for a few seconds, then collapsed to the floor, now just an empty husk.

"You have gotten your wish, Al-Ron of the Boc. Your essence will live forever inside the puzzle box. In the world inside the box, you will have the unlimited power that you crave. You need only think of something, and it will appear. Anything you desire will be yours by a mere thought. Food and drink, gold and silver, all yours.

"You can become the mightiest of dragons and soar high over mountains that you have created with a simple nod of your head, or you may turn yourself into the smallest mouse, running through the field. You will be a god. But you can never leave the world inside the box. It will be your home...for eternity."

The screams of the dark elf echoed off the walls as the billowing mists surrounded him and drew him down into the box.

Chapter 29

The spirit of Eldred waved a transparent hand, and all the chains and bindings holding the three fell away. He turned to Cooper with hollow eyes.

"Cooper, the human. You were my student long ago, when I was mortal. Do you also seek immortality?"

"No, Teacher, I do not."

"That is a wise decision. Immortality is a curse, but I sense that you have many questions."

"You are correct, Master. If I may ask, were you imprisoned in the puzzle box by the wizard, Darkon Rhee, and is it possible to free you from it? Do we need to seek him out and try to defeat him? If he was powerful enough to entrap you, how could we possibly prevail over him?"

The shade slowly shook his head.

"Your intentions are admirable, but I no longer have any mortal form to return to. Search no further for the dark wizard. He is imprisoned here with me and, even if it were possible to set me free, you could not do so without also releasing him. We are one and the same person. I was Darkon Rhee. At least part of me was. He is my darker half.

"I must reveal the secret of the Barrier for you to fully understand. Trapped behind the Barrier are the most dangerous and powerful of the demons, possessing strong dark magic that is steeped in evil and banned long ago. Their entire essence is hatred and an appetite for destruction on a scale that humans and elves can barely fathom. This fuels their power. They draw strength from the darkness. For centuries, wizards and conjurers of all types have tried to subdue these creatures using what you call white magic. Though many of these conjurers were very powerful, none succeeded for very long. The demons used their power to attack any white magic that would be used to imprison them, and they would be relentless in their onslaught. As even the strongest wall built from the hardest stone will eventually crumble under the constant steady blows of a hammer, so, too, would any spell used to ensnare these creatures.

The only thing that could permanently hold these creatures would have to be created from that same dark magic that they utilize. Rather than resist their onslaught, such a barrier would absorb their attacks, channeling their force back into the wall and constantly reinforcing it. The more they attack it, the stronger it becomes as it steadily drains them of their power.

"But, as Eldred, I was unable to master the dark magic needed to weave such a spell. It would require a being without a shred of conscience or humanity. Someone who considered every other living creature to be beneath him and of no more importance than an insect crawling on the ground. Only an individual more evil than the demons themselves could accomplish it. Thus, Darkon Rhee was born. I created a potion that would allow my dark side to rule. Every shred of decency and compassion was separated from my soul and locked away in the deepest recesses of my mind. Only the most heinous qualities remained. In this form, I saw the demons as rivals to my dominance of all things and, as such, they needed to be eliminated. Thus, I was able to control the dark forces needed to create the Barrier.

"With the help of the Spirit of the Golden Willow, I attempted to reinforce the Barrier and create a stronger and more permanent solution. She allowed me to take a cutting from her branches and plant it near the Barrier. Our hope was that, like the Golden Willow, the new tree would slowly absorb the magic, filtering out the evil and steadily weakening those creatures held within the Barrier. We believed that the young tree, combined with the great strength of the forest giants that make up the Dark Woods, would dissipate the evil, rendering it harmless. In time, the creatures would become so weak that they would no longer pose a threat.

"Alas, the young tree had not the strength to resist the evil. It has become the dark mirror of its mother, the Golden Willow. Although blue amber has existed for centuries, it's magic wasn't necessarily evil, just wild and unpredictable. The young tree began to focus and concentrate the evil, producing blue amberstones, powerful talismans infused with dark magic. The blight caused by this Dark Willow extends further into the forest every year.

"The potion that allowed me to become Darkon Rhee was only supposed to last for a short time, enough to accomplish my task and then return me to what I was before, but I foolishly underestimated his influence. When the potion wore off, a portion of Darkon Rhee remained. I had released the evil genie from deep in my soul, and now I could not return him to the bottle from whence he came. I placed barriers around my memories to keep my darkest secrets from him, but Darkon Rhee was a part of me and possessed the same will and determination. He worked relentlessly to break through my safeguards.

"Initially, he was weak, but he became stronger every day, slowly taking on a life of his own. I would sometimes awaken to

191

find that I had lost time, days that I could not remember, and then discover that some terrible act had been wrought nearby. The methods that we use to control our inner demons, the skills we learn during the kuri-aken, were no longer adequate. I brewed antidote potions designed to weaken him, to send him back to the dark corners of my soul from whence he came. Each time, his resistance to the potions grew stronger. They became less and less effective. He would come to me in my dreams and try to wrest control from me. He broke through some of my defenses, learned dangerous secrets and recorded them in his journal, the Codex Stygia that lies on the table before you. In the wrong hands, the secrets contained in the Codex could bring about widespread death and destruction.

"Finally, in desperation, I constructed the puzzle box, convincing my darker self that it would be a source of even greater power and the key to unlocking all of my remaining secrets. It was not an easy task concealing my thoughts from my other self. My last act of free will in your world was to trick Darkon Rhee into entering the box. Inside the realm of the puzzle box, we exist as two separate entities where neither one can harm the other, but we can never leave this prison that I have made for us.

"I made a bargain with the Boc. I created the Boc Passages, portals that allowed them to escape the newly formed elf nation, in exchange for their blood oath to guard and protect the puzzle box and, more importantly, the Codex Stygia. You have seen the trap I set inside puzzle box, but once inside, I could do nothing to guard the Codex Stygia. My greatest fear was that if the book was found and it's riddles solved, all that I had done to contain the evil in the world could be undone. That fear was realized when the journal was stolen by one of the Boc who was charged with keeping it hidden, and eventually allowed to fall into the hands of one such as Al-Ron.

"I must go soon. My time in your world is limited. The safeguards that surround the box will return once it closes and seal off this room and all its contents. You should take your friends and go. Leave this terrible place and never return. Tell no one of its existence. The surrounding walls will eventually crumble and bury the box forever. That is as it should be. In this form, I can no longer feel emotions, but I still retain some vague memories. I believe that the Eldred of old would be proud of his student's courage and the courage of his companions. Farewell, Guardian."

With his last words, the wraith slowly began to fade and shrink as the mists, once again, rose up to encircle him, then withdrew back into the box as if drawn in by a vacuum. While the three watched, the box closed and the sides turned and spun, locking the box closed. As promised, a shield of magic began to slowly encircle the box and protect it. The floor beneath their feet shook as the enchantment that protected the box slowly began to spread outwards.

"Time to go," said Cooper, grabbing both his staff and Shirell's from where they stood.

"What about the books?" asked Shirell.

"Too late for that. Look, they're already sealed inside the bubble, and we will be, too, if we don't go right now."

Shirell darted forward and snatched the ring off the dead finger of the dark elf.

"It's not too late for this."

The three of them made a dash toward the entrance as the walls of the room began to crumble and bits of the ceiling started to rain down.

Chapter 30

As they ran down the hall to escape the collapsing tower room, Cooper turned the corner and nearly bowled over Bodkin and Stiv.

"Back the way you came. Quickly! This whole end of the tower is starting to collapse."

Bodkin hesitated.

"We just came from there. It only leads down into the lower levels. We can't get out that way in time."

"We have no other choice," exclaimed Cooper. "We just have to hope that the tower holds together long enough for us reach the ground level."

Stiv spun on his heel and sprinted back down the hallway, placing two fingers in his mouth and letting out a sharp whistle.

"This way. Come on!"

The floor beneath their feet shook again, only this time it was caused by a section of the wall directly in front of Stiv crashing inward which was immediately followed by a huge reptilian head filling the opening.

Stiv skipped nimbly across the rubble and leaped onto the neck of the wyvern.

"Climb on behind me and hang on to each other. All of us together are too heavy for her to carry far, but she should be able to get us down and away before the whole tower collapses."

Bodkin, Susan and Cooper scrambled onto the back of the creature, but just as Shirell reached the opening in the wall, the stones beneath her feet collapsed and gave way. She toppled forward, her robes billowing out as she fell.

Cooper had both feet locked in behind the wings of the wyvern, and both Bodkin and Stiv instantly grabbed Susan to keep her from being thrown off as Kana dove after the plummeting orcanus.

Halfway to the ground, the wyvern caught Shirell's robe and swung her up and backwards. As Shirell came spinning back towards him, Cooper somehow managed to wrap an arm around her waist and drag her onto the back of the creature as it twisted and hurtled headlong at the ground.

Miraculously, Kana managed to avoid the massive tree trunks in her path, but she slammed down hard in a tiny clearing that was barely big enough to accommodate her length. Unable to slow herself due to the weight of her passengers, Kana's impact dug a furrow a foot deep, and all five riders were thrown into the underbrush.

Stiv was on his feet in an instant, racing back to where the wyvern lay crumpled in the grass, unmoving.

"Kana! C'mon girl. Tell me you're all right."

The others picked themselves up and approached slowly as Stiv continued to plead with the wyvern to wake up. No one spoke for a tense moment, unsure whether the creature was alive or not. Slowly, one eye opened, and then the other, and her head lifted slowly off the earth.

"Yes, that's my girl!" shouted Stiv, jumping up and hugging her neck. "I knew you were okay!"

"Is everyone else all right?" asked Cooper.

"Grandfather! Over here," called Susan as she ran toward Shirell.

Shirell was leaning hard on her staff that she had, by some miracle, managed to hold onto on to during their escape from the tower. Her face was ghostly white, and her arm hung in an unnatural position.

Cooper scooped her up and carried her to a large rock where she could sit. Gingerly, with Susan's help, they peeled back Shirell's robe to reveal a shoulder that was already swollen and bruised. Cooper gently probed the area.

"She didn't mean to hurt you," said Stiv. "She saved your life."

"Yes, she did. Thank you," said Shirell with a weak smile. "Bodkin, you haven't introduced us to your new friends."

"This is Stiv, and that's Kana," answered Bodkin, nodding toward the wyvern. "She's a wyvern. Kind of like a dragon. They saved me from the ant creatures back in the ruined village."

"The arm's out of the socket," stated Cooper. "I going to have to pop it back into place. This is going to hurt."

"It already hurts, but it's still better than being smashed on the rocks. Do what you need to do, Cooper."

Shirell let out a shriek as Cooper pulled and set the arm back into place.

"Sorry, it's back where it belongs now, but we'll need to get a sling on that arm. And we should get far away from here as quickly as possible."

"I have a shelter," said Stiv. "It's not far, and I have a few supplies. If the lady's able to walk, I'll take you there."

"I'll carry her if I need to." said Cooper. "Lead on, son."

Cooper hoped that his trust in the boy was not misplaced as Stiv led them back in the direction of the ruined village, returning through the woods on the exact same trail that had brought them to the keep. But just before they reached the outskirts of the village, he veered off onto a barely discernible side path. As promised, the young Boc led them to a hidden shelter that was similar to, but much larger than, the one where Bodkin had been. Once inside, Stiv disappeared into a dark corner, returning a moment later with a piece of coarse fabric that Cooper was able to fashion into a sling for Shirell's arm.

"It's not much, but I have managed to scavenge some stuff from the village," said Stiv. "It's tricky business; you have to be quick before the gants come to drive you away. We're far enough away from the hive here that they won't bother us."

Stiv produced a sack of small fruits and began to pass them out.

"My parents were farmers. I have a small garden, but it's hard to grow fruit. You have to pick it quickly when it's ripe or it turns rotten. Bad magic from the castle contaminates everything."

"Thank you, Stiv, for all your help and your hospitality," said Cooper. "I think that right now we could all use some rest before we proceed."

An hour passed before Cooper touched a dozing Shirell on her uninjured arm. The two adults approached Stiv quietly, leaving the two sleeping girls undisturbed.

"Could we speak to you outside?"

Stiv nodded his consent and followed.

"We'd like your help," said Shirell. "We'd like you to take us back to the keep."

"You want to back there?" exclaimed Stiv, a look of disbelief on his face. "Are you crazy? We just barely got out of there alive. That place is pure evil, and half of it just collapsed, almost taking us with it."

"Yes, you're right, of course. But while we were there, we discovered that there's a dragon chained up in the lower gallery. The tower collapsed, but we believe that that section of the keep may still be intact. We can't just leave the poor beast there to starve. Prax is our friend just as Kana is yours. He's been searching for other dragons for some time. This creature is one of his kind. If Al-Ron was telling the truth, it's been injured and abused. If we can release it, Prax may be able to help it. Either way, at least it will be free. You wouldn't abandon Kana if she was trapped there, would you? Please, will you help us?"

"I know the place you describe," answered Stiv, shaking his head. "We've seen it from above. I don't know what's in there besides what you've just told me, but whatever it is, it's enough to frighten Kana. I've never seen her scared by anything else, but she's terrified of that place. I think she smells death in there. If there is a dragon trapped inside there, you're right, he deserves to be freed. All right, I'll take you back there. But I'll stand watch outside. I won't go in."

"What about the girls?" Shirell inquired of Cooper.

"They followed us through the Ice caves. Do you think they'll let us go back there without demanding to come along? We might as well just agree to let them come and save ourselves a pointless argument. At least then we'll know where they are, and we stand a better chance of keeping them safe if they're with us."

"You're probably right. How soon can we leave?"

"Soon," responded Cooper. "We'll want to have enough time to get there, do what we can, and return before dark."

"We could maybe rest another hour. I wouldn't wait any longer than that if you want to get back by sunset," said Stiv.

"Good, we'll leave in an hour."

Chapter 31

As expected, the instant they were told of Shirell and Cooper's plans, both girls insisted on returning to the keep to try to free the captive dragon. Neither one wanted to wait, so Stiv produced a few torches — the only supplies that they expected to need — and they set off, back in the direction of the keep.

The hike back to the ruined castle took less than an hour, and there was no sign of the wyvern as they treked.

"Where's Kana?" asked Bodkin. "Was she badly hurt?"

"No," Stiv answered. "She says that she has a few bruises, but she'll be fine. She would tell me if she was really injured. She's not far away. She doesn't like this place we're going to, so she's watching our backs, protecting us from behind."

Just as the crumpled towers came into view through the treetops, Stiv veered off in a different direction from the way that they had come earlier.

"The entrance that you're looking for is on the far side," said Stiv. "We'll have to circle around to get there."

Ten minutes later, they came out the trees to face a part of the keep that couldn't be seen from the side where the towers stood.

"That's where you want to go," said Stiv, pointing towards a dark arch set into the wall. "I'll wait here. If you're not back before dark, I'll have to go back to my shelter. You shouldn't waste a lot of time here. We don't want to be out in these woods after dark."

"I'll wait here with Stiv," said Bodkin with a weak smile. "Wouldn't want him to get lonely."

"That's probably a good idea," said Cooper, ignoring the surprised look on Susan's face. "We'll try to hurry."

The three moved cautiously through the entrance and into a small antechamber. Any doors that may have been there once had rotted away years ago. The room was empty except for dust and dried leaves. They passed through quickly into the great room. Small pockets of natural light filtering in from far above illuminated random spots on the flagstone floor as they approached. The dragon was huddled near the opposite end of the gallery, and they could detect no movement from the creature.

From a protected spot behind a pillar, Cooper retrieved a small piece of broken masonry and sent it loudly skidding across the floor, but the beast remained still. A small ball of light sent arcing past the dragon also got no response. Finally, Cooper lit a torch and began to slowly approach the beast.

"Be on guard," he warned. "Not all dragons are as intelligent and articulate as Prax, or as friendly. Some of them are little more than wild animals. Al-Ron said that this one was blind and dangerous. It could also be crafty enough to be playing dead to try to lure us in close."

At twenty yards out, the light of the torch cut through the gloom enough to illuminate the area surrounding the beast. What they saw shocked and saddened them. The face of the dragon looked like old leather stretched over bones. Al-Ron had lied to them. This dragon was long dead. As they got closer, they could see that the poor creature was little more than a bag of bones covered with hide.

Cooper drew in a sharp breath as he circled the corpse.

"Great Mother of Dragons! How could anyone be this cruel?"

Enormous chains were embedded into the stones and shackled to the dragon's hind legs. Broken scales littered the ground beneath him. The hide was crisscrossed with scars and gashes. The left eye had been gouged out. This dragon had been tortured and abused, then left to rot where he fell.

"Horrible," said Shirell. "To do this to such a magnificent creature is unthinkable."

"Cover your eyes for a moment," said Cooper, just before he threw a bolt of blue light at the chains. The magic exploded into a hundred tiny sparks and did little more than remove most of the dirt from the surface of the links.

"As I suspected. These chains were forged to withstand dragon fire."

"I'd like to examine them more closely," said Shirell.

Holding out her staff, she sent a large ball of light into the air to illuminate the area closest to the dragon's corpse. As the shadows receded from the light, they all gasped. At the far side of the gallery, hidden from the entrance, was an enormous pile of bones. Dragon bones.

"Shades! There must be the remains of dozens of dragons here, maybe hundreds."

Shirell cautiously approached the mound of old bones.

"When I was young, my mother told me that dragons were rare and only a few existed. Where could all these bones have come from?"

"A hundred years ago, dragons were plentiful," answered Cooper with a sigh. "Most lived in the high mountains to the far north, but they still were not an uncommon sight high overhead. Then they slowly began to disappear. When the war began, only a handful remained, and many of those that were left were lured into the open and deliberately killed by the lindworm. By the time Prax finally destroyed the monster, even he believed that he was the last of his kind.

"This poor fellow chained up in the gallery, it's impossible to say with any certainty how long he's been here, but I'd guess that what was done to him happened before Al-Ron discovered this place. If he had been left outside, his hide probably would have deteriorated and begun to fall away during the cold of winter. The dark magic here seems to corrupt nature itself. Things don't decay naturally."

Cooper moved toward the bone pile.

"Some of these bones on the top of the pile appear to be more recent, but the rest are ancient. I'm surprised that they haven't turned to dust by now. It appears that this atrocity originally began and ended long ago, but someone discovered these horrible experiments and tried to revive them. Prax needs to see this."

As Shirell continued to carefully examine the remains of the dragon, Susan spoke quietly to Cooper.

"I believe that I can contact Prax, Grandfather. When we were at Kestriana the first time, after we freed him from the cave, he told me of a secret way to speak to him, in my dreams."

"That's excellent, Susan. If he can be brought here, I'm sure it will help in his search and he may be able to provide us with some valuable information. How soon can you get a message to him?"

"While I sleep tonight, I'll try to speak to him."

"Let's hope that you're successful. I think we've discovered all that we can here today. Stiv and Bodkin are waiting, and we should head back to the shelter before it starts to get dark."

Chapter 32

That night, just as Prax had instructed her, Susan quietly whispered his name three times before lying down to sleep. There were a few small openings in the roof of the shelter, and she lay there, watching the stars wink at her for a time. She had hoped that gazing up at the night sky would help her relax and she would drift off quickly. Stiv had assured them that Kana was guarding the shelter, and nothing would approach as long as she was there.

Usually, Susan would be asleep almost immediately. It was odd that it was taking her so long tonight, especially when she wanted to sleep so Prax could contact her. Hard as she tried, she couldn't seem to stop staring at one bright blue star in the northern sky. She didn't recognize it as being from any constellation she was familiar with. It just didn't seem to belong there, and she couldn't stop wondering why she had never noticed it before. If she could just close her eyes and forget about that rogue star, she was sure that she could get to sleep.

Susan jumped noticeably when the blue star spoke to her with Prax's voice.

"Susan, my young friend, why have you sought me out? What news do you have for me?"

Susan suddenly realized that she had been in the dream world all along. She quickly recovered from her surprise and answered, "We've found something that you need to see. I won't try to describe it to you because it's not very pleasant, but it is important. We're in the Dark Woods. Can you come and find us?"

"Yes, I can follow the path of your dream self through the night sky. That will lead me back to you. I have little need for sleep, so I shall leave right away and be there with the dawn. We will speak then."

The blue star blinked once before disappearing, and Susan could sense Prax's presence fade away as the entire dreamscape began to blur. Within a moment, she drifted off to normal sleep.

The travelers awoke to sunlight filtering down through the canopy of trees and a light breakfast of fruits and nuts provided by Stiv. During breakfast, Stiv sat down alongside Cooper.

"Kana's gone off into the woods. She said that she was going hunting and would bring back some wild game for us to cook. But I think one of the real reasons that she left is that she's scared to death of Prax. Her mother brought her here to escape the lindworm, but she was also frightened of the wrath of the other dragons. She believed that many of them wanted to destroy anything touched by that horrible creature. Kana's never had any contact with other dragons. Please don't tell Prax about her just yet. Let her see him from a distance. She needs time to get over her fear of him."

"All right, we'll keep her secret for now. We certainly owe her that much for all that the two of you have done for us. Be sure to tell the others so no one accidentally mentions her."

Cooper was examining Shirell's arm and adjusting the sling when Prax's huge shadow passed overhead. Cooper moved out into a small clearing and sent a ball of blue fire high into the air to signal the dragon. A moment later, Prax landed; Cooper quickly explained to him what they had found. Prax took to the air once more as Cooper returned to the group.

"I've described the keep to Prax," stated Cooper. "He said that he's seen it, and even from high above, it reeks of death. He'll circle nearby until we can get there, and I can signal to him. If everyone's ready, we can go."

Susan and Bodkin had already shouldered their backpacks and helped Shirell to her feet. Stiv carefully spread some large ferns over the entrance to his shelter, and it became indistinguishable from the underbrush.

"We're all ready," said Stiv. "Let's go."

The trip back to the keep took less time than the day before as the path became more familiar. Once again, when they arrived, Stiv and Bodkin remained outside on watch while Cooper, Shirell, and Susan proceeded into the gallery where the dragon graveyard lay. Once inside, Cooper sent a signal light up through one of the openings in the canopy, then all three moved back away. Bits of debris rained down as Prax forcibly enlarged one of the openings to accommodate his bulk and allow himself access from above.

Upon landing, Prax slowly approached the corpse of the chained dragon. His nostrils flared as he sniffed the air, but he showed no other emotion as he slowly took in the devastation that had been inflicted on his brethren. He circled the corpse, eyes flaring as he scrutinized the abuse imposed on his unfortunate kin. When he finished, he left out a mournful wail.

"Prax, do you recognize this dragon?" asked Cooper quietly.

"He was what you would call my half-brother," responded Prax. "We had different she-dragons for mothers, but we were sired by the same drake. My half-brother's name was Carr. You can see where the corner of his right ear is missing. When he was just a hatchling, it was bitten off by one of our older siblings. Young dragons play rough. I had always believed that Carr was lost in one of the attacks of the lindworm."

"The Dark Woods are a mystery, but they weren't always that way," said Cooper. "I believe that this was done before Al-Ron came here. You've lived for centuries. Have you ever heard rumors of a place like this? Do you know who could have done this?"

"I believe that I may know," answered Prax with a nod. "Your assumption was correct. This structure was built by the old race, the ones known as the Galtians, but this atrocity happened long after their departure. First, I must ask you something. You are well-versed in lore, Cooper. What do you know of the eye of Bangor Khan?"

"Not a lot. It was created centuries ago by the wizard Bangor Khan. It is a jewel-like stone said to resemble the eye of a cat. When activated, it can neutralize all magic within a certain area. The Guild of Conjurers, realizing it's dangerous potential, kept it locked away for safekeeping. Only the most senior members of the Guild knew its location. Then it mysteriously disappeared from its hiding place shortly before the start of the Gremlin Wars. Some say that Eldred, unsure if he could trust some of the Guild members, stole it himself. Its location, and whether it even still exists, was believed to be unknown for over fifty years. The truth is that Eldred did steal it, gave it to me, and I threw it into a volcano in my world."

"A wise decision. I have long suspected that Eldred disposed of the artifact. All else that you have said is accurate, except that it is not the eye of a cat that it resembles, but that of a dragon. But what do you know of its creation? Of how it came into being?"

"No one knows. It's always been assumed that the secret to its creation died with Bangor Khan centuries ago."

Shirell spoke up, "But you know, don't you, Prax?"

Prax gave the witch a toothy grin.

"Clever girl. Yes, I know. First you must understand how my kind came to be. We were not always as you see me now. We did not just evolve naturally. Dragons were bred and crossbred to be what we are.

"Originally, we were just simple creatures. Very similar to the lizards in your world, Cooper. Until two powerful wizards, Anwar Khan, father of Bangor Khan, and Bela Khan, his brother, decided to attempt to create a creature large enough and strong enough to protect them from other wizards. There was no Guild back then. Wizards in that day were constantly at war with one another, each trying to destroy their rivals and become the most powerful.

"They experimented with various animals before settling on lizards. Nightshade dogs were the result of one of their failed attempts. They tried spells to make creatures grow large and strong, but it tore the poor animals apart. They were living beings, and the change was too sudden. They couldn't control them. Some subjects grew two heads or huge back legs and tiny front legs. And they all died within hours.

"Then the brothers decided that they were being too impatient in their efforts. Perhaps a gradual change might work better. That produced some limited success. Physically, they were able to make adaptations to the creatures, but all of them went mad, their simple minds unable to adapt quickly enough to their new bodies.

"When the brothers stumbled upon a clutch of eggs, they decided to try a different approach. They wove a spell that allowed them to pass through the eggshells and place a tiny sliver of blue amber into the very bodies of the undeveloped hatchlings, infusing magic into the very essence of the creatures in the eggs.

"The wild magic possessed by the blue amber was much more unpredictable than that of the yellow amber. Their hope was that when they hatched, the newborn creatures would still grow and develop naturally, but that the magic would help mold each generation into a newer and different version.

"The first clutch contained eight eggs. Five of the hatchlings were so twisted and deformed that they died before the first day was out. But three survived and grew larger and stronger than normal. The brothers deliberately chose lizards that matured and reproduced quickly for their experiment, and within a few months, they were able to breed their new hybrids.

"They repeated the process with a new clutch of eggs and, once again, produced an improved version of the parents. Within two years, they had a dragon-like creature the size of a dog. Each new generation provided an opportunity to refine the process, trying pieces of blue amber of different sizes and shapes.

"A year and a half later, they were as big as a horse and starting to grow wings. As the developing dragons became larger, they took longer to mature, and there were many failures. Some went insane from the close breeding. Fortunately, the natural order of nature took a hand. The weak and deformed rarely survived more than a short time and were unable to reproduce. But almost every clutch produced one or two improved offspring from the previous generation. It took over twenty years to develop the dragons that you see today, and the changes became increasingly more subtle in the last five years.

"As the 'wild magic' became more and more a part of each new generation, it began to produce a myriad of results. Many were born in colors that had never been seen before. Some grew long and thin, wyverns able to ride the wind currents for hours on end. Drakes, some of whom could breathe fire while others breathed ice. A select few grew large and powerful. Most gained intelligence to one degree or another, and a few, like myself, even gained the ability to speak. It is said that Bela Khan wet himself the first time one of his dragons spoke back to him.

"Anwar Khan believed the dragon's size and strength protected them from attacks of magic from rogue wizards, and even though the changes in the dragons seemed to level off and the clutches of eggs became much smaller and less frequent, they continued to breed and study their creations for many years to come.

"It was Anwar's son, Bangor Khan, who discovered that magic had become such an integral part of a dragon's essence that when a rival wizard or conjurer tried to use some form of sorcery against them, the inbred dragon-magic absorbed the attack, weakening it and often rendering it harmless.

"He set out to try and find a way to harness that ability. A talisman that could cancel magic would make any opponent helpless. He became obsessed with the idea and began to perform terrible experiments on my kind in his quest to create such an artifact. He dissected many of my fallen brethren, eventually discovering that the strongest concentration of magic was in the eyes. His final atrocity was to remove the eye of a live dragon. As the unfortunate victim of his experiments shrieked out in pain, his captive comrades broke free and rose up against Bangor Khan, destroying the tower and ending his reign of torture. The wizard narrowly escaped with both his life and the stolen eye, which he eventually succeeded in transforming into the powerful artifact that it is today.

"The remaining dragons fled to the high reaches of the Yurt Mountains. Since that day, this tale has been passed down to every young hatchling as soon as they were old enough to understand it to remind us to never be subservient to a wizard or any other master again.

"It is clear to me that we stand in Bangor Khan's workshop. As you have already guessed, the unnatural nature of this place prevents these old bones from crumbling to dust as they should have ages ago. Someone has been trying to duplicate his unholy work and create a new eye. When they couldn't find and steal the original, they tried to create their own."

Chapter 33

"There is one other thing that you need to know," Prax said. "I have only told the story of our beginnings once before, many years ago."

"Who did you tell this to?" asked Cooper ominously.

"The wizard, Eldred!"

"Darkon Rhee!" both Cooper and Shirell said in unison.

Prax looked at them quizzically.

"I am not acquainted with that name."

"Darkon Rhee was Eldred's evil alter ego. If Eldred knew, it's possible that Darkon Rhee may have also known. He must have been trying to recreate the eye."

"Tell me what you know of this Darkon Rhee," said Prax. "If he still lives, I will seek him out and make him pay dearly for what he has done to my kin."

"There is no need for that," explained Cooper. "Eldred lured him into a magic puzzle box where he will remain, trapped for all time."

"You said that they were one and the same person. Has Eldred suffered the same fate?"

Cooper answered with a nod.

"Eldred's magic released Darkon Rhee, and rather than allow him to wreak havoc on the world, Eldred accepted the same imprisonment. As ruthless as Eldred could be at times, he possessed a certain nobility and accepted responsibility for his actions."

"I have many times wondered about the wizard's fate," said Prax. "It is good to know that it was a noble one. There is one last thing that we should do before we leave this wretched place, Guardian."

"Destroy the keep?" asked Cooper.

"We think alike, my friend. I will honor my fallen comrades by incinerating their bones. It is as close to a funeral pyre as we can provide. Then we must smash this evil place into a pile of rocks. Perhaps the orcanus would be kind enough to assist us."

"I would be honored," answered Shirell.

"You should return to your young friends outside. I am immune to the fire, but you three cannot stay. I will complete my task and leave through the roof. Then, together, we will turn this place into rubble."

Bodkin hurried forward as the three approached. Before she had the chance to ask what they found, flames shot up through the roof of the keep, followed by an orange glow shining through the glass-like ceiling of the gallery.

"Prax is cremating the dragon bones," explained Susan.

An instant later, the dragon was silhouetted by the flames as he crashed through the ceiling and flew high overhead.

"Our turn," said Cooper, as his staff began to glow with bright blue fire. "Aim for the base of the walls. The foundation is so old, it shouldn't be able to withstand much. If we can weaken it, the whole structure should collapse under its own weight."

Ancient stones cracked and shattered as Shirell and Cooper battered the walls with a barrage of blue fire. At Cooper's direction, they doubled up and hit the same spot simultaneously. Suddenly, the corner nearest them visibly shuddered, and loose stones fell from the parapets.

Cooper paused, had Shirell do the same, and then signaled to Prax, who had been circling slowly overhead. The dragon instantly tucked his wings in close to his body and dove, picking up speed as he plummeted down. At the last instant, he spread his wings wide, doubled up, and using his powerful hind legs like a battering ram, slammed into the already weakened corner with the full force of his momentum. With a groan, the wall slowly began to crumble. The devastation spider-webbed outward in both directions from the corner, picking up speed as the outer walls began to fall like dominoes in a row. For the next ten minutes, they watched, spellbound, as the earth shook beneath their feet and an enormous cloud rose, obscuring their view. When the dust finally settled, a twenty-foot-high pile of broken stones was all that remained of the once mighty keep. They stayed a few minutes longer, making certain that the collapsing walls had smothered the flames and there was no possibility of setting the forest afire, before returning to the clearing near Stiv's shelter.

Prax landed nearby and stayed just long enough for Cooper to relay their plans to return the way they had come, through the Ice Caves, passing quickly through the ruins of Stiv's old village before the giant ant creatures could become aware of them and attack. With a nod to Cooper's companions, the dragon became airborne once again, returning to his ongoing search for his kindred.

Chapter 34

Upon returning to Kestriana, it was decided that Cooper should ride alone to Finhaven, proceed to Ramses Marsh, seek out the lurker, and inform him of everything that happened at the keep. Crall had been promised the Boc book if it could be recovered. Having it buried under tons of stone made that impossible, but Cooper had also sworn to return and inform Crall of the book's fate. Shirell's injured arm would make riding very painful, and the king's personal surgeon had strongly advised against her accompanying him.

Princess Ashley, with Cooper's approval, had personally restricted Susan and Bodkin to the castle grounds for defying Cooper and following them through the Ice Caves. Even though they were no longer children and were both rapidly becoming young women, their rash decision could have easily cost all of them their lives. In light of the fact that Al-Ron had been stopped and the fairies released from their imprisonment, Ashley had shortened their punishment to a mere two days.

No longer having any real home in the Dark Woods, Stiv agreed to come to Kestriana, at least for a short time. His family was gone, and he had no wish to remain anywhere near either his old village or the ruins of the keep. The fact that there was clearly some attraction between him and Bodkin, though neither one was willing to admit to it, undoubtedly helped to influence his decision.

After spending her whole life hiding in the Dark Woods, Kana was very reluctant to leave and allow herself to be seen. Passage through the Ice Caves was impossible for her. She would have to fly. The knowledge that there were other places where she and Stiv could go and they wouldn't have to struggle just to stay alive every day was a strong argument. It took Stiv some time to convince her, but their bond was strong, and in the end, she agreed to fly him to Kestriana, though she would only travel after dark.

Early the next morning, Cooper set out for Ramses Marsh. Riding alone with his staff strapped across his back and unencumbered with any bulky supplies, Cooper felt completely relaxed for the first time since he and Susan had arrived. He had had enough excitement and adventure to last him for quite some time.

The stable master, an old acquaintance who knew Cooper and his taste in mounts, had given him the same big mare that Ashley had brought for him on their first day here when she met them by the Gnome Door. The horse remembered him and seemed to instantly pick up his mood. Though he was in no real hurry to get to Finhaven, when he came to an open stretch of fields, he gave the horse its lead and let her run. Leaning low over her back, the breeze whipping his hair, he was reminded why he loved coming to this land. In spite of the hidden dangers, it's unspoiled beauty always captivated him. Compared to the modern human world, it was like taking a few steps back in time.

Ashley wanted him to stay, she had made that quite clear. Shirell also tried to persuade him to remain, but for entirely different reasons. If he was being honest with himself, he had to admit that he still had some very strong feelings for the princess, but his love for Susan and his daughter Elana took precedent. Elana would never agree to live here, and he could never abandon Susan. So, the matter was settled in his mind.

Besides, he was riding a fine horse on a fine day with a warm sun and a pleasant breeze. He put all thoughts of the last few days aside and allowed his mind to wander to simpler, more pleasant things.

Fren, the innkeeper of the Stone Hearth in Finhaven, remembered Cooper. He especially remembered the fact that when he was there last, he had paid in advance with elven silver coins. He quickly had a boy take the mare into the stable, rub her down, and be certain that she received the best of care. After a simple lunch provided by the innkeeper, Cooper set off at a brisk pace for the marsh, arriving in less than an hour.

Cooper was hopeful that Crall would be waiting for his return and the instant that he set foot on the path, the lurker would know and come. He had no wish to travel any further into the swamp than necessary. Luckily, Crall appeared on the trail before he had gone a quarter mile. How anyone as deformed and twisted as Crall could move so swiftly and silently amazed him. One minute, the path was empty. An instant later, the lurker loomed before him.

"You have...returned, Guardian," said Crall, in his halting whisper. "Follow me...to my shelter...where we can talk."

A few moments later, Cooper stood, once again, in the earthen structure that the lurker called home. Despite the short distance from the path, Cooper knew that he would never be able to find his way back here without Crall to lead him. Near the center of the room, the Boc book from Kestriana's archive room lay on the large, flat stump that acted as a table. Next to the stump, two tall flat stones had been placed to serve as chairs. How Crall had gotten the stones there was a mystery to Cooper.

"Please sit...Guardian," wheezed the lurker. "I am unaccustomed...to having guests. But you are a...man of your word. You have come back...to tell me of...the book and the dark tower...where it resided."

For the next hour, Cooper related everything that had transpired at the keep in the Dark Woods. Crall listened intently, only occasionally interrupting to ask Cooper to clarify some small detail.

"I was aware of the...disappearance of the fairies," said Crall, when Cooper told him of their rescue from the blue amber. "It is curious...that young Bodkin...was able to perform red magic."

"Prax seemed to believe that you are the source of all knowledge and keeper of all the secrets. Perhaps you can tell me how she did that."

"Perhaps I can," responded Crall. "Or perhaps...Prax gives me too much credit. But, for now...please complete your story."

With a nod, Cooper resumed his narrative, including the imprisonment of Eldred, the fall of the tower, the discovery of the dragon graveyard, and the subsequent destruction of the keep itself.

"I am sorry," he said as he finished. "But the Boc book was in the tower when it fell. If it's still intact, it's now buried under tons of stone and debris. I was unable to bring it as promised."

"I suspected...something of the sort," responded the lurker. "When I used this book," he waved a skeletal hand at the book on the table before them, "An image appeared...the book was not...totally destroyed. But the image...was one of total darkness.

That book is...beyond recovery...for both you...or any others. But I fear that I...have bad news for you, Guardian. Come...see for yourself."

Using a boney finger, Crall flipped the book on the stump open and extended the hand wearing the silver ring over the open page. A blurred image began to slowly focus above the book. The image was dark. A fine line of light peeked out in the bottom corner of the image and Cooper realized that he was looking at the inside of a cupboard.

"The one remaining book, abandoned...in a lost Boc outpost, is lost no more. It has been...recovered and moved. I know not...who has done this. I only know...that the threat remains. Someone now possesses that last book...and could use it to open a gateway...for the creatures behind the Barrier."

Chapter 35

Shirell could hardly contain herself. She had to keep reminding herself that she needed to maintain the dignity of her position. Cooper had returned from Ramses Marsh two days ago with the news that there still remained one more Boc book that had to be sought out and dealt with, and she would deal with it...tomorrow.

But, today was Festival Day, the anniversary of the end of the Gremlin War. A huge gala was being held, and she was one of the honored guests. The king's surgeon had said that her arm was recovering nicely, and she felt better than she had in quite some time.

In the life she had so long ago, before she went off to the Hall of the Guild of Conjurers, when it was just her and her mother, Kiri, she had loved the festivals in the village. The food, the music, the dancing. Even the boys in the village who normally teased her for being a half-elf were nice to her during festival days.

The glade just outside the north gate was filled with colorful tents and bright streamers. As she moved through the center of the festivities taking it all in, she could smell the delicious aromas of the food vendors. At one of the booths, she had sampled a local favorite — a dish made with catfish freshly caught from the river Equus, lightly grilled in butter made from goat's milk, and seasoned with just a sprinkling of herbs. It was exquisite.

The hearty scent of cheese drew her toward the center of the celebration. Many of the local farms had their own personal recipes for cheese which they fiercely guarded. There was to be a competition to determine the best cheese, and Shirell, along with Cooper, had been asked to be a judge.

Shirell had promised to meet Susan and Bodkin in an hour, but for the moment, she was on her own. With Susan's help, Bodkin was getting ready for the archery competition. There was a friendly rivalry between Bodkin and the princess. Princess Ashley was the reigning archery champion, but many believed that Bodkin might just be good enough to unseat her. Bodkin had nearly succeeded once before. King Marinus had let it be known that he was personally looking forward to overseeing that match.

Resisting the temptation to sample some of the cheeses so as not to prejudice her opinions later, Shirell stopped at one of the winemaker's booths. While she admitted to being hopelessly ignorant of the subtleties of a good wine, she felt that the sample of deep red wine that the woman gave her was one of the finest she had ever tasted.

Glancing over the woman's shoulder at the open area behind the festival booths, Shirell saw Princess Ashley with Stiv and Kana at the far edge of the glade, near the trees.

After considerable coaxing, Stiv had convinced Kana to come out into the open and allow the people to see her. Word of their adventure in the Dark Woods had spread quickly, and Kana was a bit of a celebrity. Everyone wanted to see the wyvern for themselves. Even many of those old enough to remember when dragons were a common sight had never seen a wyvern. But after

226

a lifetime spent in hiding, Kana was still very reluctant to be seen. Stiv had finally persuaded her to come to the edge of the trees where people could see her from a distance. A rope line had been set up along the rear of the festival tents and a few dozen individuals stood by the rope, marveling at the wyvern and the elf boy with red hair.

The woman at the winemaker's booth had just offered Shirell a sample of a sweet-smelling golden wine when a large shadow passed over the booth. Prax circled once and then landed fifty yards from where Ashley and Stiv stood, and from the instant that his feet touched the ground, it was clear that something was wrong. The scales down his back were raised. Rather than folding his wings in close on his back as he usually did upon landing, he kept them spread wide apart, making him appear much larger and more menacing. Both teeth and claws were fully exposed, and his voice was a low growl.

"Take the boy and move away from that creature, Princess."

"Prax, what are you doing?" Ashley stared at him in disbelief. "What's the meaning of this?"

"This creature has the stench of the lindworm on it. I don't know how it managed to escape years ago, but it is one of his vile offspring! It is an abomination of evil and must be destroyed. Step aside now, Princess!"

"No, Prax. Kana has helped us. We know of her lineage. She has shown herself to be our friend and ally. Her mother was a she-dragon. She is one of your kind." Ashley caught a glimpse of movement from the corner of her eye.

"Lies and deception. Evil is part of this creature's very nature. Look for yourself, Princess. See that she most certainly is not one of my kin."

Ashley quickly glanced to her left to see Kana holding herself upright, wings spread and hissing. Two dagger-like fangs protruded from her mouth, and yellow, foul smelling poison dripped onto the grass in front of her, instantly burning it black.

Ashley stood her ground in the face of the dragon's rage. "Stop, Prax. I don't see a creature of evil. I see one prepared to defend herself when threatened. We will listen to your concerns and address them in due course. But until that can be arranged, she is under my protection as princess of the nation of the elves, and I demand that you stand down."

"I do not take commands from elves!" bellowed Prax, as he launched himself at the wyvern.

Stiv dove to the right and rolled clear, but Ashley was a split second too slow. Prax's wing caught her full on as he lunged and lifted her completely off her feet, flinging her like a rag doll to land thirty yards away.

The dragon and the wyvern clashed with an impact that shook the ground beneath their feet. The much smaller wyvern was thrown backwards, and the battle would have ended before it began if not for Kana's speed and agility. She slipped past Prax's next onrush, leaving him clawing at empty air. Time and again, Prax lashed out at her, only to miss by scant inches as the wyvern dodged and weaved.

Though Kana was faster, she could not begin to match Prax's size or strength. She had no claws to attack with and, even if she could get close enough, her fangs were useless against Prax's thick scales. Hers was a purely defensive game. If she couldn't outlast Prax, she was lost. She was a house cat trying to battle a tiger.

It quickly became clear to those watching that Kana had no experience in battle. She was fighting on pure instinct.

Despite his rage, Prax quickly realized that a frontal assault would not be effective against the lightning speed of his opponent, and he paused in his attack. As the two behemoths faced each other, snarling and growling, he was devising a new strategy. He feinted left, and then with a leap to the right that defied his bulk, Prax overwhelmed the wyvern, pinning her to the grass with one huge claw and preparing to deliver the final blow.

Chapter 36

Prax's arrival had drawn many in the crowd toward the rope line, including Cooper, Susan, and Bodkin.

While the battle raged before them, the crowd scattered. Cooper and Susan sprinted across the grass to where Ashley lay crumpled in a heap. The princess was badly battered but still breathing. Cooper examined Ashley for a moment before turning to Susan.

"Place your stone in her hand and hold it there."

Susan instantly produced the amberstone from beneath her tunic and did as she was asked. Cooper spoke a few words from a language long forgotten, and Ashley's breathing became stronger and more regular as the stone glowed blue.

"Stay with her," said Cooper.

As he rose to his feet, his face took on a look that was like nothing Susan had ever seen before. For the first time in her life, she was frightened of her grandfather. He turned away quickly, but not before Susan saw that his eyes had turned jet black. His staff quickly began to shine so bright that Susan could not look upon it without covering her eyes.

The blast of blue light from Cooper's staff caught Prax square in the chest, knocking him completely off of Kana. The backlash of Cooper's strike shook the trees at the edge of the forest. Prax rolled thirty yards across the grass before coming to his feet, shaking his head, stunned by the unexpected blow. The wyvern was momentarily forgotten as his head whipped around, searching for the new attacker. His eyes lit on Cooper's glowing staff.

"Guardian?" Prax's bewilderment quickly turned to rage. "How dare you! You have no right to interfere!" Prax shrieked at Cooper.

"If the princess dies, you will not see the next sunrise, dragon," responded Cooper, as he sent a second blast at Prax.

Prax attempted to block the strike with his wing, but the power of the blow still forced him backwards two steps and left his wing smoking.

"Very impressive, Guardian. Your magic is stronger than any that I've seen in two centuries, but you are still a fool. Even Eldred did not have the strength to stand against me!" said Prax, an instant before a fifty-foot tongue of flame shot from his mouth.

With a wave of his hand, Cooper threw up a wall of blue magic that scattered the flames into a harmless shower of sparks.

"I've had a few years to practice while you were sleeping, dragon!"

Prax attempted to become airborne, but Cooper's blast hit him high in the chest, somersaulting him backwards onto the grass.

"Go on, take to the air, dragon. It makes you an easier target." Cooper taunted the behemoth.

"Grandfather, stop!" shouted Susan, but to no avail.

Prax rolled quickly to his feet and circled slowly, looking for an opening to rush Cooper and overwhelm him with his sheer size. But the guardian was prepared and thumped his staff on the ground. Instantly, Cooper vanished as fog rose from the grass and filled the clearing. A blast of dragon fire quickly dissipated the haze. As the smoke cleared, Cooper reappeared at the far edge of the glade.

Prax was a crafty old veteran of many battles and knew this tactic. The next strike would most certainly come from behind, and he was ready. He was crouched low and swung his tail in a wide arc. He would have broken Cooper's legs had the guardian not anticipated the move and leapt straight up in the air. As it was, the tip of Prax's tail did succeed in catching Cooper's heel and knocking him off his feet. He rolled and was up in an instant, but not before Prax changed direction and charged toward him, spitting fire.

Only now, there were four identical Coopers, each one throwing bolts of blue magic at the dragon from a different direction. Dragon fire struck the Cooper on the far right and it vanished into smoke. The real Cooper ran toward the trees as his staff glowed bright, preparing for another massive strike. Blue lightning and tongues of fire flashed across the glade, crisscrossing each other as the dragon and the guardian lashed out at each other.

Without warning, a brilliant flash of red light exploded in the space separating the two adversaries.

"Enough!" A commanding voice shook the glade. With long, silver hair flying wildly behind him and the royal scepter glowing with red magic held in one hand, King Marinus rode the wyvern into the center of the fray directly between the two combatants. Both Cooper and Prax were momentarily stunned by the voice that they both knew well but hadn't heard in decades.

This was the Marinus of old, the mighty and noblest of kings who had fearlessly led his people in the war against the gremlin army.

"Stop this, both of you! You are in the kingdom of the

elves and, as such, you are subject to its laws. Only the king can decide if someone's actions warrant death. Cooper, if you truly care about my daughter, go and use your skills as a healer. And you, Prax, while you are on my lands, you will respect my laws, or I will have my army hunt you down and drive you from my kingdom. Even the mighty dragon, Prax, cannot stand against the strength of the elven army."

Cooper's staff went dark instantly. He blinked twice, and his eyes returned to their natural gray. His anger at Prax was immediately forgotten as he turned and sprinted across the glade to where Susan and Shirell knelt beside Ashley. He passed his staff to the orcanus who eyed it with renewed interest. Quickly, Cooper scooped up the princess in his arms and started toward the castle as a team of healers and their assistants hurried to meet him.

Marinus landed directly in front of Prax, whose blind anger had also subsided to be replaced with remorse.

"My rash actions have injured the princess, old friend. I beg your forgiveness. How can I undo the harm that I have done?"

"I think that you've done quite enough for one day," answered Marinus. "Go to your home in the mountains. Remain there until noon, three days from now, when we will know the extent of my daughter's injuries and Cooper has had time to regain his senses."

Marinus gestured toward the wyvern.

"I will assess whether this creature can be trusted or not. But she will be treated fairly, not judged by the crimes of the one who sired her. I swear it. Return three days hence, and we will speak then."

"I shall do as you ask, King Marinus," responded Prax, bowing his massive head. With a leap, he was instantly airborne and heading away toward the high mountains.

Marinus turned toward where Shirell and the others, took two steps, and collapsed onto the grass.

Chapter 37

Ashley slowly opened her eyes. Next to her bed, sitting upright in a chair, Cooper slept. She reached over to touch his hand, which sent a jolt of pain shooting up her arm. Cooper woke instantly at her touch.

"You look terrible," she said weakly. "How long have you been sitting there?"

"You've been here for three days."

"And you've been sitting there that whole time?"

Cooper answered with a nod.

"People will talk."

Cooper ignored her comment. "How do you feel?" he asked.

"Like I got kicked by a whole herd of those wretched horses that you seem to like so much. Every square inch of my body aches. Even talking hurts. I remember Prax attacking Kana. Everything after that is a blank. What happened?"

"Your father stopped them, but then he collapsed. He is gravelly ill."

"And I've been here for three days? Shades! The High Council must be in total disarray. Chancellor Adronis will try to seize control. Where are my clothes? You need to help me get dressed."

Ashley tried to rise, but the room spun before her eyes as

pain struck her like a club to the back of the head.

"No, lay down and be still." Cooper placed a gentle hand on her shoulder, and she found that she had no strength to resist.

"You have at least two broken ribs and possibly some internal injuries."

"But the council..."

"That's all under control. Your aunt is seeing to things there."

"What?...My aunt?...Zaneth? You're joking. She swore that she'd never set foot in the council chambers again."

"Apparently her distrust of her husband is stronger than her dislike of politics. She has taken over the council until one of you is back on your feet."

"But how did she know? She severed all ties with the family years ago."

"It seems that Marinus's valet, Macilon, has had a crush on her since they were teenagers. He's been secretly corresponding with her and keeping her up to date on important events, particularly, the king's health, for many years. Despite all that's happened between them, she still cares about her brother. Macilon sent word to her, and she came."

"But...I'm sorry, I just can't believe that Zaneth is here. I need to speak to her."

"No, you need to rest and recover. She has stopped to look in on you a few times. I'll let her know that you're awake only if you promise to stay here and let yourself heal."

"All right, I'll stay put, but only if you promise to go and get some sleep yourself," Ashley promised, secretly telling herself that she would go and find her aunt just as soon as she could get the room to stop spinning every time she tried to rise.

Cooper's gait was slower and more measured than usual as he walked down the corridor toward Shirell's rooms. Ashley was right. He was bone tired. He had only allowed himself a few snatches of sleep and almost no food over the last three days. Even though the healers had assured him that none of the princess's injuries were life threatening, and his own skills had confirmed their diagnosis, he just couldn't bring himself to leave her side until she woke and he was able to see, first hand, that she would recover. Now that she was finally awake, he had just one small task left before he would allow himself some much-needed sleep.

Shirell's temporary quarters, guest rooms for visiting dignitaries, were in the northwest corner of the castle, affording her full view of both the surrounding countryside and the main road leading up to Kestrina.

The door opened immediately at his knock, and Shirell beckoned him quickly inside. She had changed out of the imposing robes and high boots that were the customary garb of the orcanus and wore a simple tunic and pants, similar to that worn by the people who lived and worked near the castle. Cooper had almost forgotten how small and petite she was. And even though Shirell had been a teen during the Gremlin Wars some forty years ago, people aged differently here, and she looked like a young woman in her thirties.

"How's the princess? She must be feeling better if you're here."

"Awake and impatient to be up and about."

"Exactly what I would expect. I'm glad to hear it. You look like you could use some sleep."

"It has been mentioned," answered Cooper with a smile. "How's the arm?"

"Feeling much better. The king's personal surgeon has

239

examined it and assured me that in a few days, I can get rid of the sling."

"Excellent. You're in good hands. Borr is the finest healer in the land. His skills far exceed mine." Cooper motioned toward her attire. "Sneaking out?" Dressed as she currently was, with her hair down and in a loose ponytail, she should be able to walk freely through the open market in the square. Humans were a common sight in the marketplace, so even her raven hair would barely be noticed. There was little chance of her being recognized.

"After all the excitement of the last few days, Susan and Bodkin said that they wanted to just relax and go shopping. They invited me to come along. It sounded like a wonderful idea. I so rarely get to spend much time with the two girls, and I'd kill for a day away from official duties. That valet fellow keeps hovering around me and insists on accounting for my every minute. Besides, you can learn a lot wandering around in an open-air market and listening to the local gossip. You won't tell anyone where I've gone, will you? I'm meeting the girls in an hour."

"Macilon takes his duties very seriously," answered Cooper with a bemused smile. "And he is at a bit of a loss since the healers ordered him out of the king's quarters so Marinus can get some rest. The king is getting the best care possible, and Ashley is recovering. Go and have fun with Susan and Bodkin. You've earned it. A girl's day out sounds like a good idea for all of you. If anyone asks, I'll tell them that you're under doctor's orders to relax, and I don't know where you've gone. You were right about one thing. I do need to get some sleep myself. I only came for my staff."

"Well, I wanted to talk to you about that," said Shirell nervously. "I'm sorry, but in my official capacity as orcanus, I'm confiscating that staff."

"What? You can't do that!" said Cooper, a trace of anger

creeping into his voice. "I'm not a member of the Guild. I don't even live in this world. Besides, you already have the dragon staff."

"That's true, I do hold the dragon staff. But there's something different about yours. I'll return it to you on one condition. You tell me how you were able to use it to generate such power while you were battling Prax. I've experimented with the dragon staff, tested its limits, but I've never been able to achieve anything close to the magnitude of power that you were throwing at that dragon. I know that you would never use it for anything evil and I trust you more than anyone else in this world, even with my life, but I can't allow you to use such a powerful artifact without at least knowing how it works."

Cooper left out a deep sigh. "I've feared that we would have to have this conversation sooner or later. Bring me my staff and I'll show you."

Shirell crossed to a small closet across the room and returned a moment later with Cooper's carved staff. She silently breathed a sigh of relief. She knew that attempting to keep his staff was risky. Cooper was a friend and had always been one of her strongest supporters since she assumed the mantle of orcanus. She was gambling on that friendship and cooperation. After witnessing his battle with Prax, she was certain that she wouldn't be able to force him to do anything that he didn't wish to do. As she handed it to him, he grasped the staff at its center and held it out horizontally.

"Watch the ends of the staff."

Cooper closed his eyes, and a look of intensity came over his face as the carvings began to glow with a blue light. Intertwined vines formed the carvings at the upper end of the stick, and as Shirell watched, they began to slowly move and writhe like snakes. The vines shifted, separating until Shirell was

241

able to catch a glimpse of yellow concealed within their entangled fingers. A piece of amberstone lay hidden in their center.

"Of course," said Shirell. "I should have realized that your staff held a talisman."

"Keep watching," answered Cooper, in a harsh whisper.

The amberstone disappeared from view as the vines constricted back to their original locations and the blue light traveled down the length of the staff to the bottom end. The base of the staff formed a claw holding a globe. As Shirell continued to watch, the fingers of the claw flexed and opened. The dark walnut brown globe faded into a transparent ball. Suspended in the center of the ball, another stone resided. A blue amberstone.

Shirell watched speechlessly as Cooper allowed the light to fade and the carvings returned to their normal appearance.

"A blue stone?" stuttered Shirell. "But...how?"

"Eldred's genius," responded Cooper. "Let me explain. When John and I first arrived here in this land, we worked at making barrels for your old friend, Quisp."

"Yes, you've told me about that."

"He also kept us secluded from the locals so they didn't find out that we were humans and weren't really supposed to be there. So, to pass the time when we weren't working, I did woodcarving. After experimenting with a few different local species, I discovered that this particular wood grew straight and tall, carved easily, and held details well. So, I made myself a staff. It was just an ordinary walking stick then. I didn't really need it, but the more time I had, the more detailed it became.

"Some time later, we came to Kestriana. That's where I first met Eldred. He was fascinated with my staff, captivated by the intricate designs and details of the carvings. He offered to tutor me in magic if I would create a staff for him. He had a very detailed design in mind. There were Guild members who had been trying for years to get Eldred to take them on as his apprentice, and here he was freely offering it to me. I, of course, agreed instantly."

"So, you created the dragon staff?"

Cooper nodded his assent.

"I did the carving, but just like my staff, it was simply a decorated walking stick. Eldred was delighted with the results and showed it to everyone he met. Then one day, after a lesson, he said that he had something special for me as a reward for my fine work. I assured him that being his student was a great honor and I didn't need anything else, but I had learned early on, you didn't argue with Eldred.

"He asked me if he could borrow my staff, so I gave it to him. He held it out and made the carvings move, as I just showed you, and then he set the stones in place. I was quite familiar with the yellow amberstones, but I had never seen a blue one before and knew nothing of its nature at that time. He explained that the stones were perfectly matched, precisely balanced against each other, and would amplify any magic many times over. He said that my staff and his new dragon staff were the only two in existence. If you bring me the dragon staff, I'll show you."

Shirell handed Cooper her staff and, once again, the blue light glowed as the carved dragon slowly unfurled it's wings to reveal a yellow stone embedded in its chest. As the eldritch light moved down the length of the staff, the dragon's tail moved aside to uncover a blue stone. After a moment, Cooper allowed the magic to dissipate before returning the talisman to her.

"Are you telling me that I've had the kind of power that you showed a few days ago in my hand this whole time that I've been orcanus?"

"Yes, you are the first orcanus since Eldred himself to glimpse the true strength of the dragon staff. As you know, every talisman slowly attunes itself to its user. It may take you a few tries, but now that you know they exist, with a little concentration, you should be able to reveal the stones yourself. Fortunately, the secret to their creation was lost with Eldred."

"But I've tested it, explored its limits, and never achieved anything near the power that you threw at Prax."

"I did the same thing. Eldred actually charged me with testing it, working with it. I believe that he was unsure of its limitations. Even though I was his student, Eldred could be ruthless in some things and had no reservations about using me as his guinea pig. I didn't discover the staff's full potential until much later."

"Why did you say 'fortunately' the secret was lost?"

"Because the risk is so great, and the price of such power is too high. The yellow amberstone focuses power drawn from the better half of human nature. Things like love and kindness. Qualities that all of us, even someone as despicable as Marcus, possess.

"The kuri-aken ritual allows us to tap into some of our undesirable attributes and use the magic for less noble purposes, but it just scratches the surface. The driving force behind the magic that we all employ is still the good in you. In contrast, the blue amberstone, is its polar opposite and feeds off of the darkest depths of humanity. I didn't understand any of this at the time, and I used my staff just as you use yours, with similar results.

"It was years later. Eldred had disappeared and the Gremlin War had just ended. There were still small groups of gremlins hiding in the forest, terrorizing the locals. I was working with the forest wardens, rooting out the stragglers and driving them back to their homeland. I was alone and lost in my own thoughts when I came upon a stream. I bent down to get a drink. When I looked up, I found myself face to face with a gremlin on the opposite shore. I thought that he was part of a group trying to ambush me, and I lashed out in panic. I threw a bolt of magic at him, blowing a gaping hole in his chest.

"Once I realized that he was alone and unarmed, I knew that I had overreacted. He didn't have any weapons, and he hadn't threatened me in any way. I should have remained calm, warned that he needed to immediately return to his own country or face imprisonment, and sent him on his way. I dashed across the stream, praying that there was something I could do to help him. As I rolled him over, I saw the triangular medallion he wore. The emblem of a healer.

"I had just attacked a caregiver, a gremlin surgeon who was following the retreating army, tending to the wounded. I tried to stop the blood with my hands, but the damage was just too great. There was nothing I could do but helplessly watch as he died.

"Gremlin custom is to cremate their dead. Once I was sure that he was gone, I rose to go collect wood for a funeral pyre. It was the least that I could do for him. His blood was still on my hands when I touched the staff. It erupted in fire. The blood of an innocent had unlocked the hidden power of the blue stone. I was dumbstruck by the transformation, and the gremlin was momentarily forgotten. I could feel the surge of power flowing through my hands, captivating me. I directed it toward a large elm. The tree exploded into splinters. I hadn't just doubled the staff's power; I had increased it many times over. Even now, I honestly don't know if there is a limit to its power.

"But the change wasn't just to my staff. A wave of indifference came over me. Suddenly, I felt no remorse for the dead gremlin, no guilt or anguish over what I'd done, only a mild annoyance over having to deal with a corpse. With the newfound power of my staff, I burned the body, bones and all, to ash, even melting the stone medallion that identified him as a healer. I called up a strong wind and blew the ashes into the stream to be washed away. The only evidence of my terrible act was a small patch of charred grass. And I was pleased.

"When I woke the next morning, I felt like it had all been a bad dream. But in the following weeks, I found myself being more and more drawn toward the urge to destroy and burn, to abandon the things I loved. My very humanity was being usurped by evil. The power of the blue amberstone had released my personal demon, and it was trying to seize control."

"But you're nothing like that now," said Shirell. "You're one of the kindest men I've ever met. You saw some good in me when I was the witch from the Dark Woods, former student of the evil shadow mage. You helped me become orcanus. You must have found a way to resist the evil."

"You're right, I did. I found Princess Anna. More accurately, she found me. She stood by me, married me against her father's wishes, and went with me to live in my world. She became my anchor. When the evil began to manifest itself and stealthily creep into my thoughts, her love gave me the strength to send it back into the dark reaches of my mind. The demons will always be with me, but I've built barriers to keep them imprisoned where they can do little harm. When Anna died, I feared that the evil would return and overwhelm me. That I would become lost. I didn't know how I could resist without her strength."

"Somehow you did," Shirell stated.

"Susan and her mother, my daughter Elana, have filled that void."

"But the battle with Prax?"

"Apparently, my feelings for Ashley are somewhat stronger

that I've been admitting, even to myself," Cooper said sheepishly. "The loss of Anna was hard. It stayed with me for a long time. The thought of losing Ashley, too, was almost more than I could bear. My distress turned to blind rage and allowed the darkness to overwhelm my control. Prax's actions had seriously injured her. In that frame of mind, I believed that he needed to pay for his carelessness. Marinus's timely intervention was enough of a shock for me to regain control.

"Now do you see why I kept this from you? Could you knowingly murder an innocent just to unleash that power? I know that your will is strong, but do you believe that you're strong enough to fight off evil that's many times more powerful than the influence of the shadow mage? I wasn't able to do it alone. Neither was Eldred. Darkon Rhee was the manifestation of his darker side. I'm certain that Darkon Rhee came about because of the dragon staff."

Shirell stared at Cooper, unmoving, for a long time before she spoke.

"You're right. About everything. I couldn't knowingly kill an innocent. Even when I was the shadow mage's student, I never believed in his vision of destruction. All I was interested in was revenge against those who I believed had wronged me and my mother. But Kiri was a kind woman. I couldn't tarnish her memory by hurting those who had never hurt me. That's one of the main reasons why I eventually abandoned Marcus.

"But you're also right about the fact that I've been alone for many years. Unlike you, I have no family. Just the Guild and a few good friends like you and Susan. And, like Eldred, I would have little to cling to if faced with my own darker side. You were right not to tell me. I think we would also be wise to never let this secret go beyond this room."

"I was hoping that you would feel that way."

"There is one thing that you will have to do something about. You attacked Prax because he injured the princess. You might as well have openly professed your undying love for her in the public square. She's not going to forget about that."

"I know. I think fighting Prax might have been easier. I can only hope that her recovery takes longer than expected."

"I look forward to watching you try to keep her at arm's length after this," said Shirell as a huge grin spread over her face.

Chapter 38

The council chamber erupted in a cacophony of shouting once again as neither party was willing to compromise on how to proceed. Amid the chaos, few noticed the silver-haired woman who quietly entered from a side door. She was tall and statuesque, with her hair pulled back in a loose ponytail. Her plain brown frock was a stark contrast to the refined demeanor with which she carried herself, and her only adornment was a small pendant on a chain around her neck. Debate at the outer edges of the room fell silent as she was recognized. Calmly, she proceeded toward the center of the chamber.

By the time she reached the dais, only Chancellor Adronis and Lord Quin, who were locked in a heated debate, were unaware of her presence.

The Chancellor's back was to the woman. Quin instantly fell silent as he glanced over the Chancellor's shoulder and made eye contact with the woman.

"My Lord Quin, I must insist. We need to appoint an interim regent until...what are you staring at?" The chancellor spun around to find himself face to face with the woman.

"Gentlemen," she said quietly, "perhaps I can be of some help."

"Lady Zaneth, we had no idea..." Adronis stuttered.

"That I had returned to the castle?" she said, smiling

gently as she completed his sentence. "Calm yourselves, gentlemen. My presence here is only temporary. I shall only remain until either the king or Princess Ashley is recovered and able to resume their duties here. In the meantime, perhaps we should call a short recess for the chancellor to fill me in on all that's happened lately and give everyone an opportunity to regain their composure. Then we can proceed with the business of the day. Shall we meet back here in, let's say, an hour?"

There were murmured words of assent as the council members were all too anxious to exit the chamber, some of them leaving together and barely making it into the hallway before voicing their thoughts about this latest turn of events.

Once they were away from the council chambers, Zaneth suggested that they walk outside, through the open market, while they talked.

"I used to love the marketplace here at Kestriana," said Zaneth, as they walked. "It's one of the few things that I've really missed."

"Yes, I remember that you always enjoyed walking through here. I had almost forgotten how lovely you are, Zaneth," said Adronis.

"Save your charms for someone else, Adronis. I know you far too well. I'm only here long enough to prevent you and your trained lackeys on the council from attempting to steal the throne before either my brother or my niece has had the chance to recover. Then I will return to my home in the north, and you can go back to your schemes and the young women that you so love to seduce."

"You wound me with your accusations, my dear. You have always been my greatest love. And the welfare of the elven people

250

has always been my greatest concern."

"Spare me the dragon scat, Chancellor. Power and ambition are your greatest concerns. And you would gladly toss me or anyone else aside in a heartbeat if it helped you achieve your ends. As I've said, I'll only be here a short time, but in that time, I will be overseeing the council. Remember, Adronis, I know too many of your secrets. And I've kept your secrets all these years. But I warn you, it would be ill advised of you to oppose me now. I'm sure that your position on the high council would be in jeopardy if they were to discover how you bleach your hair to hide its true color. While I'm here, I will make every effort to remain cordial and respectful towards you. I will expect the same in return. Is that understood?"

Fire burned in Adronis's eyes as he answered through clenched teeth. "Yes, m'lady. It's understood."

"Good, then I will see you back in the council chambers within the hour. And do go change that horrible robe you're wearing. You always did have a terrible fashion sense."

Stiv fidgeted as he watched Susan and Bodkin comparing fabrics. A dozen questions ran through his head: "Why was it so much trouble for girls to choose one? Was it a strong, well-made cloth that wouldn't tear the first time you brushed against a branch? Why should anyone care that much whether it's light green or dark green? And, the most puzzling question of all, why had he even agreed to come with the girls to the marketplace?

"Now they're showing the cloth to Shirell and asking her opinion," he thought. "You would think that, being a little older and holding the office of orcanus, Shirell would at least be a little more sensible, but she was just as bad as the other two. Did they have to stop and look at every single stand?"

Stiv had just about decided to slip away and visit the fruit stand where at least he could get something sweet to eat when he noticed the tall woman and her well-dressed companion.

Stiv tugged on Bodkin's arm and whispered in her ear, "Who is that, the older couple standing over by the fruit seller?"

"That's Lady Zaneth, the king's sister. She's been a recluse for many years. Talk in the castle is that she's only returned because the king's ill."

"Not her, the man with her."

"That's Chancellor Adronis. He's head of the Elven Council. I think the two of them used to be married to each other."

"I've seen him before. In my village when I was younger."

"Impossible. You must be mistaken."

"No. He was dressed differently, but I swear it's the same man. I remember because I knew everyone in the village, and he was a stranger. He spoke with the elders, and then left the village to visit the keep. I had forgotten that anyone besides the dark elf ever went to the keep until I saw him just now.

"When I asked my parents about him, they crossed themselves and told me that he was a practitioner of the old dark magic that had destroyed most of the Boc. They said that the elders were duty bound to him in some way. Then they told me to forget that I had ever seen him and never mention him again. I'm sure it was him, though."

"If you're right, that means that he could have been in league with the dark elf. I've heard rumors that Adronis can be a very dangerous man. But we can't go making accusations like that without proof. Keep it to yourself. When we get back to the castle, we'll talk to Cooper and the princess privately the first chance we get."

Susan came up behind the two.

"What are you two whispering about?" she asked with a grin.

"Nothing special," said Bodkin. She gave Stiv a quick glance over her shoulder and put a finger to her lips as she grabbed Susan by the hand and dragged her toward one of the stands. "Oh, look at that beautiful red fabric."

After a moment, Stiv followed, shaking his head and thinking to himself, "If it was up to me, we'd skip the rest of the marketplace and go find Cooper right away. Girls and shopping. I think that I was better off when all I had to worry about were gants and nightshade dogs."

Chapter 39

After an afternoon at the market, the girls had promised to stop and visit the princess. Cooper had already relayed to Ashley his version of their encounter with the dark elf, but she was anxious to hear about it from Susan and Bodkin's point of view.

Stiv was all too glad to be excused. He had had more than enough of the city, all the people in the marketplace, and especially the noise. He had been offered a room in the castle but had turned it down, preferring to stay near to Kana; so, the forest wardens gave him some supplies and a small tent and found him a secluded spot a half mile from Kestriana where he could establish a campsite far away from the bustle of the castle.

An hour later, after washing off the dust of the marketplace and changing back into her robes as orcanus, Shirell joined the two girls in the hallway leading to the princess's quarters.

"I thought it would be better if we all went together," she told the girls. "I know that I'll be much more relaxed in Ashley's private quarters than if I had to stand in the throne room and relay what happened."

Lady Coramina opened the door immediately when they knocked, and she escorted them in. Ashley was on the bed, propped up into a seated position with a number of cushions.

"Susan, Bodkin, thank you for coming. I'd get up, but Cora has threatened to tell my surgeon and they'll make me stay here an extra week if I even try to get out of bed. And you've brought the orcanus with you. Wonderful, I can't tell you how glad I am to see all of you. I'm bored out of my wits being stuck here.

"Please, sit and be comfortable. I've asked Lady Coramina to be here and record everything you can tell us about your journey to the Dark Woods. The more that you can tell us, the more accurate the archives will be. Susan, your grandfather has already told us his version, but I was hoping that the rest of you could fill in some details, especially regarding what happened after you got separated. Bodkin, we want to hear all about your time with Stiv and the wyvern, Kana. And Shirell, anything you can add would be helpful."

For the next hour, Susan and Bodkin relayed everything that had happened on the way to the keep in the Dark Woods and their subsequent meeting with the dark elf, even the part about disobeying Cooper and sneaking through the Ice Caves.

"Princess, how is it possible that Bodkin can do red magic?" asked Coramina after Bodkin had finished telling of the release of the fairies.

"She has to somehow be related to the royal family, but I can't imagine how," said Ashley.

"I believe that I can answer that."

They all turned to see Lady Zaneth standing in the doorway. She had changed into a plain blue dress. Her long, silver hair still hung in a simple ponytail down her back. Anyone who didn't know her on sight might easily have mistaken her for a servant or just a woman from the village who had some business at the castle. Only her bearing and the jeweled pendant she wore gave any indication of her identity.

"Aunt Zaneth!" exclaimed Ashley.

"Hello, Ashley, dear. Once I was told that you were awake, I came as soon as I could get away. I'm sorry I couldn't come any sooner, but things have been a bit hectic around here lately.

Zaneth crossed the room and kissed Ashley on the cheek.

"It's so wonderful to see you. And to meet all of you ladies."

"M'lady," said Bodkin, dropping to one knee.

"Oh, stop all that, child," said Zaneth. "I hate fancy titles. I'm just an old lady from a small village up north."

"Well, you're still my favorite aunt," stated Ashley, squeezing Zaneth's hand.

"That's sweet of you to say, dear. Of course, I'm your only aunt."

"And that makes you special," added Ashley with a grin. "What did you mean when you said that you can explain Bodkin's ability to do red magic?"

It's quite simple. You were schooled in the family history. Don't you remember being told about Deana?"

Ashley looked carefully at Bodkin for a moment and then smiled.

"Of course, I knew there was something special about her. She has dark eyes. I noticed them, but it's been so long, I never made the connection. She must be descended from Deana. It has to be twenty years since anyone has even mentioned that name. I had all but forgotten about her. We were always told that her child had died, but the rumors must have been true."

"So, who's Deana?" asked Susan. "Some long-lost sister that no one's ever spoken of?"

"Not exactly. She was a wanderer," answered Zaneth. "Similar to the Roma in your world, Susan. They come around from time to time to trade and get supplies. They've always had a bad reputation as thieves and scoundrels, but they're a noble people with strong traditions. They're nomads, never staying in one place for long. Ashley, you should remember your mother telling you about Deana when you were a child. She was beautiful and exotic with chestnut brown hair that came down past her waist. And captivating dark eyes. Your Uncle Marcus fell head over heels in love with her from the first moment that he saw her.

"But the old queen, my mother, would never allow a prince of the elven royal family to openly associate with a lowly wanderer girl. Marcus used to sneak out of the castle and see her in secret. Everyone knew about it and just quietly looked the other way, knowing that their little romance couldn't last. It was common for a member of the royal family to have an affair as long as it was discreet. It also helped considerably that Marcus was always on his best behavior when Deana was here. It was in between one of their visits when Marcus fell from the horse and was injured.

"When her troupe returned a few months later, Deana was carrying Marcus's child. Her family demanded that Marcus marry her and support the child, which was their custom, but that was now impossible. Reluctantly, the queen agreed to let Deana stay, hidden away in a far corner of the castle, mind you, until the child, her grandchild, was born. Deana was passionately in love with Marcus and was devastated by his condition. She insisted on helping in his care and spent every moment by his side, often neglecting her own health. The pregnancy became increasingly more difficult, and by the time that the baby was due, she was a shell of her former self. The labor was long and difficult, and during the night, she began hemorrhaging. The baby survived the birth, but despite the best efforts of the healers, Deana couldn't be saved. The child was small and frail, having arrived two weeks early. No one was surprised when the next morning, the queen quietly announced that the child had died overnight. Deana and the child were quietly buried together in a secluded corner of the castle graveyard with a small headstone. Despite her reservations, my mother treated her with dignity, then made it clear that we should never speak of her again."

"But what does any of this have to do with Bodkin?"

"There were quiet rumors that the infant had actually survived. The day after the birth, the midwife unexpectedly left Kestriana and moved to a village far from the castle. It was whispered that the queen had secretly arranged to give the baby to a childless couple to raise. The queen already had an invalid son. The last thing she wanted was the embarrassment of a half-breed grandchild. But despite her pride and concern over her royal image, she was still a kind woman and a mother. She couldn't bring herself to abandon a helpless infant. That child grew up to be Bodkin's grandfather."

Bodkin had been attentively listening to Zaneth's story.

"That all makes sense. My grandfather was adopted, but he knew almost nothing about his real parents. His adopted parents told him that he was part wanderer whose mother was unable to raise him. We were told that she was penniless and alone after being disgraced and abandoned by her family, which was common among wanderers if a girl did not marry within the clan. He was raised as an elf. Do you mean to say that I'm related to that horrible Marcus?"

"Yes, I'm afraid so," replied Ashley, with a gentle smile. "But it also means that you're related to me and that Susan is your cousin."

"Remember what the lurker said?" asked Susan. "He called us both princesses. He must have known."

Ashley turned a harsh gaze at her aunt.

"Aunt Zaneth, none of us know how the lurker gains his knowledge, but how does someone who lives a simple secluded life in a far village come to know all this?"

"That's no great mystery, dear. I always suspected that the rumors were true and that Deana's baby had survived. I learned early on that when my mother said that we should never mention something again, she was usually hiding something. After she died, I went searching. It wasn't too hard to find out the truth. I've had people secretly watching over Bodkin and her brother for years, especially after their parents died."

"But you never came forward and told them," said Ashley.

"And throw their lives into turmoil? They were happy where they were, and I felt that they were much safer that way. A pair of long-lost heirs to the royal family training to be wardens of the forest? Perhaps they would have an accident? Lost in the forest, never to return? It is just the sort of thing that my former husband would be capable of. All of their adopted family is gone. I'm the only one who knows of their true lineage. I put it to you, Bodkin. Do you think I made the wrong decision?"

"Well, I do like being treated really well at the castle," answered Bodkin after a moment. "But I think that I'd get tired of it soon. I truly love being a forest warden, and I know Pen feels the same. I hate being cooped up inside. I love the freedom of the trees and the open air. I think you did the right thing. Thank you for watching over us. So, do I get to call you Aunt Zaneth?"

Zaneth laughed heartily. "I was hoping you would."

The conversation in Ashley's quarters continued for another hour before there was a knock at the door. Bodkin was closest to the door and opened it to reveal the king's valet, Macilon, who entered and approached Princess Ashley.

Zaneth instantly came to her feet.

"Macilon, what's wrong? You're white as a ghost."

Macilon cleared his throat and addressed Ashley.

"I bear terrible news, m'lady. Your father has died. You are now queen."

Chapter 40

Adronis led Mikel through the woods, finally stopping in front of a stand of large birch trees. Mikel had been a loyal servant of the chancellor for a number of years, but he couldn't remember Adronis ever asking him to accompany him into the woods before.

"This is the place," stated Adronis.

"If I may ask, why have we come here, m'lord?" inquired Mikel.

"I have a task for you, Mikel, and I will need you to return to this exact place to perform it. As you know, King Marinus's funeral is tomorrow. It will be held in the glen in front of Savalin's Oak, just outside the north gate of the city."

"The glade that we passed through a few moments ago on our way here, Sire?"

"The very same one. It is a fitting place for a king's funeral, beneath the massive branches of the mighty oak planted by the finest king ever to sit on the elven throne. Many important people will be attending King Marinus's funeral. Since the end of the Gremlin War, some forty years ago, peace has reigned, and Marinus has received considerable praise for maintaining that peace. Representatives from the other races have already begun to arrive to pay homage to him. Prince Pander of the gnomes rode in with his entourage this morning. The highland trolls are due later today. Even some of the surrounding human communities have sent an envoy to pay their respects. And although they were the enemies of the elves, tradition requires that the gremlins send an emissary. After their defeat, Marinus treated the gremlin scum honorably rather than wiping their stain from the land once and for all." Adronis turned away from Mikel and spat in the grass. "I intend to remedy that mistake when I sit on the throne."

"I'm not sure I understand, m'lord. Won't Princess Ashley ascend to the throne after her father's death?" Certain questions were risky when dealing with the chancellor. Mikel hoped that this would not be one of them.

"Yes, normally that would be true."

Mikel breathed a silent sigh of relief that Adronis's anger was not redirected at him.

"But what if our dear princess doesn't survive long enough to attend her own coronation, Mikel? Perhaps there could be a gremlin assassin smuggled in with the emissary's guards. What could be more horrifying than for an injured princess to be brutally cut down while the entire castle is attending the king's funeral? The treachery of gremlins is well known. A rallying cry would go up. Justice for the murder of the beloved princess. A strong leader will be needed.

As the head of the High Council and the king's former brother-in-law, I could be swept onto the throne in a rush of anti-gremlin fervor. I would become king and be charged with the task of removing the blight that is the gremlin race all in one fell swoop. That is a charge that I would gladly undertake."

"A bold plan, Sire. But I am still unsure why we are here or how I may help in this plan," stated Mikel.

"You will play a key part in my plan. In keeping with tradition, at high noon, Marinus's body will be carried past all who came to bid him a final farewell, then placed atop a funeral pyre. Anyone who wishes to offer their thoughts or relate some story from the past will then be given the chance to speak. As a member of the High Council, I am required to be in attendance. Due to her recent injuries, Princess Ashley's surgeon had forbidden her from leaving her rooms, so she will be observing from her balcony. This is where you come in."

"She will have guards by her quarters. I am no coward, Sire, and I will undertake any task you ask of me, but if I am to kill the princess, it will be very difficult at that time."

"Relax, Mikel, I don't need you to kill the princess. That is a pleasure that I reserve for myself. Your job is equally important. I have, in my possession, an artifact. A book that will open a passage and allow a creature from behind the Barrier to be released."

"A creature from behind the Barrier?" exclaimed Mikel, aghast. "But, m'lord, the creatures behind the Barrier are monsters."

"Yes, but that is what you will do on this very spot. Don't worry, the army garrison will be able to deal with a single creature," Adronis assured him.

"At exactly three o'clock, after everyone has had time to say what they will and eulogize Marinus, you will open the portal using the book, and then slit the throat of a young goat that you will need to secretly bring and secure here early on the morning of the funeral. The smell of the blood will lure a creature through the passageway. Once it has finished with the goat, the beast will be drawn toward the glade. It will attack the guests at the funeral, causing widespread panic. The guards in the castle will be called away, leaving the princess unguarded. In the confusion, I will be able to dispose of her."

"But Sire, what if the creature should wander off into the

woods?" asked Mikel. "Would that not ruin the timing of your plan?"

"You wound me with your lack of faith, Mikel," Adronis answered, an unpleasant smile crossing his countenance. "You should know by now that I leave nothing to chance, but your question is a legitimate concern. There is a very good reason why I chose this exact spot. Look closely at the stand of trees behind you. They are tall and strong. At their base, shrubs with long, sharp thorns were deliberately planted many years ago. Passage is nearly impossible. This section of the forest is part of the castle's natural defenses. No army or large group could approach without fighting their way through the briars. What keeps an army out will also keep the monster in. The beast may be a mindless brute, but it will understand pain. It will avoid the thorns and move towards the glen, especially when it smells another easy meal.

"Once the creature is gone from here, you will quickly return and close the book so none of the monster's companions can follow. Then you will return the book to me. The army will destroy the beast, and no one will be the wiser as to how it escaped. You need only to follow my instructions exactly and you will be well rewarded. Now, we should return to the castle. If anyone should ask about our presence in the glade, just tell them that I was checking the preparations for the funeral."

Chapter 41

Stiv batted at an unruly strand of hair. He hated formal affairs. The servants at the castle had given him a fine tunic and breeches to wear. He had to admit that his old clothes were rather worn and frayed. But this new tunic was stiff, and the embroidered design around the collar constantly tickled the back of his neck.

Bodkin jabbed him in the ribs with her elbow.

"Would you please sit still?" she whispered. "You're at the king's funeral, and we're in the front row with the honored guests. Everyone can see you, so *please* stop squirming."

"I'm sorry," responded Stiv. "I am trying. How much longer will this last?"

"Not much longer. Prince Pander is next, and then Lady Zaneth, the King's sister. She's the last one to speak. Then you can get up and walk around. At six, the banquet will be held to celebrate the king's life. Finally, at midnight, a small group of the king's family and closest friends will return to the pyre, which will be lit by a family member. Princess Ashley is still confined to her rooms, so Zaneth had agreed to light the fire and sing the litany. I've been over this with you three times already. Now, would you please be quiet?"

Stiv knew that Bodkin was right and hoped that the last two speakers would keep their remarks brief. Many of the visiting dignitaries had already told tales of Marinus's adventures over the years. Some of the stories were somber and respectful, and others were bawdy and amusing. The king had lived a full life and made many friends. Fortunately for Stiv, gnomes are rarely long-winded, and Prince Pander was no exception. Within minutes, Zaneth was on her way to the podium to speak.

As Zaneth rose from her seat, Bodkin nudged Stiv and nodded toward the members of the High Council seated to their right. Chancellor Adronis was quietly slipping away as most eyes were directed at the king's sister.

"Now, I wonder where he's going," said Bodkin.

"Well, we can't follow him without being noticed," whispered Stiv. "We'll just have to wait and tell Cooper as soon as this is over. I wish that we could have approached him earlier, but there just wasn't an opportunity."

As Zaneth began to speak, Bodkin reluctantly agreed that Stiv was right.

"As many of you know, my brother and I didn't always agree. But he was still my brother, and I loved him. I was with him on his last day. We talked for a long time about many things. We talked like we did years ago. He told me that it was glorious to ride the wyvern, like riding into battle when he was young. His eyes sparkled as he spoke of it. It was the happiest that I've seen him in many years. Then he gave me a note and asked me to read it to all of you gathered here today."

Zaneth slowly unfolded the paper and began to read.

"I, Marinus Samarian, ruler of the kingdom of the elves, wish to thank all who have come here today. It has been my great honor to serve as your sovereign for these many years. There are no finer people in all the lands than those that dwell in the kingdom of the elves, and I hope that I will be remembered as a fair and just ruler.

"My one regret is that after the passing of my queen, I allowed myself to become angry and brooding. I drove my family away, and I must now beg their forgiveness. My dear sister, Zaneth, who has come back to me in my last days. Princess Ashley, who has tolerated my anger for many years. And my other daughter, Anna, who stands next to my queen and awaits me on the other side. Words cannot express my regret over my actions. Anna married the finest human I've ever met, and I drove her away because of it. I was a fool and missed so much of your lives.

"To the Guardian, Cooper, I owe the greatest debt. You have defended my kingdom against armies from without and evil from within. I have one final request, though I have no right to ask it. Have the dragon, Prax, fly you high above castle Kestriana and spread my ashes to the winds so they may settle on the land that I love. That is all I ask. And know that I have loved you all. Farewell, my friends."

Zaneth wiped a tear from her cheek before carefully folding the note and returning to her seat.

As the memorial ended, Prax, who had been in attendance at the north end of the glade, launched himself into the air, circled the castle grounds, and began to climb high into the air. Once he had become a small speck, he sent a tongue of fire hundreds of feet into the air, the flames announcing to anyone within miles that Marinus Samarian, king of the elves, had passed into the next life.

Chapter 42

Mikel was waiting when Adronis returned to his rooms.

"Is it done?" Adronis asked the man the instant the door was closed.

"Yes, m'lord. Everything exactly as you instructed. I took the book into the woods while the king's funeral was underway. Then I slit the throat of the goat, and I opened the book using the ring and the words that you taught me. I hid and waited until a creature appeared, lured by the blood of the goat. The creature appeared, devoured the goat, and then left in the direction of the glade where the ceremony was underway. Everything happened just as you said it would. When I was certain that the monster was gone, I retrieved the book and returned here with it. As you can see, the book and the ring now lie on the table before you."

"Excellent, you've done very well, Mikel."

"Thank you, m'lord. But how will you control that creature? I did not expect it to be so large. It's nearly the size of a dragon, and it savaged the goat like nothing I've ever witnessed before. I'm not ashamed to admit that my hands are still shaking just from the sight of it."

"Well we can't have that. Let me get you a drink to calm your nerves."

Adronis retrieved a flask of golden liquid and two glasses

from a cupboard. He deftly poured two drinks and offered one to Mikel.

"It was impossible to know exactly which creature would come through the portal, but we have nothing to worry about. There are plenty of soldiers at the funeral. Everything is under control."

As Mikel stepped forward to accept the drink from Adronis's left hand, the chancellor plunged the dagger, concealed in his right hand, deep into the unsuspecting man's midsection. The glass shattered as it fell from Mikel's hand onto the hard floor.

"I am sorry, Mikel. You have been a loyal servant, but your body, found in my quarters, will help confirm the story that the princess was not the only target of the assassins. Their goal must have been to destroy the leadership of the elf nation. By mere chance, the murderers killed the wrong man, and I escaped unharmed. Your death will prove my innocence. Besides, you know a little too much, and I can't go leaving loose ends now, can I?"

Adronis finished his drink and waited until Mikel was still, then he calmly wiped the blood from the blade onto the inside of the dead man's tunic where it wouldn't be seen.

"I am glad that you stepped off the carpet, Mikel," Adronis callously said to the dead man. "Blood is so hard to get out of fabric, and those rugs were expensive."

Adronis locked the door from the inside. He couldn't have anyone finding the body before he finished what he had to do. He crossed the room, turned the hidden knob in the carving on the wall, slid behind the tapestry, and was gone.

Chapter 43

The crowd of well-wishers was slowly beginning to return to the castle when a scream pierced the glade. All eyes turned to look as the underbrush at the far side of the clearing parted and the creature, droll and droplets of goat's blood dripping from slavering jaws, entered the glade, slowly stalking toward the crowd of onlookers.

"Shades, It's the scree!" exclaimed Cooper. "It's been released from behind the Barrier."

Korin and a half dozen of his guard instantly surrounded Lady Zaneth, the remaining dignitaries, and their entourages. A squad of twenty soldiers, part of the honor guard, quickly formed a wedge and bravely charged the monster as panic-stricken spectators scattered. The soldiers surrounded the monster, but their spears snapped like toothpicks against the creature's dense hide.

"Your weapons are ceremonial," shouted Korin. "They're not designed for combat. Fall back!"

But his warning came too late as the beast savaged the soldiers. The squadron was quickly swept aside, barely slowing the beast down enough for most of the crowd to run for the castle. Korin grabbed one of his soldiers by the arm.

"Fetch the garrison! Quickly! Alert the castle!"

The man took off running toward the castle, shouting a

call to arms.

All that stood between Lady Zaneth and their friends were Cooper, Shirell, Korin, and a handful of his guards armed only with long knives.

Bolts of blue slammed into the scree as both Cooper and Shirell attacked it simultaneously. The monster paused momentarily, shook its head, then roared its defiance and continued advancing toward the small group of elves and humans.

Horns sounded announcing the approach of the garrison from Kestriana, already alerted by the citizens scrambling for the safety of the castle gates, but they were still too far off to arrive before the creature butchered everyone in sight.

Cooper and Shirell continued to throw fireballs at the scree, but it shrugged them off like mere pinpricks. The beast crouched, preparing to leap into the midst of the defenders when a serpentine blur slammed into it like a runaway train.

The speed and ferocity of the attack took the scree by surprise, and the two behemoths rolled fifty feet across the grass. With Cooper and Shirell protecting their backs, Korin instantly seized the opportunity and had his charges bolt for the protection of the castle and the approaching garrison.

The scree twisted on the grass, attempting to get to its feet, but Kana had wrapped two coils around it's midsection and was driving the breath from the creature's lungs as she constricted. Kana attempted to drive her fangs dripping with poison into the neck of the monster, but it's hide was too tough to penetrate, and one of its forelegs was still free. Kana shrieked in pain as a vicious swipe from the scree tore part of her wing off. The wyvern's coils rippled, and a perceptible snap was heard as bones broke, yet the scree continued to batter Kana.

Finally, with one devastating blow to the side of her head,

Kana went limp and the scree quickly freed itself from her grasp. The beast screeched out its anger as it raised a razor-sharp claw, intent on delivering the fatal blow to the wyvern, when a wall of fire erupted between the two combatants and drove the scree backwards. Prax had returned.

The trees shook as the mighty dragon roared, challenging the monster. An instant later, Prax set a portion of the grass ablaze as he engulfed the scree in dragon fire. For a moment, the scree vanished in the conflagration, only to emerge unscathed. The creature had been born in demon fire, and the dragon flames had little effect on him. The scree charged Prax, who attempted to take to the air. But the scree had anticipated Prax's maneuver and launched himself high into the air, slashing Prax's wing and bringing him crashing to the ground.

The instant Prax hit the ground, the scree attacked again, slashing and tearing at him. A powerful swipe of Prax's tail sent the scree rolling across the grass, giving Prax the moment necessary to regain his footing.

Prax and the scree circled each other, feinting and darting back and forth, each looking for an opening that they could exploit. A battered and savaged Kana lay motionless in the grass. From where Cooper stood, there was no way to tell if she was alive or not. It was impossible to tell how much, if any, damage the wyvern had inflicted on the monster.

The scree seemed impervious to attack. His strength appeared to be nearly equal to Prax's and, as fast as Prax was, the beast was faster. The demon creature darted under Prax's wing and swiped viciously at the dragon's underbelly. Broken scales flew across the grass, and Prax was thrown sideways by the sheer savagery of the attack. The scree lunged again and again, each time to be beaten back by Prax's powerful wings and sharp claws. Both the scree and Prax dripped blood from a dozen places, but the scree seemed barely slowed by its wounds.

Cooper watched in horror. Prax was tiring, though the demon creature showed no signs of fatigue. If the scree was able to defeat Prax, it would ravish and destroy every living thing in this world. Mighty as Prax was, he was only one dragon. It had taken over a dozen of his brethren to drive the scree inside the Barrier. They had to do something.

Cooper grabbed Shirell by the arm, whispered in her ear, and sent her running to the other end of the clearing as Prax and the scree continued to clash and circle each other. Once Shirell was in position, Cooper threw a small fireball at the scree. The attack bounced harmlessly off its snout, but for an instant, the demon creature was distracted. Although he had no way of communicating to Prax, Cooper prayed that the wily old dragon would realize that a second, more serious attack, was imminent.

Prax crouched down in what appeared to be a defensive posture, but before the scree could attack again, Prax used both his wings and his powerful legs to unexpectedly launch himself straight up into the air. Instead of clashing with the dragon, the leaping scree passed underneath, missing Prax by mere inches and landing face first in the grass. The monster instantly came to its feet roaring its frustration, and a split second later, both Cooper and Shirell sent balls of brilliant white light, pinpointed at the scree's eyes, to explode on either side of the creature's head. Blinded and disoriented, the scree lashed out, clawing and slashing at the empty air. Prax landed next to the monster and, swinging the massive weight of his tail, slammed the scree with a blow that would have snapped a tree trunk.

The scree was lifted completely off its feet and thrown forty feet across the grass. The ground beneath their feet shook as the monster bounced once and then lay still. Prax landed ten yards away, wary of any movement. For two full minutes, the scree remained motionless.

Shirell sprinted across the grass.

"Cooper, we did it!"

Cooper turned and started toward Shirell, but he spun back instantly as Prax roared.

The scree still lived. The instant that Prax drew near enough, the demon creature lunged forward in an attempt to eviscerate the dragon. But the beast stumbled. Kana had wrapped her coils around the hind legs of the scree and, arching upward, buried her fangs deep into a wound that Prax's claws had opened on the shoulder of the beast. The scree spun round, and with a vicious slash, ripped open a long savage gash down Kana's side. Kana's hold loosened as she screamed out in pain and with a quick roll, the scree managed to, once again, free itself from the wyvern's grip. It rose to face Prax once more.

Prax had withdrawn twenty yards and held his ground. The staffs of both Cooper and Shirell shone brightly with the magic's blue light. But no attack came. After taking a few steps, the scree's movements became clumsy and unwieldy. The scree screamed out its defiance as Kana's venom coursed through its veins. The creature's knees buckled and, though it tried to rise, it's muscles no longer responded. Prax circled behind the beast and, with a leap, pinned it to the ground with his massive bulk. The scree continued to snap and snarl viciously as Prax raised one powerful foreleg and delivered a crushing blow to the side of the beast's head. An audible crack was heard as the scree went still for the final time, its head contorted at an unnatural angle.

Chapter 44

Before the dust had even settled, Stiv was racing across the grass, shouting for Kana. Bodkin followed a few steps behind. The wyvern's side was torn to shreds, and there was blood in her mouth.

"She's still alive. Please, you have to help her!" he implored Cooper and Shirell.

"There's so much damage," said Cooper, carefully examining the wyvern. "I may be able to stop the bleeding. Beyond that, my healing skills are limited to humans and elves. I don't know if I can do any more for her."

"You must save her!" pleaded Stiv, tears openly running down his face.

Though he was still breathing hard from the exertion of the battle, Prax approached and peered over Cooper's shoulder.

"Do as much as you can, Guardian," he said. "Close her wounds as best you are able and give her water. Then lash her to my back. I will carry her to my home in the mountains. If you can keep her alive for a few hours and she is truly my kin, I will be able to induce the dragon sleep. Her body will heal itself. I'm afraid that I have misjudged her. She fought bravely. Worthy of any dragon. We must do all we can to save her. If she survives, perhaps she will forgive my poor judgment of her." A puddle of blood was steadily spreading under Prax from the gash in his underbelly made by the Scree. "And perhaps I may need to join her in that sleep."

"You'll never reach the mountains bleeding like that," stated Cooper. "Shirell, quickly. I've shown you the process of using the magic to sear the wound closed. Do you remember the procedure?"

"Yes, I remember," Shirell answered. "What do you want me to do?"

"Tend to Prax. Seal up that belly wound. I'll help Kana. Her injuries are far more serious."

"Prax, this is going to hurt," said Shirell.

"Do what you must, Orcanus."

Zaneth and Macilon separated themselves from the gathering crowd.

"How may we help, Cooper?" asked Zaneth.

"Have water brought for her to drink, cloth bandages to stem the bleeding, and I need a nurse. See if there is a healer in the crowd. They can't be squeamish. I need someone who can hold pressure on the wounds and clean them after they're sealed. Move the people back away."

Zaneth nodded to Macilon "Get them everything they need."

"Right away, m'Lady." Macilon hurried into the crowd, issuing orders and sending people scurrying. A moment later, four young elves presented themselves at Cooper's side, one of them carrying an armload of clean bandages.

"We're apprentices at the Guild of Healers. We watched the dragon battle the demon. We want to help," the tallest of the group stated.

"Excellent," said Cooper, addressing the young elf that had spoken. "You go with the orcanus, she'll tell you what to do. The rest of you, grab some bandages and stop the bleeding everywhere you can. Then we'll have to seal and clean each wound. Some of these wounds are severe. Be careful, she may thrash around a bit."

The apprentices quickly began to clean and dress the wyvern's injuries as best they were able.

"Cooper," said Bodkin. "There's something important that we need to tell you. We're certain that Adronis is behind everything that's happened here. He must have the last book. He slipped away just before the demon appeared. He knew that it was coming. When we were in the marketplace a few days ago, Stiv recognized him. Adronis visited Stiv's village years ago. He's a Boc. He must have been the one who released the demon."

"That explains a lot," said Cooper. "We were sure that Al-Ron had a confederate in the castle."

Zaneth, who had rolled up her sleeves and been helping the apprentices, stopped and addressed Cooper.

"I overheard what Bodkin said, and she's right. He bleaches his hair, but its true color is red. Adronis is descended from the Boc. If he did release the Scree, his next move will be to try to kill Ashley and steal the throne. It's exactly the sort of thing that my former husband would do. I knew that he was treacherous, but even I didn't expect this. But you cannot leave to try and stop him, Guardian. If you do, Kana will die. Stay and try your best to save the wyvern. I'll go and have the guards seal the castle. They'll listen to me. If Adronis escapes, he could use the book to release more creatures from behind the Barrier. We can't allow that to happen. He must be stopped."

She nodded to Stiv and Bodkin.

"You two, go find Korin. Get to the princess's quarters and protect her. Hurry!"

Shirell stooped under Prax's right wing, examining the gash in his underside as the young healer approached.

"How may I help, Madam Orcanus?" the healer asked.

"We need to stop the bleeding. You are familiar with the process of sealing an open wound with a hot iron?"

"Yes, but it is a very crude procedure, m'lady, usually done only in emergencies."

"I think this counts as an emergency. But we'll do this a little different than usual. We will use a tiny spot of magic rather than a large hot iron. It requires pinpoint control, but if done correctly, we can stop the bleeding without damaging the surrounding flesh in the way that a hot iron would. I will need you to keep the area around the wound as clean and dry as possible."

"I have assisted with numerous surgeries, m'lady, I understand what you propose and, I'll admit, I'm anxious to observe this technique. I will do my best to help."

"Good. One other thing. We don't have time for formalities. My name is Shirell. What's yours?

"I am Timas."

"Nice to meet you, Timas. Let's get to work and make your teachers proud."

For the next twenty minutes, Timas cleaned and dabbed at Prax's wounds as Shirell sealed them with surgical precision. Slowly, the strain began to show on Shirell's face and, time after time, Timas carefully wiped her brow to keep the sweat from her eyes.

Suddenly, Prax flinched violently and both Timas and Shirell were knocked to the ground. Timas was back on his feet in an instant.

"Shirell, are you hurt?" he asked as he helped her to her feet. "What happened?"

"Oh, Prax. I'm so sorry," Shirell said tearfully.

"I burned him, Timas. I recently injured my shoulder. I thought that we would be done quickly, but the pain in my arm is becoming too much. My hands are shaking, and I can't hold them steady any longer. I don't think that I can continue, but we must. We're only half finished. Cooper can't help us. He's too busy with the wyvern."

"Can you maintain the magic, Shirell?" asked the young apprentice.

"Yes, I think so."

"Then let me steady and guide your hand. As I said, I've assisted in surgery, and I've observed your technique. Together, we can do this."

Shirell looked up into the eyes of the dragon.

"What do you say, Prax? I can't finish on my own."

"Let the young healer try," answered the dragon, turning his head to face Timas. "I trust my fate to you."

Timas quickly grabbed two of the buckets that had provided water and turned them upside down.

"Sit here," he said to Shirell as he pointed to the closest bucket.

Timas sat down behind Shirell and gently took her arm, supporting it with his own and allowing her to cradle her shoulder against his.

"Now, summon the magic and let me direct your hand."

Shirell slowly called up the magic and focused it into a single point of light. Timas's hand was steady and precise as he continued where Shirell had left off. For the next hour, the young healer expertly guided her hand while supporting her injured shoulder. Finally, he sighed deeply and said, "That's the last of it. We're finished."

Chapter 45

Susan, Coramina and Princess Ashley watched the activities below from the balcony of Ashley's quarters. The head surgeon had forbidden the princess from leaving her rooms, and Susan and Coramina had agreed to stay, keeping her company during the king's funeral and also ensuring that she followed doctor's orders.

"Susan, what's going on down there now?" asked Ashley. Coramina gently held the princess's shoulders down as she tried to rise from her chair for the twentieth time. "I can't bear to be cooped up in this room while so much is happening. I should be down there."

"Princess, please be still," Coramina scolded her. "You'll do no one any good if you re-injure those ribs or puncture a lung. Our friends are there, and they're all very capable."

"Cora's right, Aunt Ashley," said Susan. "The monster's dead and Grandfather is attending to Kana. He has a few helpers. They look like healers. Shirell is tending to Prax. I can see the blue light of her magic. I don't think that he's badly hurt. That funny little man, Macilon, is directing servants, and Stiv and Bodkin are coming this way, probably to check on us."

"It sounds like things are under control," said Cora.

"And your Aunt Zaneth is down there also. If you promise to move slowly, Susan and I will walk you over to the railing and you can see for yourself. Susan, would you get Ashley's robe?"

"Certainly," said Susan.

She crossed to the far side of the room as Cora gently helped the Princess get to her feet.

"Cora..." Susan's voice trailed off abruptly.

"Susan?"

Cora and Ashley turned to see Adronis clutching Susan, a vicious looking blade pressed against her throat.

"Adronis!" cried Ashley. "What is the meaning of this? How did you get in here?"

"My dear Princess," answered Adronis, grinning, "you grew up in this castle. You should know about the hidden tunnels."

"They haven't been used for so long that I had almost forgotten that they existed. I should have guessed that you would have a hand in all that's happened today. Is there no limit to your treachery? What was your plan? To murder me in the confusion caused by that creature and claim the throne as my grieving uncle?"

"How astute of you," sneered Adronis. "I'm sure that you recognize this blade as a kav, the traditional weapon used by gremlin assassins. It's made from obsidian and its unique shape cuts like no other blade. When you three are found murdered with the tell-tale signs of a kav, it won't be hard to convince the High Council that the gremlins must have been in league with the shadow mage Al-Ron. Even though he was recently defeated by Cooper and the orcanus, he must have given them the book and the knowledge to summon the demon creature who now lies dead in the clearing below. What better time than the funeral of the king to stage an attack and assassinate his successor, throwing the whole ruling family into chaos. Representatives from other lands are here. On such an occasion, it would be easy for an assassin to sneak into the castle, hidden in one of the delegations. I shall have little trouble making the case that we must unite against this old enemy. I will easily be proclaimed regent. I have already convinced one of the fools on the High Council to propose exactly that if you should prove unable to resume your duties. War will be declared, and we will finally wipe the gremlin scum off the earth. I will achieve both goals in one fell swoop."

"You're mad!" cried Coramina.

"Not at all, Lady Coramina, and I must apologize. I do regret having to kill you and the girl. I've always found you to be one of the more pleasant individuals in the court. And the girl is just a bystander. I was expecting to find the princess alone. But your deaths will add to the outrage of the people. I will try to be quick and not make you suffer."

Adronis raised his hand, prepared to plunge the knife into Susan's chest, but before he could carry out his task, the door crashed open.

Korin stood in the doorway, sword drawn, with Stiv, Bodkin and three armed guards behind him.

"Let her go, Chancellor. It's over."

"No!" snarled Adronis. "This is Susan, Cooper's granddaughter and a direct descendant of the king. I know you too well, Korin. You won't dare put her life at risk. Put down your sword, or I'll slit her throat from ear to ear."

"If you harm one hair on that girl's head, you'll die in a heartbeat."

"And you'll still have to explain to Cooper how you let his granddaughter die. No, you won't kill me. Besides, if you did, you'd never find that Boc book. I have confederates who I've instructed in its use. In the wrong hands, all the creatures behind the Barrier could be released. Can you take that chance?"

"You know that I can't let you go, Chancellor. Release the

girl. Even if I did agree to let you leave, the guards have been alerted. You will never get out of the castle."

"Don't be so..." Adronis's voice trailed off as the arm holding Susan slipped down off her shoulder. The gremlin knife clattered onto the floor.

A red stain slowly began to spread across the front of Adronis's tunic as his eyes rolled up toward the ceiling. Susan shook free of his grasp as his knees buckled and he crumpled onto the carpet.

Zaneth stood behind the fallen chancellor; the long knife held in her right hand dripped red. "I couldn't let him escape into these hidden passages. They weave through the castle walls like a maze, and there are a number of hidden exits if you know where to look. You would never catch him once he was in there. I used to play in them when I was a girl. He must have forgotten that I was the one who showed him where they were. The Boc book is in his quarters, along with his murdered lackey. Another victim that he planned to blame on the gremlins."

Chapter 46

The next morning, Cooper rose early and went directly to examine Prax and Kana's wounds. Guards had been stationed overnight with orders to summon him immediately if there was a change in either one's condition. He had just completed his inspection of Kana's injuries and was examining Shirell's work on Prax when a small group made up of Lady Zaneth, Macilon, Bodkin, Stiv, and Shirell approached from the castle.

"How are your patients, Guardian?" asked Zaneth.

"The wyvern Kana is breathing strong and steady. None of the wounds that were closed and sealed yesterday have reopened. She has been given water to drink, and I believe that she is as fit for travel as I am able to make her."

"That's excellent news. And our friend Prax?"

"You may ask him yourself, m'lady. I was just about to do that."

"Mischievous little Zaneth," said Prax, and though his voice was hoarse and weaker than usual, he still managed a lopsided grin. "The king's troublesome little sister."

"That was a very long time ago, Prax," answered Zaneth, with a slight smile. "We are greatly indebted to both you and Kana. But are you well enough to travel?"

"Your man, Macilon, arranged for water to be brought for me to drink and a leg of mutton from the kitchen to help me regain my strength. And I am grateful. I believe that am recovered enough to make it to my home in the mountains. Kana will be strapped to my back. Once there, I will induce the dragon sleep. If she survives the journey, she will recover, but it will take time."

"I'm coming with you," announced Stiv. "We've been together for a long time. Kana trusts me. Besides, you'll need someone to untie the straps when you arrive. Once I know that she's safe, I'll journey back here."

"Do you know what you're saying, son?" asked Cooper. "Those mountains are treacherous and unforgiving, even for experienced climbers. Under the best of conditions, it will still take you weeks to make the trek back."

"That's why I'm going too," chimed in Bodkin. "I've been trained by the wardens to survive anywhere. And it'll take two of us to get Kana down from Prax's back without reopening her wounds. It'll be much safer if the two of us travel together."

Prax spoke up. "It will be a dangerous flight. I believe that I can carry the two of you, but my strength is limited. The winds in the mountain passes are relentless and frigid. You may very well freeze to death before we arrive or be blown from my back. Are you certain that you still wish to accompany me?"

Bodkin reached over, took Stiv's hand, and together, they nodded their assent.

"Well, it appears that your minds are made up. You're both very loyal and brave, and we wish you a safe journey," said Zaneth. "Macilon, please take them to the stable master. Have him outfit both them and Prax with bridles and straps to keep them secure on their flight. And straps for the wyvern. Also, get them warm clothes and food. But pack as light as possible. It will be a difficult flight for Prax as it is."

"Right away, m'lady. Come with me, you two." Macilon

290

scurried off in the direction of the stables with Stiv and Bodkin in tow.

"He's a good man, madam," stated Cooper as he watched the three leave. "You do have an opening on the High Council. Have you considered Macilon?"

"Oh, by the gods, no," answered Zaneth. "Politicians do nothing but hem and haw and debate endlessly. Macilon knows every servant by name, every tradesman and the names of all their children, every guard and how long they've served. He is the grease that makes the wheels turn at Kestriana. He is perfectly suited to be exactly where he is. He's also a very old and dear friend. Why would I punish him by asking him to be a politician?"

Cooper couldn't help but laugh at her candor.

"I take your point, madam."

"Please just call me Zaneth. I gave up titles many years ago. On the way here, I had the opportunity to speak with Shirell. She has an interesting idea. I think you'll approve."

Shirell had been checking the missing scales near Prax's wounds and turned to speak to Cooper.

"Timas has suggested that we find young healer apprentices with an affinity for magic and try to teach them the methods that we used on Prax. I would not have been able to finish sealing Prax's injuries without his help. His steady hands, trained for surgery, allowed me to treat Prax's wounds. If healers could be taught this, it would be an invaluable skill, especially in accidents or emergencies."

"I did notice the precise work on Prax and was going to mention the fine job that the two of you did. The cleaner the wound, the faster it will heal. One of the other apprentices told me that Timas was helping you and that he was the best surgeon in their class. As far as his idea, it's not a bad one, though it's not a new one either. Eldred suggested the exact same thing years ago, even proposing that we invite healers from the other races. He felt that training together would promote mutual respect and understanding among the races and that the craft of healing was far more important than petty prejudices.

"The triangular emblem that identifies healers was one of Eldred's ideas. A simple medallion that is now recognized everywhere and allows healers to treated with respect and dignity. A shrewd diplomatic move. Sadly, after the destruction of the Conjurer's Guild, there was no one left to teach this method, and the Healers Order was too busy rebuilding its own ranks. The idea was forgotten. As orcanus, you could revive the idea. If you wish, I'll mention it to the princess when I see her later today. Will you be returning to the Guild Hall today?"

"Tomorrow morning. For the rest of today, Timas has offered to treat my shoulder and then give me a guided tour of Kestriana. Please tell Susan that I'll join the two of you for dinner, though."

After Shirell left, Zaneth asked, "Guardian, am I right in believing that Shirell has been the new orcanus for some time now?"

"Yes, that's correct."

"Then she must have visited Kestriana numerous times and be quite familiar with the layout of the castle."

"That's also correct."

"Then why would she need a guide to show her around?"

"Because, m'lady," chuckled Cooper. "The young man doesn't know that."

"Oh, I see," said Zaneth, with a faint smile. "Perhaps, I should ask Macilon to give me a guided tour. I have been away from the castle for quite some time."

"I believe that your 'old and dear friend' would be more

292

than happy to oblige."

Epilogue

The air shimmered above the Boc book. An instant later, Crall appeared. The protective spell surrounding the puzzle box had created a bubble that prevented tons of stone from collapsing onto the box and burying it for all time. Crall silently thanked the dark elf for leaving the book close enough to the puzzle box for it to be encased inside the bubble. Moving quicker than his emaciated frame would suggest possible, he snatched up the puzzle box and the Codex Stygia, then darted back through the portal opened by the Boc book.

Without the puzzle box to sustain it, the bubble quickly began to weaken and dissipate. With a thunderous crash, a mountain of broken masonry and splintered timbers smashed down, ensuring the final destruction of what had once been the dark elf's laboratory.

When Crall emerged from the other end of the portal into his home in the swamp, he was wheezing terribly. But he still clutched the puzzle box in one bony hand and the Codex Stygia in the other. His twisted limbs were unaccustomed to such rapid movement. He had gambled that the spell surrounding the puzzle box would hold for a few precious seconds after the box was removed. If he had guessed wrong, he would have been crushed in the blink of an eye. He had guessed correctly.

The Boc book in the keep was lost forever, and now only

three of the original thirteen books remained — the one that had belonged to Adronis, now securely locked up by the orcanus at her Guild Hall, the second one dangerously located inside the Barrier, and the last one that lay open on the floor directly in front of him. But they were no longer of any consequence to him. He had what he desired.

Carefully, Crall closed the book before him and, along with the Codex Stygia, returned it to the hidden room with the other artifacts that he had gathered. Dangerous artifacts that he had collected over the decades in an attempt to protect innocent lives and, in some small way, redeem himself for the evil he had caused before his own arrogance released the forces that turned back on him and changed him into the creature known as the lurker.

Some of the items were things that he himself had created. Other artifacts were lost to him, having been discovered by Eldred before he could retrieve them. Many were safely locked away in the vault beneath the ruins of the old Guild Hall. It was some consolation to him that both he and Eldred had the same goal and the number of people who knew of the existence of Eldred's vault could be counted on one of his boney hands.

After reassuring himself that both books were secure in their proper places, he returned to the main room and placed the puzzle box in the center of the flat stump that served him as a table.

With one last sigh, Crall extended the hand wearing the silver ring and began the rite that would open the box. The box spun and turned, the top separating as he knew it would, finally releasing the mist that accompanied the shade of Eldred.

"Who has called me forth?" the specter of the wizard asked.

"You know me...ghost of Eldred...I am Crall the Lurker."

"I do know you of old, Crall. But what does the lurker

wish of one such as me?"

"I have opened...the puzzle box...Give me its prize!"

"You know the price. Why would you ask for such a curse?"

"Am I not...already cursed, spirit? I have lived...in this world, suffering the torment...of this broken body for too long. I have only one wish...To make the one responsible...for my pain pay for his deeds. The one known as...Darkon Rhee. He exists in...the world inside your box."

"That is so. But he can never escape. Darkon Rhee is imprisoned here for all time."

"That is not enough...He is free inside your world...Take me into your world...where I can seek him out and bond with him...I will make him...suffer my vengeance for all eternity...His crimes deserve no less."

"If that is your wish, then so be it. You know that I cannot refuse, but you know the rite. You must ask to join me in my world."

"I, Crall," the lurker began.

"No!" The shade of Eldred cried, stopping him before he could finish. "You must use your real name. The name you possessed before you became the creature known as the lurker."

Crall wheezed once.

"Very well, spirit. I, Bangor Khan...have opened the puzzle box. I demand...the gift of immortality...that is my reward."

Crall's contorted hand reached up to touch that of the specter. As promised, the spirit of the twisted creature known as the lurker was drawn up beside Eldred's shade. But the face of the spirit was not one of crooked hideous features. Instead, it bore the countenance of Bangor Khan. The mist instantly returned to envelope the two shades and draw them back into the box.

Moments passed before the lump of tattered clothing on the floor stirred. Muscles and limbs that had been twisted and bent for years screamed out in protest as the figure used the stump/table to slowly drag itself to a seated position. He was free. The creature known as the lurker was gone from inside his head, taking with it the voices of all the former hosts. His mind was clear. He was alive and he was Brin once more.

About the Author

Tom Dillman started writing about a dozen years ago — he had stories in his head that he had to tell. *The Legacy of the Boc* is the second book in his *Gnome Door* series. The first book, *The Gnome Door Chronicles*, was published by Crave Press. Dillman is retired and, when he's not writing, he enjoys woodworking. He is also a long-time runner and student of karate.

www.ingramcontent.com/pod-product-compliance
Lightning Source LLC
Chambersburg PA
CBHW020231260626
47156CB00002B/625